# RISING STAR

# EMMANUELLE

USA TODAY BESTSELLING AUTHOR

# SNOW

Smart Lily
Publishing

SAM STEVENS
ECHOES WORLD TOUR
FEBRUARY 16, 20
#1
Dad
SAM STEVENS
SAM STEVENS

# CARTER HILLS BAND UNIVERSE
### (SUGGESTED READING ORDER)

**Carter Hills Band series**
False Promises

HEART SONG DUET
Blindsided
Forevermore

**Whiskey Melody series**
Sweet Agony

SECOND TEAR DUET
Cruel Destiny
Beautiful Salvation

BREATHLESS DUET
Wild Encounter
Brittle Scars

**Upon A Star series**
Last Hope

Midnight Sparks

**Love Song For Two series**
<u>Lonesome Heart Duet</u>
Fallen Legend
Rising Star


<u>Two of Us Duet</u>
Snowbound


Wicked Love


All titles available at
emmanuellesnow.com


*For the best experience, read in the order as shown above*

# BECOME A VIP

## TO NEVER MISS A THING

**Snow's VIP**

Join **Emmanuelle Snow's VIP newsletter** for all the cool stuff, promos, new releases, giveaways, and gifts.

emmanuellesnow.com

**Snow's Soulmates**

Join Emmanuelle Snow's Facebook VIP group, **Snow's Soulmates**, to chat with her and other readers, get updates, and more bonus content.

facebook.com/groups/snowvip

# Chapter 1
### Madison

While sipping champagne with Sam after his successful album launch, I was completely absorbed in the intimacy of the night—especially when he spoke about his ex-wife—and couldn't help reaching for his hand. How was I to know the sparks of our attraction would shoot right through me? A buzz arose where our skins touched, and my breath caught somewhere between my lungs and throat.

I hadn't planned on hinting at my childhood… It just came out in the heat of the moment. An invisible vise strangled my heart when I confided in him, and I prayed Sam wouldn't pry about my past any further. That's when *he* intertwined our fingers together, sending a bulk load of mixed signals to my body.

I pulled my hand away, unable to process how the minor gesture had such an impact on me.

After what felt like hours, Sam reached back for my

hand. Of his own volition. Shooting addictive heat through my blood and more confusion into my mind, as if he couldn't *not* touch me. As if the small connection was meaningful to him too.

Right there, sitting beside him at his kitchen counter, I melted for him even more. And my stupid heart imagined scenarios that couldn't exist in real life, only in my mind.

Hours later, I was lying in bed, unable to rest my mind long enough for sleep to claim me. After an hour of tossing and turning, I got up and decided that sinking into a hot bath would help me relax. The scorching water did miracles to untie the knots in my back, but it did nothing to ease the one around my lower abdomen. Moving to my knees, I reached for the phone I'd placed on a folded towel on the floor and did something I'd sworn I'd never do. I put Sam's new album on, the one I bought the moment it got released. Setting my device back down, I immersed myself deeper in the water and closed my eyes, the sound of his voice erasing the remnant jitters waltzing within me.

How could a voice be powerful enough to appease my body, heart, and soul all at once? As if it connected us in a way no other words could express.

Rocked by every word he sang, I ventured one hand between my thighs, imagining those were his fingers. The ones I had never gotten to experience in the way I craved the most.

My breasts pushed out of the water, my back arching when I touched myself the way he would if he were here—with me. Not sleeping a flight of stairs above, unreachable.

I cursed at myself. Pressing on my clit with the heel of my hand, two of my fingers found their way to my throbbing center, and a crazed sensation zipped through me.

Sam's voice sang about love. And lust. My hand moved to the rhythm of his guitar, playing my own body like he played his instrument. With ease and abandon. With purpose and conviction.

My movements turned frantic. I increased the pace. My vision blurred. My breath spasmed with every exhale. My lower belly filled with pools of lava.

I pictured him in the country bar that night when he had sung on a stage for the first time in two years. Cooking on the grill, sending heated glances my way. His hands on mine when he had taught me to play the guitar. That irresistible grin that tugged at his lips whenever we argued, knowing he was right and I wasn't. The vulnerability he didn't hide when we had opened our hearts to each other, retelling the stories of our lives earlier tonight.

My head tilted back. My thighs spread apart giving me more space. I had no more conscious control over my body. It was only regulated by the pleasure building in its depths.

I strangled the edge of the tub with my free hand as the orgasm hit me. It rippled from so deep inside my core, that for an instant, I believed the ride would never come to a stop.

**...Baby, I'm holding ya  
Baby, you can count on me  
I have your back, now and  
forever...**

The song ended, and tremors shook every fiber of my being as I landed back into my physical body.

I had touched myself dreaming about Sam in the past, but this, the images of him invading my head, the sound of his voice, the words he sang, it had never felt so real. He was with me, touching me, without even being here.

Breathless and relaxed, I toweled myself dry and

ignored my reflection in the mirror. I wasn't ready to assess how pathetic I had become. Not even taking the time to put any clothes on, I slipped under the covers, chasing sleep.

A part of me still hoped Sam would walk in and relieve us both of the pent-up tension that was impossible to ignore whenever we stood close to each other, and touch me until his skin was branded on mine for the rest of my life.

Within a minute, I passed out, ready to continue the fantasy in my dreams, promising myself this would never happen again and knowing I would have a hard time resisting if temptation called my name again.

———

The next morning, I woke up early. I had my bedroom to set, some of my boxes to unpack, and my clothes to hang in the closet. I still wasn't sure why I had agreed to move into the Stevenses' home, other than it made sense to prepare the girls for their new adventure. No doubt, I would have to adjust too. When I'd lived on a yacht last year, it had taken my stomach two weeks to adjust to being on the ocean twenty-four-seven, the swell of the waves becoming more perceptible whenever I lay down at night.

The sound of little feet padding in my direction brought a curl to my lips. In no time, Mikaella and Justine stood in my doorway, wearing matching PJs and grins, fawning over every piece of clothing spread on my bed when I invited them in. None of the outfits were spectacular, but they ran their fingers over the material of the jeans, T-shirts, blouses, and summer dresses as if they were priceless pieces. Justine, spread on her front, took a whiff of one of my cardigans.

"Do you wear perfume?" Mikaella asked, now standing next to me, her big sparkling eyes traveling over my few possessions.

"Sometimes."

"Can I try it?"

That was when I realized Mikaella never got the chance to do just that, wear her mother's perfume. Or try her heels and jewelry. Tiny needles pierced my heart as I watched her.

I neared her and tucked her hair behind her ear. "Absolutely. Let me find it first. I think it might be—"

Sam's voice reached us. "Girls, ready for breakfast?"

Justine jumped to her feet. "Maddie, come, come," she singsonged. She curled her fingers around my digit and pulled me after her, the sound of her laughter contagious.

I choked on a gulp of air when we stepped into the kitchen and I came face to face with Sam.

"Good morning," he whispered, his eyes locked on mine, an unreadable expression crossing his features.

"Morning." I coughed out the single word.

"Sleep well?" he asked with one tipped brow, a hint of a smile curving his lips.

"Mm-hmm."

Could he guess, just by staring at me, I had given myself an orgasm while my mind overflowed with images of him last night? While he sang to me? Oh. My. God. Was my face turning crimson? Were my eyes betraying me?

I swallowed, pretending to be immersed in something Mikaella said as I replied, "You?"

His throat worked, and he said nothing for a beat. "Yep." He pinched his brows together, shook his head, his smile still anchored to his mouth, and turned around, humming. A new buoyancy, I'd never noticed before, trailed behind him.

Something had happened. Sam Stevens wasn't the chirpiest guy on the planet. And now he looked rejuvenated. And in the best of moods I'd ever seen him.

I cleared my throat, wiped my moist palms on my jeans skirt, took a cleansing breath in, and offered, "Want me to make my special chocolate and strawberry waffle recipe?"

"Yes," the girls screamed at the same time.

Sam and I burst into a chuckle, and it filled the room with a lightness I couldn't resist.

Just like that, I became a full-time presence in their household, and for some reason, it felt strangely comfortable as if we'd all been living together forever.

# Chapter 2
### Sam

**B**reakfast, the first one we shared with Madison, turned out to be much more of an enlivened experience than usual. The girls, in a cheery mood, couldn't stop chatting and laughing. At their request, as if she was a new shiny toy they had to carry around everywhere, Madison helped them get dressed before Riley and Devon picked them up and drove them to the zoo. I loved the idea of giving Madison some much-needed time and space to unpack and make herself at home, without my little chatterboxes asking hundreds of questions and creating additional cacophony to the task. We had almost two months left before leaving for the tour. The four of us living under the same roof was the final test to prove to me that we could do this—all of us, together.

"I'll be in my office if you need help with anything," I told Madison after I carried the rest of her boxes from the garage to her bedroom.

"Thanks. I should be fine." She offered me a warm smile. When she lifted her arms to pull her hair into a high ponytail, her shirt lifted from the front, giving me a peek of her toned midriff.

I swallowed hard and forced myself to look away.

After last night, I wasn't allowed to look at her in any way other than my daughters' nanny or the hired help. My dick and I had reached an agreement, and I was adamant about it, even though my body had hummed with bliss after I relieved some of the tension that had been crippling it. Now I felt like a new man. One who'd broken through some of the chains holding him in place.

I retreated to my office slash music studio before Madison could notice how I ogled her, and locked myself for hours, not risking a foot out, even to get lunch. Sure, last night had helped to get rid of the edginess, but I was a weak bastard when it came down to Madison Prescott. Truth be told, now that no children could walk in and break whatever moment we shared, I feared I couldn't be trusted to contain myself. Or that my willpower would snap if presented with an opportunity to kiss her sweet mouth without any lingering distractions.

When the doorbell rang around five, I put my guitar on its stand and rubbed my fists over my eyes, wiping out the exhaustion that weighed there. The front door opened before I had time to get to it. Two small tornados rushed in with blue cotton candy and sugary smiles.

"Daddy, I saw a monkey. And a giraffe. And a *pota-lalamus*. Uncle Riley told me we could go back again another time. With you and Maddie. Where's Maddie? Where's Maddie? Where's Maddie?" Justine hopped all around me, unable to stay put for more than a few seconds, her eyes round and glistening and her pigtails bouncing on either side of her head.

I looked behind me. No trace of Madison. I would've thought she would come running at the commotion. She never resisted the lure of my daughters' innate enthusiasm.

I pinched my brows and shrugged. "In her room… huh…I think. Don't go in. Knock and wait—" My baby girl disappeared before I could finish giving her instructions.

Justine wasn't very good with personal boundaries. I'd have to tell Madison to lock her bedroom door when she didn't wish to be disturbed. Or maybe I could buy her a doorknob sign that said *Unavailable* or something funny to keep the girls out.

Mikaella inched closer. I lifted her up and dropped a kiss on the top of her head. "How is it going, sweet pea? Had a great day?"

My daughter sighed. "Yeah. I wanted to stay till late, but Uncle Riley said it was time to go, and if I stayed behind, I'd have to clean the elephants' cage." She scrunched up her adorable face. "Ugh, it's disgusting. Not cleaning elephant poop. It's huge and smelly. Yucky. Big no."

Riley, Devon, and I all started laughing when teen-Mikaella made a face that spelled *It's not funny Daddy*.

I swallowed my chuckle. "Sweet pea, you're right. I'm glad you decided to come home." I ruffled her hair, and she disappeared upstairs after saying goodbye to my friends.

"How did it g—?"

"Daddy. Come. Quick. Maddie is sick," Justine screamed from the other side of the house where the guest bedroom was.

My eyes traveled between Riley and Devon, and I lifted a finger. "Gimme a sec." I followed the sound of my daughter's voice that pleaded, "Hurry, Daddy."

"What's wrong, baby girl? I—" My words died on the tip of my tongue when I entered the room.

Madison lay on the tiled floor in the adjoining bathroom, her face ghostly white and her lips trembling.

I moved closer and crouched down beside her, combing the loose tendrils of her hair away from her face. "Hey, talk to me. What's going on?"

"I'm…I'm sick. I've been…I've been throwing up for the last hour." Her eyes were glossy and her hands shaky.

I felt her forehead with the back of my palm. "You're burning up. Why didn't you tell me?"

"You…you were busy. I-I didn't want to bother you. I thought it might just be indigestion."

"Want me to drive you to the clinic?"

She shook her head, and it took everything I had not to pull her into my arms and kiss her fever away. "Nah. It's probably a stomach bug…or…or the flu. I'll rest tonight. I-I should be fine by the morning."

"Your skin is gray," Justine said, framing her face with her little hands.

"She's right. You don't look so fine to me. Wait here. I'll bring you something for the fever."

Devon was standing outside the bedroom after I gave Madison the medicine. "Listen, Sam. Riley and I talked. We don't want the girls to catch something. If it's okay with you, we'll take them home with us tonight."

I sighed and nodded. Even if I knew she was right, I couldn't help my stomach from free-falling at the thought. My girls had only ever had a handful of sleepovers in their lives, and only with their grandparents. It wasn't exactly how I'd pictured their first real one to be. But honestly, what choice did I have? "You sure?"

"Affirmative."

I huffed. "Okay. Let me pack their stuff."

"I'll help you. Come on, sweetie," Devon said to Justine, tugging at her hand. "Let Maddie rest. Your daddy will take good care of her. Now we should get ready because Mika and you are having a sleepover at our place tonight. Isn't it exciting? I bet Hope will be ecstatic to have friends over."

Justine bounced on her feet, her smile growing larger by the second. She singsonged, *"Sleeporver. Sleeporver. Sleeporver."*

I shook my head with a grin. That girl.

I buckled Justine in her car seat, kissed both my daughters, and made them promise to be on their best behavior.

Mikaella stared at me, a wrinkle forming across her forehead. The tiny-teenager version of her had made a comeback. She waggled a finger before me. "You better not catch the flu, Daddy. It's gross when people vomit. Dis-gus-ting. Sabrina threw up in art class once, and it stank *soooo* bad."

I raised my hands. "Pinky swear. I'll do my best, sweet pea."

With my heart leaping in my throat at the idea my kids were experiencing a new milestone without me, I waved at the car pulling out of the driveway. My lips tilted up at the sight of Riley in daddy mode, driving Devon's SUV instead of his usual red sports car. Yeah, the family-man vibe kinda suited him. Once inside, I rushed to check on Madison.

Heaves rocked her body. She flushed the toilet, looking even paler than before. "My-my stomach didn't appreciate the medicine." A timid smile graced her lips, her eyes shadowed by dark circles. She rubbed her upper arms, chills shaking her body.

"Tell me what to do. I'd heat some soup, but I'm not sure you'll be able to keep it in."

Her teeth chattered.

"How about a blanket?"

She nodded. "Please. I'm *sooo* cold."

I returned to the room minutes later with a pile of blankets in my arms, helped her to bed, and wrapped one around her shoulders. "Better?"

"I'm sorry, Sam. I'm supposed to care for Justine and Mika, not the other way around."

"Get some rest and stop worrying. The girls left with Ry. Sleep. I'll check on you later." I half-closed her door so I could hear her if she needed me.

How could I have been so stupid, locking myself in my studio all day, to have missed Madison being sick? "See what you did?" I hissed at my dick. "All your fault. You can't behave, and now we're hiding from temptation. Nice job."

I fixed dinner, and for the first time in forever had to eat by myself. No sound filled the lonely silence. I was so used to living in squabbles and giggles that I had forgotten what quiet sounded like.

For a fleeting moment, I savored the calm. I knew the girls were safe, yet my insides still coiled at the thought of them being away.

Restless, I checked on Madison for the millionth time. The sight of her when I cracked open the door broke my heart. She was awake now, curled up on herself, knees drawn to her chest, shivering and her teeth chattering.

"Fuck. That bad, huh?"

She lifted her eyes, and her gaze pierced mine.

"Wanna take a bath? I know that's what I do when I'm not feeling well," I suggested, hands shoved into my pockets, not sure how to approach the situation…or her.

"Yes," she murmured. "Please. Can you—?"

I nodded. "Gimme a few minutes. I'll come get you when it's ready."

Hiding in the en-suite bathroom, I exhaled the tension swirling in me. I honestly had no clue what I was doing, and deep down I knew I wasn't the right person to help Madison. But who else would care for her when it was just the two of us left here?

Why didn't I insist Devon stay and help her out? That would have made much more sense. I sighed because I was an idiot, but not *that* much of an idiot. I would never risk Devon getting sick on my behalf just because I was too stubborn to keep my hormones in check.

I shook my head, chasing the dreadful thoughts away, and turned on the faucet. Once the bathtub was full and the water was slightly more than lukewarm, I went to get Madison, who hadn't moved from her position on the bed. "Still up for that bath?"

She nodded.

With careful steps, I helped her to the other room. I placed a clean towel by the bathtub. "You got everything you need?" I asked.

She whispered a low "Yes".

"Think you can manage on your own or do you need me to…you know…help you?" The words exited my mouth before I could analyze them, and I wanted to slap myself for being so absurd.

*And now I was volunteering to help undress my children's nanny. Absolutely fucking great.*

"I-I can manage. Thanks…for…huh…offering."

I rubbed my nape, keeping my focus on the water. "I'll be in the other room. Just call me if you want anything… or whatever… I'll be over there if you… Anyway, I'll let you do your thing now," I said, pointing behind me with my thumb. *Way to go, Sam. Real, smooth.*

After twenty minutes, I heard the distinctive sound of bathwater being drained and moved to my feet. Seconds later, Madison reappeared wearing only a purple terry cloth robe she adjusted at the waist.

"How are you feeling?" I asked, taking tentative steps in her direction.

"A bit better. But I'm still cold." As if summoned, chills traversed her, and she wrapped her arms around herself.

"I called our family doctor while you were in the tub. There's a stomach bug going around town. He said to call him back if the fever doesn't break within two days."

Madison returned to her previous position under the covers, and I tucked two more blankets around her.

"Want water?"

She nodded.

I left the room and came back seconds later with a full glass. She took small sips before discarding it on the bedside table.

Her teeth chattered.

I sat on the edge of her bed, and the voices in my head hollered that I'd regret what I was about to do. But damn it. Madison looked like shit, and if I could do anything to make her feel better, I wouldn't miss my chance. Ignoring the way my heart banged against my ribs, I raked my fingers through my hair and spoke the thing I feared I'd regret the moment the words escaped my mouth, "Scoot over. I'll warm you up." She shifted to her right, and I stretched my legs over the pile of covers. With one arm around her shoulders, I pulled her against me. My hand found her forehead. Warm as a furnace against me, her fever hadn't broken. "I got you," I whispered against her hair, my lips dying to kiss her right there.

Madison nestled in the crook of my arm, her head

resting against my chest, and her body grew heavier as she fell asleep.

A long while later, her chills abated, and her breathing evened out.

Half-seated, a pillow behind my back, I refused to move, not willing to wake her up.

The scent of her perfume permeated my nostrils. Citrus and Madison.

My eyelids fluttered, and my head hung lower. Before I realized it, I dozed off too.

"No, Mama, no."

Gut-wrenching sobs and a death grip on my upper arm jolted me awake. In the darkness, I had a hard time recalling where I was or if it had all been a dream or reality.

"No, please. No. Stop. It hurts."

The grip on my arm tightened, fingernails digging into my skin through my shirt.

*Madison.*

I cocked my head to watch her, the light from the hallway casting a soft glow on her tear-drenched face. With my thumb, I brushed away the wetness on her cheeks, noting that her fever had dropped a little. "Hey, it's okay. It's just a bad dream. You're safe. Nothing will happen to you."

Her glossy eyes captured mine, and for a second, I got lost in them. Her lips shuddered, and she blinked as if to reset her brain. "Thanks," she whispered, her voice rough.

"Still freezing?" I asked.

"*Yesss,*" she said, her voice carrying the remnants of fear.

"Want me to stay?"

"Please."

I reached for her hand, and she relaxed in my

embrace. With a quiet peace stirring in my core, we both drifted back to sleep.

The sound of my phone vibrating on the nightstand pulled me out of my slumber. It took me a moment to come back to a conscious state.

Still asleep beside me, Madison's head was pressed against my chest. I brushed my fingers across her forehead and realized her fever had dropped

I stretched my arm to grab my device and look at the time. *Nine o'clock.* My limbs felt so heavy that I would have sworn it was much later. Many notifications filled the screen. The first one was a text from Riley, sent over three hours ago. I clicked it open.

RILEY

We're fine.

Along was a picture showing him, Devon, and the girls at a pizza place, all grinning.

The latest one was of my girls deep asleep in his guest bedroom, Hope, their dog, squeezed between them.

RILEY

See? More than fine.

I smiled at this sight and typed back.

ME

Enjoy. They turn into monsters on day three.

RILEY

No, they're adorable.

ME

I know. Kiss them goodnight for me.

RILEY

Will do. I'll call you in the morning.

I placed my phone beside me and tilted my head back. Madison muttered something in her sleep, and I froze to avoid disturbing her rest. I held my breath, waiting awhile, wondering if the nightmares would make a comeback.

They didn't. She mumbled some more until she fell back into deep sleep.

Her company filled a void I never knew existed in my heart.

I missed that. Having a woman to cuddle. To care for. To love. Sure, I had my daughters to keep me fully busy and fill my heart with butterflies and magic, but I missed having a woman in my arms. In her sleep, Madison circled my waist with one arm like she could read my inner thoughts, and I was a goner.

A part of me yearned to stand and run away, to leave the room, but I couldn't because the rest of me longed for her comfort as much as she required mine.

Hating myself for not being strong enough to do the right thing, I removed the pillow behind my back and lowered myself onto the bed, and without giving my brain room to think, I closed my eyes and drifted back to sleep.

———

The early morning sun's rays filtered through the drapes and blinded me as I forced my eyes open. I fastened my arm around the woman splayed over me. Until my brain caught up and I remembered it wasn't just any woman, but Madison, my children's twenty-one-year-old nanny, wearing only a bathrobe.

*Fuck.*

The realization I'd slept in her bed, our bodies entangled, chased the last traces of sleep from me. I could feel the softness and warmth of her legs and stomach against my skin. What did I do? How could I have been so careless? This was a ginormous mistake. A big setback. Putting the tour at risk. If it went to hell, I'd never forgive myself. And Riley would kill me. My kids would never forgive me if Madison decided to leave us. They loved her. They needed her. I depended on her…and needed her too. Much more than she'd ever know.

Why was I acting like a hormonal teenager instead of a grown-up man around this woman?

Just as traitorous as usual, my morning wood stretched tall and proud, and her hand moved too close for comfort. My breath wheezed when I tried to squirm out of her hold. I failed. Her eyes sprang open, and I flinched internally at my predicament. I cursed all the saints I could remember the names of in my head.

Just when everything in my life almost made sense again, I screwed up the fragile balance by sleeping with the nanny. Well, not sleeping with her, per se, but beside her. As if that changed anything. We slept in the same fucking bed. In each other's embrace.

"Hey," I said, to break the awkward silence, running a hand over my face, unable to look at her just yet. "Listen… Huh… I'm sorry. I tried to warm you up, and I kinda fell asleep. This wasn't planned. Won't happen again." My body vibrated at the excitement of her not being in a hurry to escape my arms and the situation I'd put us in. It was like she belonged there.

The mishap woke up a thirst inside me.

For the first time since Lisa had left, I wondered when I'd let myself find love again. One day. Maybe when the girls would be old enough to understand and ready to welcome another woman into their lives.

Trying to conceal my more-than-obvious erection, I pulled the blanket over my lower body.

Madison detached from me and sat beside me, her hair disheveled, and her lips a dark shade of pink. The sight reminded me of that morning after we'd kissed, a lifetime ago.

I focused on her face. Sporting flushed cheeks and shiny eyes, I wondered if she was still feverish. "How are you this morning?" Small talk was something I didn't excel in. We had broken so many of our own rules yesterday. So many boundaries. So many everything. I had cared for Madison with the goodness of my heart, without any ulterior motives, but right now, in the light of a new day, our night together seemed to mean an awful lot more. No matter how hard we tried to stay apart, we always ended up entwined in each other. I'd be lying if I said waking up with her in my arms didn't feel incredible, and I hadn't slept this soundly in years.

"Better. I think." She nibbled on her lower lip, leaving tiny indentations I wished I could erase with a kiss.

"Good."

I stirred to rise when her hand reached for mine. "Thanks. You know…for making sure I didn't like…you know…be alone." She paused, her gaze trained on our joined hands. "And for warming me up."

I nodded. "I couldn't let you freeze to death. Ice blue isn't your color," I said in a teasing voice. I cocked my head to the side and ordered my entire body to stay put. "Now that you're doing better, I…I should go."

She nodded her agreement while fastening the tie of her robe around her waist and resting against the headboard.

"Listen, I know you told me once to never try to fix you or anything, and it's not what I did…or what I'm doing here. You were having nightmares last night, and they sounded kinda scary. I just… It would make me feel better if I knew they aren't memories. The other night, you mentioned being neglected as a child. Call it father's instinct…but I don't know… It sounded serious. Like you feared something—or someone."

Great, now I was rambling, trying not to sound like a patronizing idiot.

Madison cleared her throat. "I did? Oh, I'm so sorry. This is embarrassing… It used to be a daily occurrence when I was a kid. I haven't had those in years."

"Are you okay?"

She offered me a tiny curl of her lips. "Yeah, no need to worry. I'm fine. I've never been beaten up or anything. It's all in the past… Nothing to worry about."

"You'd tell me if it weren't the case?"

"Yes."

Without another word or look in her direction, I left her in the middle of the bed, closing the door behind me. Scratching my temple and pondering her words, I hurried to my bedroom upstairs.

# Chapter 3
### Madison

When I woke up, the scent of fever clung to me. My eyelids weighed tons, and I couldn't seem to open them. My body felt sluggish, my limbs unable to follow commands. Disjointed memories of the previous day overtook my mind. I recalled being sick and Justine screaming for Sam. And then, blackout. The fever had messed with my brain. I remembered feeling cold—teeth-chattering cold. I forced my mind to work so I could figure out if I had made a fool of myself. Or thrown up somewhere I shouldn't have. How did I even make it to my bed? I couldn't even twitch a muscle when I had laid down on the bathroom floor.

I swept my tongue across my upper teeth in a faint attempt to dissipate the bitter taste in my mouth.

A slight movement on my left startled me.

Oh no, had one of the girls joined me in bed in the middle of the night?

If so, we'd have to discuss it. Sam would never agree to this, and I wouldn't too. Talk about blurred lines. Also, the idea of them walking down the stairs in the dark was enough to send a wave of panic through me.

My heart banged in my chest at the thought of it.

The deep breaths couldn't belong to Mikaella or Justine.

Someone—a male someone—was lying beside me. Oh God… What did I do last night? Worse, I had no recollection of any of it.

My body recognized him before my mind had time to catch up.

His scent, a musky mix of woodsy aftershave and something exclusively him, filled my nose, and the realization hit me. I wasn't entangled with just anyone. I was entwined with Sam Stevens. My boss. And the man I was madly in love with, however much I tried to convince myself otherwise.

A nightmare. It all boiled down to this.

I messed up. *We* messed up. Something must have happened, because why else would we be sharing a bed?

I raked my brain, but I could only recall him talking about blankets. What did I miss? I sucked in a hefty dose of oxygen. *Think, Maddie.*

There must have been a logical explanation for this… huh…situation, for lack of a better word. No matter what, we were sharing a bed. A bed. My arm was around him, my legs tangled with his.

My breath hitched on its way out. Tremors rose in the depths of me—not the feverish kind this time.

My mouth filled with acid. Would I be sick again?

Could this be a hallucination? Perhaps my fever hadn't broken, and my brain was making up stories based on my fantasies. Perhaps I was still deep asleep and dreaming.

I inhaled, wishing I could wake up alone in my own bed, and that all of this was just a figment of my imagination.

With renewed energy and motivation to learn the truth, I forced my eyes open, one at a time. Sam's gaze was locked on mine. My airways constricted and my chest tightened. None of it was a dream.

"Hey," he said, a tiny arc gracing his lips that depicted more anxiety than genuine happiness. His voice, sexy and rough from sleep, warmed my insides.

Feeling self-conscious, I secured the bathrobe tie around my waist. When did I even change into this? My brain was failing me. I couldn't seem to recall anything. Sam's gaze followed the movement of my fingers, and I wrapped the bedspread around me as he rambled.

After some forced small talk on his part, Sam's expression shifted from caring to worried. His next words shook me to my core. "Listen, I know you told me once to never try to fix you or anything, and it's not what I did…or what I'm doing here." He kept talking, but only every other word registered.

I wanted to disappear—this was so humiliating.

I hadn't had nightmares about my early childhood in years. These days, they manifested often. My boss had witnessed one of my *middle of the night* breakdowns. Was fever to blame, or were there similarities between my early years and his kids' reality? After all, he had confided in me about Justine's recurring nightmares.

When Sam exited my bedroom, after I reassured him I was doing just fine and he didn't have to make a big deal about my bad dreams, I resumed my breathing.

Once in the en-suite bathroom, alone, with my back leaning against the closed door, I exhaled, releasing all the agitation that churned within me.

Unwelcome heat crept along my cheeks. How could I ever face my boss again after waking up in his arms, wearing nothing but a half-open robe? We'd agreed to stay apart. And now… Now, we'd woken up tangled up. In bed.

I undressed, praying the hot shower would quiet my racing thoughts before they erupted into a full-blown panic attack. The hot water soothed some of my frayed nerves and washed away most of the leftover traces of last night's fever.

Tiptoeing out of my room, dressed casually in a pair of lounge pants and a gray long-sleeved shirt, I approached the kitchen. Unsure about what to say, I rolled my bottom lip between my teeth, flicking my still-damp hair over my shoulder, trying to look unaffected. Sam's gaze found mine the instant I stepped into his peripheral vision. The intensity in his eyes pinned me to the spot, stealing the air from my lungs and the thoughts from my brain.

The words died on my tongue. Nerves gripped me. My heart shot up into my throat, and another wave of heat rolled over me. Was the fever coming back?

Even without being able to name it, I could tell something had shifted between Sam and me after waking up in his arms earlier.

The way our bodies fit together.

The zing of electricity that had sparked from him to me.

His tousled bed hair, lending him a boyish charm.

And his eyes—now I was certain—could read me, if I let him in.

"Feeling better? For real?" Sam asked as I poured myself a tall glass of orange juice and took a seat at the island.

"I think so."

"Hungry?"

"Famished. Something smells divine."

"Good. 'Cause I've made scrambled eggs. Want some?"

I nodded.

"Here," he said, pushing a plate in front of me. "I'm heading out to pick up the girls. Need anything before I go?"

I swallowed a mouthful of food. "No. All good."

"We are spending the day running errands. Just rest, okay?"

"You sure? I can take care of them if you have work to do. I'm not at the top of my game, but I'm feeling much better than I did yesterday, and I can deal with them."

"Nah. Take it easy."

I brought a forkful of eggs to my mouth but didn't take a bite. "About last night…huh…thank you. For everything." I paused and cringed. "Are we fine?"

Sam swiveled to face me. "I am if you are. It was a lack of judgment on my part. I'm sorry I put you in an embarrassing situation. Don't want you to think I-I took advantage. I shouldn't have—"

"You were there for me."

"Yeah…then… Okay. Yes. We're good."

Sam took off, leaving me all alone with my chaotic thoughts.

"What's wrong with you?" I chastised myself. "No matter how amazing the chemistry is between you two. Get. A. Grip. On. Yourself. Girl."

Caring and longing for someone were two very different things, and right now, thanks to yesterday's fever, I was mixing them both.

"Get your groove back on. You have a job to do." After I cleaned the kitchen, I wrapped myself in the pink fluffy blanket in the den and lay down on the couch, too weak to do anything but rest, as Sam had suggested.

I exhaled my annoyance.

Every time I tried to stay away from him and felt I was making progress, some incident pulled me right back to square one.

I breathed out the last remnants of mortification writhing in my lungs.

Adjusting myself, I sealed my eyelids and abandoned myself to sleep, praying it would make me forget all the awkwardness of the morning.

I sighed. All better now.

# Chapter 4

## Sam

In a rush to leave and before the weirdness between Madison and me returned, I exited the kitchen, climbing into my SUV minutes later. Turning the key in the ignition, I savored the fleeting sense of freedom. If last night had taught me one thing, it was that this woman had the power to ruin me if I didn't keep myself in check.

Alone in my car on my way to pick up the girls, I got lost in my own mind. Images I tried to keep at bay flashed in rapid succession, my brain refusing to grant me the reprieve I begged for. Madison, with her hair loose on her back, still damp from her shower, and her cheeks now a healthier shade of pink. When she'd entered the kitchen earlier, while I was prepping breakfast. Her sea-green irises that had drawn me in, the moment she had neared me.

How we had stared at each other for a fat minute, neither of us strong enough to escape the magnetism we always fell under.

My heart thundered in my chest at the memory, the sight alone strong enough to unleash all the locked-up lust simmering inside me.

I coughed to loosen my throat and rolled my neck, my blood flowing to my groin instead of my brain.

"Daddy," Justine screamed, tackling my legs before I could lift her up as she opened the door at Riley's, a craftsman house he bought a few years back. My friend slash manager had the means to live in the most upper-class neighborhoods of Nashville, but after growing up in one of those mansions, he said he preferred living a much simpler life. Again, it suited him.

Hope came running too, and I squatted to pet her head while she licked my bare knee just beneath the hem of my khaki shorts.

Wrapping my baby in my arms, I kissed her cheek. "How was the sleepover? Did you girls have fun? Have you been nice?"

"Daddy, we're always nice." She giggled when I tickled her belly after I stood back up and kicked the door shut.

"Stop worrying, Stevens," Riley chimed in, handing me a mug of hot caffeine. "Hungry? We baked croissants."

"No. Just had breakfast before coming over." I entered the kitchen. "Hey, sweet pea," I said, nearing Mikaella and ruffling her hair.

"Daddy. I'm not ready to go. I wanna stay here with Devon. We have plans. Girls' plans."

I scratched my nape. "I understand, but I have a whole day planned for us too."

"Is Maddie coming?"

"Nah. She's gonna rest a little longer. She's already doing better, though."

Mikaella pouted and pressed her fists to her hips. "I like it most when Maddie is there with us."

*Me too, Mika.*

I pinched the bridge of my nose. The plan was to stay away from Madison all day—not to invite her to spend her day off with us. "How do you feel about the children's museum?"

Her eyes lit up. "For real?"

"Yes. But if you wanna go, you better finish your breakfast and get ready."

Riley snickered beside me as she attacked her food.

Devon joined us, and after kissing me on the cheek, she sat next to my daughter.

My friend motioned for me to follow him and led the way to his home office. "You good?" he asked.

"Yeah. Why?"

"Just wanted to check on you and make sure you were holding on. It's been an intense couple of months, and I don't want you to have a panic attack because you feel overwhelmed."

"Everything's great. I swear."

He frowned and studied me, searching my face for the answer to a silent question. "How is it going with Madison? Do you think it'll work out on the road for that long? I sensed some tension between the two of you the other day."

The tension wasn't between us. It was between my legs. All my egoistical dick's fault.

I blew out my discomfort. "All good. No tension. The girls love her. She's amazing with them, and I trust her, so that's all I'm asking for."

My friend clapped my shoulder and grinned. "Enjoy your free time then because your life is about to get a bit wild again." His cheerfulness vanished. "Stevens, I'm glad we're doing this together. I really am."

"Yeah, me too. Thanks for getting me out of my sad existence. I owe you one."

For the rest of the day, the girls and I visited the children's museum. It was enough distraction to keep my thoughts in line for a few hours.

On our way back to our car, both my daughters' hands rested in mine while Mikaella kicked pebbles and dust on my right, and Justine sang a cartoon theme song on my left.

The late afternoon sun shone through the buildings, warming my face. Birds chirped in the trees lining the sidewalk. My daughters had lasting smiles on their faces.

Life was great, and about to get even better.

We spoke about everything and anything when Justine asked, "Do you think Maddie is missing us?"

My throat worked at the mention of my forbidden crush. My daughter stopped in her tracks, trying to catch my gaze, her eyes shining with expectation.

"Yeah, I'm sure she is."

"Cool," she said, resuming her walk. As if her question hadn't just fucked with my mind and willpower to forget about the nanny for the time being. She continued, her happy demeanor never faltering. "Because I miss her too. I really don't like it when Mama's sick. It makes me sad."

My heart flipped in my chest. Beads of sweat popped on my nape. My mouth went dry, and black dots danced in front of my eyes.

Before I could object or come up with a reply, Mikaella jumped in. "Maddie is not your mama, loser. She's your nanny. You already have a mama. And you can't have two. It's the rule."

I let go of Mikaella's hand to drag a palm over my face before turning toward her once I regained some of my composure back. "Mika, you can't talk to your sister like that. It's not nice. What did I already tell you about using grown-up language?"

Justine's eyes filled with tears.

My eldest daughter's face was flushed with indignation. "I'm right. Maddie isn't her mama."

Awesome. Perfectly awesome.

"No. You liar. I don't have a mama, and I want one. And I choose Maddie to be *my* mama. No one else. She's nice. And kisses my booboos. And reads to me at night. And she thinks I'm a princess. Maddie is *my* mama." Sobs rocked my baby's body, and she hid her teary face against my leg.

I crouched down to draw her to my heart. The one about to escape my chest and leave me to deal with this mess all by myself.

Words jammed in my throat, while Mikaella continued her rant. "Your mama's name is Lisa. Not Maddie. You're so dumb, Justine. Stop being a baby. You cannot have two mommies. Just one. One. And you're not allowed to choose."

Her words shook me to my core, and I came back to my senses, holding my hands up to put a stop to the argument. "Girls, stop. Justine is allowed to wish she had a mama. It's perfectly normal. And Mika, you're right, Maddie is not your mama." How would I ever deal with this? It was bound to happen at some point. Madison and I had crossed lines. We had changed the rules. Even without realizing it, my daughters sensed it. I blamed myself for all of it. Even I had a hard time keeping up with the situation. For now, I wished the girls and I could have had this discussion later—much later. When they were old enough to get it. To understand the hues and implications.

Leading my daughters to the nearest bench, I sat with them on either side, my arms curled around their shoulders. "Listen. I know you have questions about Lisa. I do too. But I'm not sure I have the answers you're both looking for. Justine, Maddie is not your mama. She's a nice woman helping us out and taking care of you. She loves you two very much, but Mika is right."

"But I want Maddie to be *my* mama," she sniffled, pressing her runny nose against the sleeve of my T-shirt this time.

I tightened my arm around her. "I know you do." I inhaled a cleansing breath. "And Mika, no more calling your sister names. Enough with that. It's not how we speak to each other in this family. Justine is four. It's all confusing to her. Even I am confused sometimes. It's okay if you are too."

"What *confused* means?"

I let out a low snicker. "It's when you don't know something because it seems a bit complicated. And a lot of grown-up things are confusing."

"Can I call Maddie *Mama*?" Justine asked, her cheeks drenched with tears, but her eyes filled with hope.

"Let's call her Maddie, okay? Can you do that?"

My youngest daughter bobbed her head and moving to her knees, hooked her arms around my neck. "I love you, Daddy."

I pulled Mikaella closer. "I love you, girls. Now let's go home and make some mac and cheese and have a picnic in your castle. Sounds good?"

They both cheered up, and our discussion was probably not forgotten, but put aside for now. When Lisa left, she had put the burden of dealing with her departure on my shoulders. She fucking quit on us and didn't even have to pick up the broken pieces she'd scattered behind.

From that night, I'd dreaded the moment I would have to explain her actions to our children. No, *my* children. She had lost the privilege to call them hers when she forfeited her parental rights.

With my heart heavy in my chest, I made it home, exhausted by all the things I had no control over.

———

"Okay, girls. Today we're decorating the tour bus. I bought supplies to make it ours. Uncle Riley is freaking out at the idea we're painting it pink, but I'm sure it will grow on him."

They both chuckled.

Mikaella, Justine, Madison, and I were all dressed in old shorts and shirts, ready to tackle our pre-assigned tasks.

"Justine and Maddie, you're in charge of the bunk room. You're painting all four walls in the bubblegum pink we picked up earlier. Tomorrow, the artist I hired will come and paint the giant unicorn mural, so it must be done by tonight. Are you up to the challenge?"

They both nodded, their fists resting on their hips, paintbrushes hanging from their fingers.

"What about us, Daddy?" Mikaella asked.

"Sweet pea, you and I, we're doing some construction work."

"With the big saw?"

"Yes. With the big saw. And a hammer. And all kinds of power tools. Do you think you can help me with this task?"

She nodded. "Yes, Daddy."

"Great. Let's start. And grandma sewed matching comforters for your beds. She'll send them over."

"YAY." Both girls screamed at the same time.

Madison and I exchanged a glance. Things were better between us. Even after the night we'd spent wrapped up in each other in her bed. Following my conversation with my daughters that day, I had drilled into my head once and for all that Madison and I were better as friends, our relationship less confusing to all of us. The sexual tension between us had decreased from a wildfire to a blaze. Still scorching but easier to control. It seemed like Madison had come to the same conclusion because she didn't stare at me the same way anymore.

Things were great and going according to plan.

"Teams," I called out. "Ready, set, go."

Madison lifted Justine in her arms, and they hurried inside the bus. The bunk room wasn't big by all means, but with personal touches and love, it would be perfect for the girls.

"Okay, sweet pea," I squatted to level my eyes with hers, "you and I will put together the new doll house I bought, and then we'll build a small bookshelf to put in your room and a ladder so you can climb on and off the top bed. We wouldn't want you to break your other wrist, would we?" I could have bought all this, but I thought it would be more fun to do it ourselves. I wanted the girls to feel at home on the bus, and doing all the prep work with them sounded like a good idea.

She giggled, and it warmed my heart. "No, Daddy."

She had a few days left of her—against all odds—powder-blue cast, and since she was right-handed, the fracture had barely stopped her. Armed with multicolor glitter and paint brushes, Madison had embellished her cast, transforming it into a piece of art. My kid definitely had the most fashionable broken wrist in town.

"Where will Maddie live, Daddy? Is she going to stay in your room?"

A tingle I hadn't felt in a while shot up my spine. I pushed the pang of excitement down and brought all my attention back to my daughter. "No, sweet pea. Maddie will have her own bunk."

"Will she sleep on our bus?"

"Yes, she will. Don't worry about her, okay?"

Mikaella was busy applying a coat of white paint to our DIY bookshelf when Madison and Justine joined us, wide smiles on their lips and splatters of pink paint on their clothes and skin.

"We're done, Daddy. It looks beautiful. Come see," my daughter said tugging at my hand.

I followed her inside. "Wow, you did all this?"

She bobbed her head. "And we painted Maddie's bunk too. She agreed."

Could Madison ever refuse anything to my kids? A tiny smile tugged at my lips at the thought.

"It looks fierce, baby. I love it. Come on, Mika is almost done. Let's get you clean up before your nap."

The tour bus was parked in our driveway, an idea Riley had, so the girls could get used to it. We had even planned on spending a few nights on it so they'd get comfortable in their new environment before the big day. My friend was doing everything in his power to make this tour the easiest possible transition for the girls, and I would never be able to thank him enough.

After a quick shower, I tucked the girls in and met Madison on the back deck with a bowl of tortilla chips and two beers. She accepted the offered drink.

"How did Justine convince you to paint your bunk pink?" I asked.

She smiled, the sight contagious. "Oh, she didn't have to do much. The girls must have worked some magic on me. I can't resist their charm. Be honest. Have you seen them doing some voodoo lately? I suspect they are little witches in disguise. They're the cutest. Justine was so excited when she offered that I couldn't refuse."

We clinked our bottles. "Welcome to the club. I hope I'll grow a spine by the time they turn sixteen, or I'll be in big trouble." I laughed, and she joined in.

"I can already see you getting gray hair just trying to keep up with them."

"It will be that frightful, huh?"

She bobbed her head. "Just wait and see."

The sound of her laughter warmed me up inside.

"I bet they'll team up against you. They remind me of Ems and me growing up. I'd want to be here to witness it with my own eyes. The Stevens girls are a handful when they put their minds to it. They follow in their daddy's footsteps. They're fearless…and own the biggest hearts."

As if she'd just heard her own words, and the meaning behind them, she turned her head, avoiding my eyes.

I was about to settle into my chair when I spotted a dab of pink paint below her earlobe. Wetting my thumb with my tongue, I rubbed the stain before I realized the intimacy of the gesture. Madison's breathing hitched, and I hissed a quivering gulp of air.

Her hand closed over mine, keeping it in place while she closed her eyes for the longest seconds of my life.

"Sorry, you had paint right there," I said, rambling the words out in order to explain my temporary lack of judgment.

She breathed out a whispered "Thanks."

If there were any lingering doubts in my mind, they weren't there anymore. I would die a starving man.

# Chapter 5
### Madison

The voices coming from the house brought me out of my slumber.

I blinked, trying to reboot my brain and remember where I was.

How long had I been out? By the sun hanging low in the sky, I bet it was late afternoon.

Which meant…ugh…I had slept in bright sunlight for hours.

Sliding my sunglasses up onto my head, I raised my arms to inspect the damage. My green-army shorts and black tank top did nothing to cover my bare skin.

My stomach tightened. I looked like a freaking lobster.

The skin of my arms was devil red.

Another fuck-up to add to my already long list.

Since I'd moved into this house, nothing was going as planned. How could Sam trust me to take care of the girls if I couldn't even take care of myself? How could he see me as a grown woman if I wasn't even smart enough to use sunblock? Right now, I resembled a teenage girl on spring break who thought she was too cool for shade and sunscreen.

Today was my day off, and after Sam and the girls had left early this morning to spend the day at a family friend's farm, I'd decided to read on the back deck. Never did I think I'd fall asleep in the sun.

My hands flew to my cheeks, and the warmth of my skin told me everything I needed to know.

The back door slid open before I could cover up.

"Here, you are," Sam said in his rough southern drawl as he stepped outside.

Just the sound of his voice was enough to send a flight of butterflies to my belly. Damn it. *Get a grip on yourself, Maddie.* Could my resolve—not to lust after him and to keep my sanity—hold up when I needed it most?

I folded my legs and wrapped my arms around my bent knees, resting my chin on them as Sam took a seat in the lounge chair next to mine, stretching his long legs. At that moment, even his calves looked fabulous.

Stupid misplaced infatuation.

"The girls are looking for you. I told them it's your day off, but according to this"—his attention drifted to his watch—"we have about two minutes before they come barreling here." His eyes landed on mine for the first time, and I offered him a *I'm sorry* smile as his gaze trailed over the length of me, taking in the sunburn. "Shit, Maddie. Did you use sunscreen?"

I shook my head slowly, using all the strength I possessed to hold his gaze.

He swung his legs over the edge of the chair and leaned forward.

One of his hands landed on my knee, and the other

cradled my face, his thumb tracing the ridge under my lips. His eyes translated every word his mouth refused to speak out loud. My fascination with him multiplied. Sam Stevens was made of so many layers, I had still to uncover them all. He jerked away the hand cupping my face, as if the warmth of my skin had burned his palm. In a slow movement, he leaned forward, his cheek barely grazing mine, his stubble rough against my sensitive flesh. Shivers zigzagged along my back.

I gasped.

He growled.

Could he hear my raging heartbeat?

I fisted his shirt, my head spinning, as the scent of him invaded my nose, my body requiring his sturdiness to avoid falling over the edge. Our breaths mingled.

Time slowed.

"I don't like you hurting," he whispered.

"I never meant to fall asleep."

The jolt of his touch on my knee went straight to my center, and I moved my leg to the side to escape it.

Sam lifted his palm and rubbed it on the fabric of his black athletic shorts after adjusting his white T-shirt. "Sorry." His Adam's apple bobbled, and he glared into the distance before bringing his eyes back to me. "You've got to treat those, or you'll be in a lot of pain over the next few days. Do you have any after-sun lotion or aloe?"

"No," I said. "I'll go buy some." My weak voice didn't sound like mine.

"Don't be silly. I'll go. Take a cold shower while I'm gone." He moved to his feet and half-spun around to study me, his fists clenched beside him. The muscle of his jaw flexed. His eyes darkened. "What were you thinking sleeping in direct sunlight?" His tone had turned harsh. Why was he even mad? First, I hadn't done it on purpose.

I'd come out here to relax, not to get second-degree burns. Second, I'd hurt myself and no one else. "Anyway. Go shower. I'll be back." He yanked the door open, his stride long and heavy, his feet pounding on the hardwood floor. "Girls, get in the car. We're leaving." I heard some protests, but the door closed, and it drowned their words. I stood there, on the back deck, chills from my overdose of sun exposure running through me.

The front door slammed shut, and the house vibrated.

Why was Sam upset with me? We'd shared a moment. Again. He was genuinely concerned. I could tell. And then he turned ice-cold.

Feeling skittish, I rushed to my room, undressed, and locked myself in the bathroom, the cold jets of the shower cooling my cooked flesh. The water eased some of the burning sensations.

I got out, a towel wrapped around me, just in time to hear a knock on my bedroom door.

Justine stood on the other side, a tube in her hand.

"Hey, what do we have here?"

She handed me the lotion. "It's for you. Daddy said you gotta use this." She gasped. "Why is your skin red? Are you sick? Do you want soup? Daddy always makes me *chickling* soup when I'm sick."

A smile tugged at my lips. "Chicken soup, you mean."

"*Yesss. Chickling* soup. Mika's favorite. I'll ask Daddy to make it."

I shook my head. "No. Your offer sounds nice, but I'm okay." *And I wouldn't want to bother your father. He seems overly annoyed with me today.*

"Come with me," she said, pulling at my hand.

"Just a minute. I'll get dressed."

"No time. I wanna show you what Daddy got for you."

"For me?"

She nodded, her smile reaching both ears. "Yes. Come, it's a surprise."

With my other hand holding the towel firmly around my naked self, I followed her to the dining room.

On the wooden table, big enough to seat ten people, were a dozen different after-sun gels and creams.

"Whoa," I said, struggling to put my shock into words.

"Daddy said you can have them all because you have bad, bad, bad *sunbrunes*."

"Sunburns, sweetie."

She flipped her hand in the air like I was being silly.

I scanned the bottles, feeling a flush ascending my face. As if it could get any redder.

"I'll try this one," I said, picking an aloe-based gel.

"No. They're all yours. I chose the one in the pretty pink bottle. Because I like pink. And unicorns like pink too. What's your favorite color?"

I let out a snicker. "Pink is great. I love yellow too."

"Cool. Wanna play with me and Mika?"

"Sure. I'll meet you guys in about ten minutes."

"Mika is in the castle outside."

"I'll find you when I'm done here."

Justine traipsed away, a large smile brightening her face and her eyes full of sparks.

I started toward my bedroom when I noticed Sam frozen in the den's archway. Tight jaw. Flared nose. Dilated pupils. Firmed shoulders. He looked both intimidating and alluring. This version of him played with every thread of my control. He watched me. No, he undressed me with his eyes from afar. My towel could catch fire at any moment, so I tightened my grip around its edge. He said nothing and walked past me, leaving a whiff of his cologne in its wake, warning Justine not to climb on the kitchen stool by herself.

I had never felt more naked than I did right now.

In the bathroom, still shaky from the hot encounter that had me squeezing my thighs together, I avoided looking at myself in the mirror as I applied one of the cooling gels to my sensitive flesh. Shivers moved from my head to my toes, the ache slowly settling in.

After I dressed in a loose cotton shirt and lounge pants, I gathered my clothes and towel and carried them to the laundry room at the end of the hallway.

I sucked in a quick breath, and my heart fluttered as I walked in.

Bare-chested and giving me a frontal row view of his muscled abs, Sam stood there, his black T-shirt hanging from one hand.

His expression darkened, a wrinkle forming across his forehead. From up close, he looked even more daunting due to his broodiness and the six inches he had over me, but also more handsome—and lethal—to me.

"Sorry," I said, glancing down, trying to get away from his spell. "I-I should have knocked. I didn't mean to… It wasn't… I was…"

I closed my eyes with a sigh and spun on the balls of my feet, ready to bolt. A powerful hand circled my wrist, holding me in place.

With a grimace, I tilted my head back.

Sam stared right at me. The strength of his gaze punctured holes through my blazing epidermis. "Stop apologizing, Maddie." His voice had roughened up. Again, why was my name so sexy every time it rolled off his tongue? "Justine dropped her juice all over me, and I had to change my shirt."

Could I conceal all the sensations dancing inside me if I tried hard enough?

Of their own accord, my eyes traveled down his corded

forearms to the V leading into his pants. If I didn't get a grip on myself, I'd soon be drooling. I'd never ogled a man like this before, without an ounce of shame.

Whatever I told myself, I couldn't look elsewhere. My tongue darted out to lick my lips. The lines weren't blurry anymore, they had vanished.

"Are you okay?" Sam's voice brought me back to the present moment.

Was I still eating him up with my eyes while I was lost in my thoughts?

"I…I told Justine I'd play outside with her and Mika, but if it's fine with you, I'd take a nap instead. I-I feel lightheaded."

He talked gibberish.

"What?" I asked, blinking.

"Nothing."

"Are you sure?"

"Sure. I'll be out of town tomorrow. Hopefully, you'll feel better by morning. I'll come get you when dinner's ready."

We fixated on each other for another beat, way too long for my sanity, neither of us saying anything else.

Sam cleared his throat.

I blinked, trying to evade the enchantment.

"Thanks for…huh…the after-sun collection you got me. You didn't have… You didn't have to go into that much trouble. One would have been enough."

He cocked his head, looking so devastatingly handsome it almost hurt not to be able to do anything about it. "I had no idea what you usually use and what works. I didn't want to take any chances."

His tongue flicked across his full lower lip. Had he done it on purpose, or were my hormones out of control?

"Anyway, thanks. I'm sure my skin will get better soon."

Sam released his grip on my wrist, and I rushed to my bedroom, closed the door, and leaned against it until my breaths evened out.

With a heavy sigh, I fell face first on the mattress, wishing I could go back two days in time.

Whatever I did to enrage him, this angry side of my boss had never looked so dangerous.

So intoxicating.

To me—and to my body.

# Chapter 6



The night had been a series of tossing and turning. Around two o'clock, still wide awake, I went downstairs. A golden glow illuminated the kitchen, making me curious. Instead of sauntering to my music studio like I'd meant to, I ended up staring at Madison's ass clothed in night shorts while she rummaged through the refrigerator, bent forward and offering me a perfect view.

As if she could sense me lurking behind in the shadows, she closed the door and whirled around until we faced each other, handing me a bottle of water. Her eyes bore into mine, and the air between us tightened.

Hair stood on end on my arms.

Invisible magnets pulled us forward. We both took a step toward each other. The semi-darkness did nothing to conceal the delicious curves of her body or the gleam in her eyes.

I uncapped the lid and downed the cold liquid in one gulp, my gaze never drifting from the woman standing before me. She followed each undulation of my throat, her facial expressions doing nothing to hide the thirst in her eyes, the desire overpowering. Madison Prescott was the reason behind my endless nights and of my mind going haywire. That no-sunscreen stunt she had pulled earlier had sent a pang of panic through me. Her flesh would hurt. She'd need care. And I wasn't allowed to be the one providing it.

Wrath boiled in my blood just thinking about it.

Tired and upset, I refused to be a gentleman and molded my hand to her waist, while I erased the gap keeping us apart. Her breath whistled on its way in. She parted her lips and splayed her palms across my heart, the pounding impossible for her to miss. I trailed the fingers of my other hand down the length of her bare arm. She shivered. My dick got harder. A moan crossed the cusp of her luscious mouth. A guttural groan left mine. I had turned into a starving animal that had been refused its favorite meal—and I was fucking famished.

Another step forward.

I backed her against the refrigerator.

I cupped her chin, leaning in so my mouth hovered near her ear.

Tremors worked through her.

Goose bumps blossomed under my fingers as my hand met the bare stretch of her stomach—the tiny strip her tank top couldn't conceal. The one about to drive me absolutely insane. Or push me past the line I'd been careful not to cross so far.

My thumb lingered over her juicy lips.

I pushed myself further into her space and smelled the faint perfume of the after-sun lotion she had put on.

In that instant, I hoped she could catch the scent of my rising desire, because I doubted it was concealed anymore.

"I'm fucking starving right now, Maddie. And I'm fucking furious with you. It's not a good mix. I can't decide if I wanna punish you right here on this countertop or hold and kiss you until that sunburn heals."

With her devilish lips, she sucked my thumb into her mouth, the vision so hot my dick grew a couple of inches in my pants, begging to be freed. Madison twirled her tongue around the tip, nibbling he flesh with her teeth. Oh, how much would I pay to have her reward my hard-on in a similar fashion? Sweat crawled along my spine. She never looked away, even when a loud moan straight from the depths of her broke the tensed silence.

The rise and fall of her chest hastened.

"You're playing a very dangerous game," I said, barely holding it together, breathless and affected in a dozen different ways. I lacked the words to describe the overwhelming sensations pulsing within me.

Madison released my finger with one last swirl of her tongue, and I thought I would combust.

She edged away and escaped the cage of my arms. With her bottle in hand, she retreated to her bedroom without a word, pausing only once to glance at me over her shoulder.

The gears of my brain, already spinning at high speed, ground to a halt at the sight. Was it an invitation to follow her or a warning to stay away? I couldn't tell, my common sense long gone.

With that simple gesture, she had reversed the roles. She was now in charge. She was the hunter, and I was the prey, a role I had no idea how to navigate, or resist.

With my forehead pressed against the refrigerator door, I slid a hand under the waistband of my pants to offer my dick the attention he was throbbing for. I couldn't think clearly anymore. What was I supposed to do?

I shut my eyes and cursed at myself.

I'd almost bent Madison over the island and got my way with her. Picturing myself ramming into her with abandon so we could move forward once and for all, and I would stop imagining the taste and feel of her every time I found myself alone with nothing but my thoughts to keep me company.

My heart pumped too much blood.

Each inhale burned the lining of my throat. I was done lying to myself and becoming more miserable with every passing day.

Minutes ago, Madison had showed me just how much she lusted for me too, not hiding behind pretenses and fake excuses this time. She'd flashed her desire right into my face, without even breaking eye contact. Fuck, that was hot. She was far braver than I was. And a lot bolder.

It was a very dangerous game she had started, probably aware I'd have a hard time resisting. And that I would never leave unfinished.

Desperate to put to rest our suffering, I padded toward her bedroom.

My fist floated inches from the door, ready to knock and kill that arousal paralyzing both of us, when I heard a muffled cry coming from inside the room. Pressing my ear to the wooden panel, I listened, unsure if I'd imagined it. Another cry, more audible this time, resonated from the other side. Oh, geez, I would die tonight. That was how I'd leave the Earth. With her gasps echoing in my mind. And my erection standing tall and proud, stiff as a flagpole.

My hand returned to my crotch, my dick relishing the idea the woman we were both obsessed with was plea-suring herself after a heated encounter with us.

"Fuck," I muttered through clenched teeth as I rubbed myself to the sounds of her shallow whimpers.

This was wrong. I had become a man I didn't recognize. I couldn't ever name all the ways my actions were wicked.

Madison's eyes, when she'd glanced at me over her shoulder minutes ago, weren't issuing an invitation or a warning, but a challenge. A dare. I'd walked straight into her trap. I had struck the match and set myself on fire.

She had won—big time—and by doing so, she owned me a lot more.

Feeling like a voyeur, or whatever listening to things I shouldn't through a closed door made me, I let go of my erection. A low curse passed my lips. I braced my shoulders, walked away, and locked myself in my music studio, desperate to find another outlet to the blaze searing within me. Since jerking off thinking about the nanny had revealed itself to be a fucking mistake in the past, I used music as my escape this time.

Much better. And much safer.

No way I was risking my sanity, or my dick—or any other part of my body—to release the tension coiling inside me.

I went back to bed around four and slept for about—I picked up my phone on the nightstand to check the time— an hour. I blinked. Could it really only be five in the morning? I was screwed. I was so screwed, I didn't even have words to describe how lame I'd become lately. My middle-of-the-night lack of judgment had proved it.

Restless, I swung my legs over the edge of the bed. No need to prolong the inevitable any longer. Getting up now would give me more time to jumpstart my day and prep breakfast. Or maybe I could go for a run. Clear my head. Get rid of the angst or whatever cocktail was simmering inside me even hours later. It'd been a long time since I'd jogged around the neighborhood to release crippling tension in me. Yeah, I should put on my runners and exercise until both my body and my brain surrendered.

With my fingers, I rubbed the sleep off my eyes and got up.

The first pink and orange streaks over my backyard treetops greeted me as I drew back the drapes, filling me with hope for the new day.

Tonight, I had a concert scheduled in Charlotte and another one in Atlanta tomorrow. The first few to warm up, test the set list, and make some tweaks before leaving for the tour.

Jitters had taken over my stomach since yesterday, at the realization that it was real and there was no turning back.

The thought of leaving the girls for two days and being back onstage for a full concert rattled my nerves—one part of me anxious, the other brimming with a thrill nothing else could match.

Dressed in cotton pants, a gray Henley, and a Carter Hills Band vintage black hoodie, I tiptoed down the hallway and checked on the girls as I passed their room. They were both deep asleep, tucked under their comforters, looking peaceful, the sound of their steady breathing enough to calm me down, or at least ease a little of the tension still gripping me.

In the kitchen, I made myself a coffee, cursing at the coffeemaker when it made grumbling sounds—something I'd been doing a lot since my little escapade downstairs in the middle of the night. I had to keep quiet. Madison waking up right now and being all adorable and sexy at this early hour would do me no good in my present state of mind, especially now that I felt vulnerable and angsty, and my testosterone had been spiking a little too much these past few days.

Asking her to move in had been both the stupidest and smartest decision I'd made since she entered our lives.

Last night's events replayed in my head, and to be honest, I had almost given in without a second thought. What Madison had done was hot as hell and had completely unraveled my composure on a whole new level. She hadn't been ashamed, and she had shown me exactly what I was missing with that little session she'd indulged in behind closed doors afterward. It would forever be etched in my memory. Her cries. Her moans. My blood bubbled like lava at the reminder.

The sane part of me wished we'd met under different circumstances so we could figure out our relationship—and the arousal reverberating between us. If she weren't working for me, this impossible-to-ignore craving between us wouldn't feel so inappropriate, would it? If that were the case, would I still feel like being with her meant stealing her youth? Yes, her age would stay the same. She was barely in her twenties. I could never ask her to skip a decade of experiences and fun times to play mommy to my daughters. Everything about the idea of being together felt wrong, even though, deep down, it felt awfully right. This was an impossible situation, one my hormones, my heart, and my head couldn't settle on. A part of me wanted to fuck her out of my system, another craved to make her mine and hold on to her, and the third knew both of the others were wrong.

With a coffee mug in my hand, I grabbed a stack of documents Riley had asked me to read, that I'd discarded on the counter yesterday, and made my way to the back deck. An hour or two of peace, witnessing the awakening of a new day should ease my annoyed self. It usually did the trick.

Just when I was about to take a sip, I halted, stumbling over my own feet, the scorching liquid almost spilling all over me when I lowered the mug in a jerky movement.

Every lingering residue of sleep left me.

My heart bounced in my throat.

I exhaled, trying to dull the new surge of fire coursing in my veins. The tension between my legs. The thunderous hammering of my heart.

Was life playing with my flimsy willpower on purpose? Was it all a test?

Despite myself, my eyes were drawn to her sculpted thighs and plump ass in those purple spandex leggings, the toned skin of her midsection, the curves of her waist, the swell of her boobs peeking from the top of the sports bra.

Bent over on the mat spread across the deck, her hands and feet planted as her hips lifted toward the sky, Madison looked breathtaking in the morning light—and sexy. And too dangerous to be in this house. In my house. Around my sex-deprived self.

My sleep-deprived brain couldn't deal with so much exposed flesh and temptations at this early hour in the morning.

Oblivious to the fact that I was watching her through the glass pane, she switched from one yoga pose to another. Her face, arms, and feet—still red from the sunburn—already looked better than they had yesterday.

Deep breath in. Deep breath out. I would rupture at the seams, and nobody was prepared for the devastation that would ensue.

My dick sprang wood. No blood irrigated my brain anymore. Many forbidden thoughts tempted me, no matter how hard I tried to lock them away. I was dizzy, barely able to stand on my own two feet.

Once I regained some composure and adjusted the crotch of my pants, I pushed some of my annoyance down and yanked the back door open.

The desire coursing through me turned to wrath. Yeah, this was the only way I could make this work. Be angry instead of a lustful mess.

All the images haunting me came back with a vengeance. Pushing Madison against the wall and punishing her with my cock for looking so young and innocent—and too fucking appealing—and finishing what we'd started mere hours ago.

My anger escalated. The images intensified instead of receding. My imagination ran wild.

If I had my way with her, I would ram into her from behind, spread her legs with my knee to get the perfect angle, and then I'd lower her to *her* knees and let her suck every last drop of cum from me until we both got it out of our systems and we rode a wave of bliss neither of us was ready to come down from.

I'd seen it in her eyes when she bumped into me in the laundry room yesterday, and again during our encounter against the refrigerator door. She was lusting for me as much as I was craving her. Yesterday, she couldn't run away fast enough from me after she bumped into me while I was bare-chested, panting, after ogling me like she was starving. Then she had closed her eyes—yep, she shut them—too weak to face me, with unmasked arousal straining her features. And then later, she had fucking sucked my thumb as if it were my dick. She knew what she was doing when she did it. She was aware it would mess with every string of my composure. She couldn't hide the glint in her eyes when she'd aimed her challenge-filled stare at me over her shoulder. Gone was the nice woman I had gotten to know in that instant. Madison had become a temptress testing my limits. And she won. She mastered that little game between us.

I had to take back the control, or it would end badly. For the both of us. We had said we wouldn't cross the set boundaries, and I was adamant about keeping my end of the deal.

As I got closer to her, my annoyance increased a couple of notches. I couldn't contain it. I had to explode, one way or another, no matter the form. So, I chose the less damaging for both of us.

Now on all fours, one leg bent at a ninety-degree angle behind her, and one stretched fully in a straight line, show-casing the curve of her ass, Madison turned her head to face me as I stepped next to her.

"What are you doing up at this hour?" I asked, my voice laced with fury I couldn't pinpoint the source of, other than my raging hard-on. She blinked, and I lowered my voice, my words still clipped. "It's too early to be doing…to be doing whatever you're doing dressed like this."

I gestured to the length of her, and she sat on her ankles, her eyes wide and full of questions. "It's my morning routine. I get up at five, three times a week."

The pink flush on her face turned a shade darker.

I put my mug and papers down, and tugging at the back of my hoodie, I pulled it over my head and threw it at her. "Wear this."

Madison's lips parted, and she murdered me with her gaze. "Are you serious?"

I crossed my arms over my chest and tipped my chin up. "Do I look like I'm joking? You can't wear these clothes. It's just…well…inappropriate."

"Pardon me?" She scowled at me, no other sound coming from her.

We both engaged in a staring contest, neither of us ready to back down—to accept defeat.

After a moment, with a glower that turned her eyes into weapons, she slid her arms into the sleeves and stood to her feet, her eyes still zeroed in on me. Too big on her, my hoodie ended just above her knees.

Something in me clamped tight.

She was supposed to look less tempting wearing more clothes. Instead, she looked even more attractive with my hoodie on.

This. Wasn't. Supposed. To. Happen.

Her long dark ponytail swept over her shoulders.

The muscle of my jaw ticked, and I clenched it until my teeth hurt.

"Happy now?" She folded her arms across her chest, mimicking my stance. "When I signed up for this job, I don't recall the contract saying anything about being treated like a child or getting a second father figure in the process."

My irritation toward her seared. She hadn't gone there, had she?

My lips pursed, but I couldn't find the words to express my ire or my thirst because, at this point, there were hard to untangle, both heating up my blood and other parts of my body and taking over me.

"Stop being a brat. I'm not your father. These thoughts I have about you are not father-daughter like, I swear. You should be aware by now."

Madison yelped, her lips parting, so ready to be kissed. Or fucked.

*No, man. Stop. Enough.*

She stared at me, her pink lips pursed, ready to speak.

*There. Better.*

"Then stop acting like you are." Her tone imitated mine now. Edgy and full of sass behind the laced-with-hunger annoyance. "You're not allowed to dictate how I should dress. And you have no right to barge out here and get mad at me when I'm off the clock. When I agreed to move in here, you promised I'd have my own space. Right now, your acting out is in contradiction to your own words. You've asked me if I trusted you before. I did. I still do. But this…this invasion of my private time is unacceptable." She ended her rant with a tip of her chin, defiant and even more alluring as she didn't back down from the fight *I* started.

My anger reached new heights.

Madison took a stand before me, and I fought with myself not to shut her up with a kiss—or a swirl of my tongue all over her soft flesh. The apex of her thighs. Or those perky nipples that were pointing at me through the fabric of her bra minutes ago.

"Commenting on my appearance is a new low for you. Better think about it twice next time before chastising me with undeserved criticism."

"Well, if you wear such little clothing in September, what do you even wear in July?" She opened her mouth, but I continued. "Don't answer. I don't wanna know. Anyway, I…I already do. Gosh, Maddie, you can't parade in spandex and think I'd be cool with that. It's distracting. *You're* distracting. Not that you can't wear what pleases you, I agree…but…" I shook my head in defeat. "No but… This whole situation is unbearable." I closed my eyes and exhaled the air screwing with all my brain cells. "Now get dressed before you catch a cold."

A cold? Was I being stupid on purpose? Damn it. A cold. Now I really sounded like a dumb teenager's father.

The urge to facepalm myself itched my arm. Instead, I stood my ground in front of the woman wrecking my world.

Right about now, I had no clue how to control this hormonal storm invading me, and I readied myself for the disaster waiting to happen. When had I transformed into this pathetic version of myself?

I used to be fun. And I loved to party and have a good time. Drink, dance all night, make love under the stars, come up with new and exciting plans, be optimistic, and dream big.

Fucking Lisa.

How long was I going to blame her for everything bad happening in my life? How long could I fault myself because she had abandoned me? My forbidden crush on Madison had nothing to do with my ex-wife. Except for the fact that I wouldn't be standing here in this aroused state I could do nothing about if she hadn't walked out on us.

Would we still be happily married if she hadn't left, though? No.

Because the attraction I'd felt for Lisa never even neared the one I felt for the girl standing in front of me. One day, it would have caught up with us. She had just accelerated the process—in the most heartless and worst possible manner.

This one, right here, was on me.

The impulsive side of me had just confirmed to my kids' nanny, in not so many words, all about the nasty things I wished to do to her. Not only had I spoken them, but I had thought them too. Been thinking them for months.

A feeling I'd never experienced before adhered to my heart. It made me feel small. Without another glance at her, I pivoted around and vanished inside, leaving a flab-bergasted Madison behind.

Now I would have to burn my hoodie because I bet the scent of her would forever cling to the fibers.

At seven, I woke the girls up, looking forward to the distraction they'd bring.

I lifted them both in my arms and carried them down-stairs, pretending to be a big bad wolf about to take them to my secret lair.

"Did you make breakfast?" Mikaella asked, her eyes half-mast from sleep and her curls tangled into a nest at the back of her head.

"It smells *gooood*," Justine sang, looping her arms around my neck and kissing my cheek.

"I did." I plopped them onto stools around the kitchen island.

"Where's Maddie?" Mikaella asked.

"I'll get her," Justine said, climbing off her seat and running toward the guest bedroom before I could call out her name.

"Wait for me," Mikaella said, running after her sister.

With my elbows on the countertop, I rubbed my palms over my face in defeat.

After I'd argued with Madison about her poor choice of clothes earlier, she returned to her bedroom and hadn't yet come out. I already feared she would parade in a tiny bikini just to disturb my mind even more—and to prove a point. That she was unattainable, to someone like me—especially to someone like me. A single dad with young children trying to resuscitate his dead music career with an attempt to tour the country. Not the perfect match for a beautiful, barely adult woman with dreams of her own and her whole life in front of her.

With my newfound caveman attitude and Madison moving in, my stupidity level around her had multiplied by ten. I had lost my mind, and I kept rolling, piling up mishaps. Starting with kissing her, sleeping in her bed, and spilling my dirty thoughts.

Everything she did or said pushed a button inside me. It messed with me. She wasn't the problem, though. None of it was her fault. I blamed the tour. It got me anxious. It would all go back to normal once I found my footing again. Or maybe I could blame Riley. For putting all these silly ideas in my head and placing Madison on my path.

Two minutes later, the girls returned, tugging at Madison's hands.

"Sit beside me," Justine said.

"No. Maddie is sitting next to me," Mikaella argued.

A wide smile lightened up Madison's face. "I'll sit in the middle. That way, you'll both be by my side."

Justine hopped around with a contagious grin.

"Who's gonna sit next to me then?" I asked, arching one brow, my eyes traveling between my daughters.

"Me." My baby girl raised her hand. "I'll sit beside you too, Daddy."

I moved one seat to my left to let the three of them sit beside one another.

The conversation flew easily, but an invisible wall had risen around Madison and me.

She had changed into dark jeans and a white tank top. Madison wearing something of mine earlier had mattered to me, and I kinda missed the vision of her dressed in my hoodie. I wouldn't object if it were all she ever wore from now on. My thoughts were conflicted. Desire tangling with reality had become a big web around my sanity I had no clue how to escape. With a heavy sigh, I made conversation with my children instead of entertaining the images playing in my head.

"Girls, Daddy is going away for two nights… Just like we discussed. Maddie will stay here with you."

"Is she gonna sleep in your bed?" Mikaella asked.

My eyebrows shot to my hairline. "What? No. She'll sleep in her own room."

"But I'm scared. I want Maddie to sleep upstairs. Next to our room," Justine said, her lips quivering, the corners of her eyes filling with tears. "What if I have a *nightlemare?*"

"Nightmare, baby," I said. "It's gonna be okay. Maddie will hear you if you wake up in the middle of the night. I found the baby monitors in a box in the garage. We'll set them up. Together."

Tears drenched my little girl's face. "No. I want Mama to sleep upstairs. With us."

Air frizzled in the kitchen.

The room fell silent.

We could only hear Justine's sobs. And my deafening heartbeats.

I closed my eyes, trying to come out with a smart reply. We already had this conversation, Justine and I, and I believed she understood.

"She's not your mama, dummy," Mikaella said, igniting the already explosive situation.

"Mika. Where did you learn all these words from? For the umpteenth time, be nice to your sister. And stop using this language."

"Whatever. Justine always wants Maddie to be her mama. It's stupid." She lowered her head. "We have a mama. Her name is Lisa."

I cursed a couple more saints under my breath. At this pace, by the end of the tour, I'd know all their names.

Why did Justine have to open that door right now? This morning, of all days?

Before a well-scripted answer could pass my lips, Madison jumped in.

The first few words left her mouth and carried away the fears swirling inside me. "Sweetie, I can't sleep in your Daddy's room because I have my own room. And Mika is right. I'm not your mama. I'm sorry yours isn't here, but I can't be her. I can be your nanny, your teacher, and your friend. I can play many roles, but not your mama's, okay? Do you understand?"

Justine threw a fit, kicking her stool and thumping her tiny fists on the counter. I'd never seen her acting out like this.

My damaged heart plummeted down my chest at a dizzying pace.

"I don't want Lisa. She's not my mama. I don't love her. She's mean. I want Maddie. I love Maddie. Maddie is *my* mama. Just Maddie."

I sprang to my feet and wrapped my arms around my daughter. "Shhh, baby. Shhh, it's okay. It's okay to be upset. Shhh." I pulled her against my heart as it fractured into more pieces inside my chest. My face rested against her head, her body shaking in my embrace.

Sitting on the floor, I rocked her back and forth, wishing I possessed special powers to repair my child's wounds.

One look at my watch told me I had one hour left before Riley picked me up.

With my thumb, I wiped the tears cascading down her cheeks. "It's okay. You're allowed to be upset. I was too for a moment. Fine, lots of moments. But it'll be all right. I promise."

I rocked my baby until the fight left her, not turning in Madison's direction the entire time, avoiding the look in her eyes. Or maybe because, in that instant, I wished she was the one healing my bruised organ.

Once the air cleared, I tried again. "Let's go and set those monitors up and see how they work." With Justine in my arms and Mikaella attached to my hand, we grabbed the devices from the garage.

For the next half-hour, the girls and I talked to one another from across the house after we plugged them in. Once they were appeased, I gathered my suitcase and guitar and everything I needed for the next two days.

"Here," I said, placing the keys to my SUV in Madison's hand.

Her eyes rounded. "Why? I already own a car."

"Yeah, but I'll be more at ease if you use mine. Anyway, the girls' car seats are in there. Take it. I don't know why I didn't think of buying you a new one, to begin with."

She closed her fist around my keyset. "It's not necessary, but it's nice of you. Thanks," she said in a strangled voice that peppered goose bumps down my back.

A strand of hair fell across her forehead, and I fought with myself the urge to push it away. Restlessness clamped my shoulders as we stood closer than we had in a long time —if you didn't count last night's refrigerator clusterfuck.

After a second, she brushed the tendril away herself.

"If you need anything, call me, okay?"

"We'll be fine, Sam. I've spent the last few months caring for Mika and Justine. I know everything there is to know. Don't worry. Do what you have to do, and don't let your mind run wild."

"Listen, about earlier"—I had no idea how to deal with the whole mama-thing situation Justine had thrown at us,

as if Madison required more reasons to bail on me—
"thanks for jumping in. I've been having this conversation with Justine a few times already, but for some reason, she has decided that my explanations aren't satisfying enough. I'll talk to her again when I get back."

The same strand of hair that Madison had pushed away seconds ago, fell over her eyes once more. This time I didn't think before I combed it aside, shaping my palm to her cheek.

Electricity, powerful and sizzling, traveled from her visage to my hand. Hair stood on end on my arms. I breathed, but my airways had gone on strike.

The temperature of the room skyrocketed.

Our gazes melded together, and everything around me stopped. She pressed her cheek into my palm.

With a strangled voice, I added, "I'm sorry. For this morning. I was out of line. And an idiot."

"Which part?" she asked.

I licked my lips to return moisture to my mouth. "All of it."

Justine ran our way and snaked herself around my leg, interrupting us. This kid had a skewered sense of timing. "Daddy," she singsonged.

I released Madison's face and dropped my hand at my side to pet her hair, and the suffocating tightness between Madison and me evaporated.

I swallowed hard.

"Come here, baby," I said, lifting her up and perching her on my shoulders. "Uncle Riley will be here soon. Let's wait for him outside." I angled my body to face the woman it hurt to leave behind.

We locked eyes. There were so many truths I hoped I could tell her.

Instead, I said, "Call me. For whatever reason. I'll be back in two days."

"Don't worry."

She waved at me, avoiding my stare as I walked away, a rock replacing my dying heart and my heels heavy as concrete.

# Chapter 7
## Madison

Sam had left about four hours ago, and already I was a living bundle of nerves. It didn't help that he called twice to make sure I had no questions or missed anything. Both times, I'd heard the anxiety lacing his voice, and it had sent a fresh batch of jitters to my stomach. I knew tonight was a big deal for him. Even bigger than his album launch. And even though my place was here, taking care of Justine and Mikaella, a big part of me wished I could stand tall by his side. Holding his hand and whispering in his ear that I believed in him and everything would be all right. That he got this. But all those scenarios were just fragments of my overactive imagination.

The girls and I had prepared a surprise for him. Something I'd planned with Riley to ensure the first show after his long hiatus would be epic. To make it super special. Unforgettable.

Now that the girls were napping, I busied myself with folding laundry and sorting tiny pairs of socks. When that didn't work to distract me, I sat with a novel on the back deck, away from any direct sunlight, and lost myself in the pages.

The rest of the day passed in a blur.

We called Sam on video chat after dinner, and I put the girls to bed soon after since they kept arguing about anything and everything. They too could sense the anticipation permeating the air.

Sitting in my favorite chair in the den with the novel I'd started earlier, I tried to keep myself busy and prevent my thoughts from wandering to uncharted territory—Sam's territory. Unable to get engrossed in the story this time, I opened the messaging app on my phone, a tug-of-war rising inside me over whether or not I should wish him good luck for his big show.

Even after convincing myself it was cringe-worthy, I still did it.

ME

Enjoy tonight.

He answered seconds later. A part of me wished he was wrestling with the same question on his end—whether or not to contact me.

SAM

Thank you. How are the girls? I felt the excitement earlier when we talked.

ME

Deep asleep.

Couldn't stay put for more than a minute.

They asked me to tell you they were proud of you.

...

For what it's worth, I am too. It's something amazing you're teaching them. To get back out there. Even if they don't realize it yet.

SAM

Thanks.

I hate being far away from them, though. It's hard. And it's just been a few hours.

ME

They're happier when you ARE happy. Want my honest opinion?

I sank lower in my seat, loving how easily our conversation flowed, now that we didn't have to face each other —or deal with the burning desire that could mess it all up.

SAM

Please. Enlighten me.

ME

You're a great dad. You're allowed to put your needs and dreams first sometimes. Don't feel bad for doing this. I promise you everything is under control. Just enjoy your night.

SAM

...

Thanks, Maddie. I needed to hear that.
Gotta get ready. Riley is knocking on my door.

Talk to you later.

ME

Night.

*Miss you*, I added in my head.

I reread our exchange a few times before putting my phone away. Not really tired, but no longer feeling like playing detective for some fictional characters, I locked myself in my bedroom. For the first time, since I'd started working here, I cried myself to sleep, feeling lonelier than I'd had in a long time.

I shed sad tears for something I could never have.

And happy tears for the man I loved who faced his fears and mental blocks to pursue his dreams.

# Chapter 8



I stepped out of the green room, my face set and my back firm. This was it, the moment when everything in my life would finally fall into place—or at least, I hoped it would.

Riley met me backstage. "Ready, Stevens?"

In the last hour, the jitters that had plagued me all day had turned into excitement.

"Yeah," I said, pulling him into a hug. "I can't believe I went through with your crazy idea, man, but I'm glad I did. Right about now, it seems right."

"Don't thank me yet. Just do your thing. Mika and Justine will be proud. I know I am."

I blinked my emotions away. "Thanks for believing in me. And thanks for kicking my ass. I needed this. Someone to believe in me again when I didn't. I'm not sure I would've gone through with it if you hadn't been the one pushing me." I coughed to release the emotional rock lodged in my throat.

"Anytime."

From our spot by the side of the stage, we watched the crowd of expectant fans. I shook my legs, stretched my arms, and cracked my neck. This was the moment I'd been dreaming about for a long time and thought would never happen again.

I blew out a long breath. "It's a full house." All my cells vibrated with a renewed zest I wasn't used to experiencing anymore.

"Make the most of it. For the next two hours, forget everything else."

I nodded and pulled my friend into one more hug. "I'm thankful you brought me back."

Riley clapped my shoulder. "Go shine out there. And have fun. You deserve it."

With my confidence back, I walked onstage, my heart so full I thought it would rupture my chest. The cheers and applauses of the crowd packed more tears into my eyes.

I raised a hand in the air, waving at all those people who came to see *me*, letting their energy course through me. The grin on my lips matched the dampness of my eyes, both mirroring the emotions surging inside me. *God, I've missed this.*

With a tilt of my head, I grinned at my manager who stared at me with overflowing pride.

"Hey, folks." The cries of the crowd intensified. My grin widened. Wolf-whistles. Applauses. People screaming my name. "Thanks for being here tonight. It's been a while." More whistles. "I can't believe I'm standing here right now. It's a dream come true to be back after over two years. I'll play some of my old stuff and new material from my just-released album tonight. The last two years have been rocky, but I've made it through. None of this would have been possible without Riley Burns, one of my best friends, and the guy behind all this. Without him, I would still be living a life that's not mine, thinking I shouldn't play music ever again. Once again, Ry, thank you."

I saluted him before strumming the first chords of "No Matter What." The crowd sang along with me. They knew every word. This song was probably the one playing the most on the radio even after all these years. Six years ago, it won the *Song of the Year* category at the most prestigious country music award show. I'd written it the day Mikaella was born.

Seated on a lone stool in the middle of the stage, I played acoustic versions of "Small Town" and "All Those Who Came Around." Flashlights from cell phones became tiny pinpoint stars in the darkness, thousands of glittering beams aimed at me.

I closed the concert with "You're My Whole World," an emotionally charged ballad I'd written to my daughters a few weeks back. In the studio version, we could hear their voices and laughter in the background.

My fingers strummed the first chord of the chorus when an unexpected "I love you, Daddy"— Justine's voice —filled the stadium, and a clip of me running around with my girls played on the giant screen behind me. Emotions I couldn't contain or define jammed in my throat. Then "Daddy, you're the best," out of Mikaella's mouth, played from the speakers.

My heart bounced in my chest.

Hot tears ran down my cheeks.

I let them roll. Up until then, I had ignored the healing power they carried.

I inhaled, closing my eyes to steady my voice and everything that screamed to be let out inside me, and after some of my composure returned, I sang with all my heart until my voice broke on the last note.

Cheers and screams mixed with my own pulse pounding in my head, deafening me in the best possible way.

"Thank you, Charlotte," I said as I walked offstage, my face drenched with all the fervor this night had brought.

Riley pulled me into his arms the moment I walked backstage. "Stevens, that was sick. Incredible. You did it. For some reason, you're even better than you were when you left. That confidence. You owned the stadium. You delivered one hell of a performance. And it's your first show. Imagine after fifty." He paused and pointed behind me with a finger. "Listen to the crowd. They never lie. It's insane. All for you, man. Bask in the recognition."

The rush of the moment warmed my blood.

My body hummed with delight.

He led me further away, but I stopped and pivoted to face him. "Did you do this? The girls?"

We both smiled.

"Yeah, we did. A while back. I'm astounded they haven't said anything to you. We wanted to surprise you."

"That was incredible. You nailed it. I thought I would collapse on the stage. How did you make it happen?"

"Maddie. It was actually her idea. She's the one who captured the video and made the montage."

"She did?"

"Yeah. All her. She respects you very much. Now go change. We have a VIP party to attend."

———

Still high on adrenaline, I entered the VIP section of the bar. I had no idea how I'd survived two years without music in my life. Tonight, I felt ten years younger, and every layer of pain around my heart had faded away. They didn't exist anymore.

Nothing could temper my ecstasy.

Now that the addiction had set in, every bit of me itched to go on tour. To be onstage most nights. To fill stadiums with screaming fans.

To be where I belonged.

The security guard at the top of the stairs stepped aside to let us in.

I froze as I entered the dimly lit room. So many people were there.

Carter and April, Dahlia Ellis—Carter's ex-bandmate and best friend—and her husband Nick were chatting with Devon in one corner. Dylan Daughtry and Trevor McLachlan, two country stars I considered close friends, were talking with Aisha and her husband Gavin by the bar. Dozens of other people from the industry were scattered all across the room.

"What are you guys doing here?" I asked as I stepped closer to my friends and hugged them, happiness waltzing through me.

"We wouldn't have missed your big comeback for anything, man. You were great up there. It suited you. As if you've done it before."

I elbowed Carter in the ribs as he let out a warm chuckle after his quip.

"Ohmygod, the last song was so emotional. Did you know about the video?" April asked. "You looked to be in total shock."

"Because I was. I had no idea."

"Well, I was a crying mess. That was beautiful," Dahlia chimed in.

"Thanks," I croaked out, another surge of emotions

building in my throat. "How have you been, Dah? It's been a long time."

"Great. I'm glad I didn't miss your big return. Next time you guys are spending time together, we'll try to be there. I'm sorry we missed your birthday."

"It's okay. I know how crazy life can get. I'm happy you came tonight. It's good seeing you. Gimme half an hour. I'll say hello to everybody and be back so we can catch up," I said, leaving them as Riley joined us.

Four hours later, I entered my hotel suite and perused the empty space around me. A set of leather couches, a small kitchen with a dining table by the floor-to-ceiling windows overlooking the city, a bar along the wall leading to what I assumed were the bedroom and bathroom. With its ten-foot-high ceilings, wooden-planked floor, and dark-colored artworks decorating the walls, the sumptuous suite —too big for one man—lacked some liveliness. Everything was immaculate, a contrast to my home where toys, glitter, and princess outfits brought a touch of life to every room. Here, the reality of my loneliness weighed heavier than ever before. In the last two years, I'd never been away from home. Somehow, I doubted I would ever get used to the pristine and superficial decor of hotel rooms again.

Being here felt wrong. My children were with a nanny instead of their parents. Their mother should have been the one caring for them. Kissing them goodnight, and tucking them into their beds.

Adrenaline still ran high in my bloodstream, not letting me close my eyes and surrender myself to sleep. I craved a diversion. Something to keep my mind busy.

Music was my drug of choice.

I doubted any junkie could go to bed after shooting their best stuff up their arm.

Dressed in a pair of washout jeans and a long-sleeved

black cotton shirt, I made my way to the hotel bar. I looked at the time. Twenty minutes until last call.

I sat on a stool by the bar and ordered a whiskey. "Make it a double," I told the bartender.

I fidgeted with the paper coaster as he poured the drink before me. I chugged half of it in one gulp, relishing the burning sensation down my throat.

Some of my nerves settled. A sense of calmness washed through me.

I closed my eyes and listened to the mellow song playing in the almost-empty bar as I nursed the rest of my drink. Slower this time.

The alcohol relaxed me.

I could breathe easier.

My thoughts moved far away from the two little girls waiting for me at home.

With a wave of my hand, I addressed the bartender, now busy drying glasses with a white cloth. "Hit me again."

"You want company?" a woman, about my age, dressed in a short cobalt dress asked as she took the stool next to mine.

"I'm fine," I said, keeping my gaze low.

"You sure? You look lonely." We exchanged small smiles. "Here for business?"

I cringed at the interruption but answered anyway. "Sorta. What about you?"

"My sister's wedding. She's the worst. I was supposed to stay at her place tonight, but she went all bridezilla at her maid of honor. Got the hell out of there before it was my turn." She let out a laugh that warmed my insides.

I raised my glass. "Cheers to getting away. Crazy brides-to-be are the worst."

The woman brought her wineglass to her lips and

pushed her long blonde hair over her shoulder before holding out a hand. "I'm Lucy, by the way."

"Sam," I said, shaking her hand.

"Do this often? Come to the hotel bar and drink by yourself?

I shook my head, mirroring her smile. "Not in a long time."

"Closing in five minutes," the bartender said, picking up my empty tumbler.

"Already? I thought I had more time. Can I get another one?" Lucy slid her credit card across the counter. "Pour Sam one too and put his tab on my card, please."

"You don't have to do this, but thanks," I said with a nod.

"It's my pleasure. You want to finish your drink upstairs?" She arched a perfectly plucked brow, her chin pointing at my glass.

Could losing myself in a beautiful woman cure me of my nanny obsession?

Lucy squeezed my forearm, her touch comforting. "No pressure. We can just talk. I'm not tired, and I could use some friendly conversation. I flew from Europe, and let me tell you jet lag is a real thing."

"Conversation. Yeah, I can do that."

She fetched her purse. "Follow me then." We both grabbed our drinks and walked to the elevator in easy silence. I cast a discreet glance toward the lobby. No doubt Brent, the security detail shadowing me tonight, was somewhere around. I caught sight of him as I stepped into the car, and he joined us just in time, before the door closed.

"Which room are you in?" I asked, for Brent's sake, and to prevent him from following me.

"Fifteen-o-seven. Why?"

I shrugged. "No reason. Was wondering if we were on the same floor."

My bodyguard gave me a subtle nod once the elevator car stopped. Before we could even shut the door behind us, he'd be standing by Lucy's room.

---

Lucy's hand landed on my thigh as she sat beside me on the mattress. Her touch warmed me up and sent a foreign buzz through me. My brain swam in a whiskey bliss, just enough that every tingle running through me electrified my body. Her floral scent, mixed with the wafts of red wine, spiraled around me. Her teeth left indents on her lower lip, and I leaned closer, ready to leave my own.

She locked her fingers behind my neck, and pulling me closer, she brushed her lips against mine. I sucked in a breath, contradictory thoughts battling inside me. Right then, I decided to turn off all the warning signals screaming inside my head.

Lucy lowered her fingers to my belt buckle. I tried to relax. To enjoy the present. To let go. But no matter how hard I wanted to relax and surrender myself to her touch, everything about this moment felt wrong. As if I was a guy cheating on the most precious person in his life. And truth be told, I'd never been the *fuck random chick on the road* kind of rock star. All my life, I'd been in steady and lasting relationships. I wasn't interested in those games. Up until now, I'd only slept with women I had genuine feelings for.

Lucy moaned against my mouth as she unzipped me, and I pushed back. She searched my eyes, lust filling hers. Something I couldn't share, however much I tried to convince myself. Even my body wasn't into it.

Before her hands could reach the waistband of my

boxer briefs, I jumped to my feet. "I'm…I'm sorry," I said, scratching the top of my head.

"It's not you, it's me? That's what you're about to say, right?"

I swallowed my uneasiness. "Yeah… There's someone else. I've been trying to move on, to forget about her, but I see her everywhere, even in my dreams."

"Lucky girl."

I let out a half-snort. "Let's just say it's complicated."

Lucy patted the comforter beside her. "Wanna talk about it?" I eyed the empty spot I'd vacated seconds ago. "I'm not gonna jump your bones. I promise. At the bar, I said we could talk. So here I am, inviting you to confide in me."

I zipped and buttoned my pants and sat next to her after buckling my belt. I had no one else to talk to about this. If I went to Riley, he would freak out. Devon would worry about me and the girls. Carter would tell me, "I told you so." And none of my other friends knew Madison, so they wouldn't be of any help. Perhaps opening up to a stranger would be best after all.

"Okay, let's see. Where should I begin?"

The woman offered me a lopsided smile. "The beginning?"

"Well, my wife divorced me two years ago. She packed her bags and left one night. No explanations other than she hated being a mother to our daughters. So, the girls and I have been alone all this time… Well, until my best friend persuaded me to hire a nanny so I'd be able to go back to work and live again…"

And just like that, I told a stranger all about my relationship with Madison without giving her too many details, just the main facts.

A weight left my back as I spoke the words out. "I'm unable *not* to think about her. All the time. And we're about to live in close quarters for six months in a RV because I have to go on the road for work, and I'm barely holding it together as it is." The RV was close enough to a tour bus, I figured. I wouldn't reveal too much about myself, keeping it vague in case she hadn't recognized me.

Her hand enveloped mine in a comforting gesture. "Sam, does she love you back?"

My head cocked in her direction at the L-word. "I'm not…huh…it's not… No one said anything about love. It-it's just a crush, but for some reason, it won't go away. Even after all this time. Even after I've told her she was too young for me. She doesn't deserve to be tied down with two kids at her age. That would be incredibly selfish to ask that much of her."

She shook her head. "Sam, did you ask her what she desires? You can't make assumptions and decisions for her. She's an adult. She deserves to make her *own* choices, to decide what's good for *her*. Whether it's you and your daughters or something else, that's not your call to make. It's hers. I'm pretty certain, with everything you've told me, that she's strong enough to deal with whatever she chooses. But either way, you gotta respect her voice. It would be a shame to deprive your daughters, and you, of this amazing woman because you can't accept where her heart stands, don't you think?"

I pressed my clammy hands onto my thighs. "But what if…what if she misses out on her youth because she dates me? What if it all goes to shit and my girls lose the only woman who has ever truly loved them?"

"What if it's the best thing for all of you? Aren't you curious to find out? Are you willing to miss out on the opportunity just because you're afraid of hypothetical situations that haven't even occurred yet?"

I shook my head, keeping my chin down. "Guess not."

"So, what are you doing here then? Why are you here with me instead of there with her? Why aren't you opening your heart to her and seeing what she thinks? Where it'll take you?"

I fought my breathing to return to normal—and the words to stay put.

My gaze met Lucy's and she nodded, waiting for me to speak the truth.

Time halted for endless minutes.

My heart drummed in my chest, unable to stay still.

"So?" she pushed.

"Because…because I'm scared. I-I'm fucking scared. Happy now? The last time I trusted someone with my heart, she walked away. She fucking left and never explained anything to me. How can I be sure that this time with Maddie, it won't be a re-run of the same saga? How can I be sure I'm not putting my heart at risk again? That I'm not the problem? That my love isn't defective?"

Lucy smiled. "You can't be. You are not the problem. Love is like that. It *is* messy. And complicated. But it is also beautiful."

Her words thrived in the space between us.

"It's late. I should let you get some sleep." I stood up, and she walked me to the door. "Thank you," I said, dropping a kiss on her cheek. "It doesn't seem much right now, but you've helped me figure things out. I'm sorry I couldn't go through with whatever we were doing earlier."

She rested her hand on mine. "I'm happy I could help. For what it's worth, and I know we've just met, I can tell you're one of the good ones. That girl is lucky to have you by her side. She'd be a fool not to trust you with her heart."

I opened the door.
"Good night, Sam."
"Night, Lucy."

# Chapter 9

## Madison

I woke up to the chime of my phone. My eyes stung from the tears I'd cried earlier. In a short span of time, I had lost my best friend and fallen in love, hard, with my boss, a man with whom I had no chance of a future. The harsh truth hit me like a freight train. And stomped on my broken heart. A new notification came through. I patted the bed around me, looking for my device. With a deep inhale, I checked the screen, not sure I was ready in case it was Sam. Texting with him, even over silly subjects, would only magnify the reality I'd forever be his friend.

Nothing more.

I relaxed my shoulders at the name flashing on my screen.

RILEY

Click the link below. It was a hit. You're a
genius. You should be proud of yourself. I
know I am. It was even more emotional
than we thought it would be. Check his
reaction. It's priceless. I filmed it for you.

Great job, Madison.

Don't have too many awesome ideas, or I'll
have to hire you full-time, working for me.
Just kidding. I recognize talent, and you're
exceptional at what you do. Working with
kids is your calling.

[link]

Tears burned the back of my eyes the instant they landed on Sam onstage, hearing his daughters' voices just as he strummed the first chord of his latest song's chorus. The one he wrote for them. He looked around as if searching for them, then found the video playing on the screen behind him. The same video I had shot of the girls running around in the backyard last summer, their faces split with huge grins, and laughter in the air. Pure happiness. Raw moments between a devoted father and his adoring daughters.

I cupped my overexcited heart with a hand as I watched the video for a second and a third time.

Even on the tiny screen, Sam looked handsome. This video, filmed by Riley or someone on his team from backstage, showed a side of Sam that none of the other clips I'd seen online revealed. A lightness. A sense of belonging. Of calm. Something that wasn't visible in his earlier career days.

ME

Thank you for sending it to me. It means a
lot. I'm glad it was a success.

An emotion I couldn't name wrapped tightly around my heart, and I sealed my eyelids, wishing sleep would claim me again so I could be free from the agony swarming within me.

By the morning, my good spirits had returned, and the girls and I spent the day making craft projects in the den, the rain outside taming their bubbling excitement.

It was almost two at night when cries woke me up this time.

"Monster. Monster. The monster is here."

I bolted up the stairs two at a time, panic rising in me when I heard Justine screaming in her sleep. It was the last night before Sam returned home. We had chatted with him earlier, and he'd told the girls he would be here after breakfast the following day. I adjusted my tank top and night shorts before pushing the door open and tiptoeing into the room. A nightlight cast a soft glow around the space. The sight of Justine, her face and neckline soaked in tears, broke my heart.

"Hey, sweetie. It was just a bad dream." I pulled her into my embrace as I squatted before her, dabbing her tears with my fingertips, and sprinkling kisses along her hairline. "I'm here. It's okay now. You're safe. I've got you."

Nightmares.

Growing up, they had been a nightly occurrence. Until they appeared further and further apart and stopped. Now that they had made a comeback, I prayed they would leave me alone soon enough.

"I'm here, and I'll chase all the monsters away."

She heaved and hiccupped, never loosening her white-knuckled grip on me.

"Want me to lie down beside you until you fall asleep?"

"*Yesss.*" Her voice shook with the remnants of her nightmare.

"Then scoot over. Let's cuddle."

We settled ourselves under the covers. I kept my arms around her, and she pressed her face into my chest.

"Sing Daddy's song."

"You want me to sing it to you or play it on my phone."

"Sing."

I coughed to loosen my voice, and the lyrics spilled from my lips. Each girl had a few favorite songs from their daddy's repertoire and without asking, I knew which one would soothe her better. Justine's eyes fluttered close, and before I was even done, she had fallen back asleep, her tiny fingers fastened around mine. A spark shone in me. I had become someone else's safe harbor. The small gesture confirmed I hadn't landed in the Stevenses' lives by chance. I was always meant to be here and help them heal. The same way people had done for me all those years ago.

I combed Justine's hair with my fingers, singing the last verse of Sam's song.

Once I was sure she was back in dreamland, I made my way downstairs toward my bedroom.

In the dark, humming the song I'd just sung, I didn't notice the silhouette lurking near my door. I bumped into a human wall and almost crash-landed on my ass if it weren't for his strong arms circling my waist just in time.

My pulse went ballistic.

"You?" I asked once the shock subsided and my vocal cords regained their function. "What are you doing here? You scared the shit out of me. I thought… I thought you said—"

He ran a hand through his hair, and my eyes followed the gesture, mesmerized. "What you did minutes ago was hot."

My eyebrows furrowed. What was he talking about? "Almost falling?" I risked.

He shook his head, and my throat worked hard to catch up with my overzealous breathing.

"What then?"

His stare moved down to his hands still holding me in place. I drew in a shaky breath. Heat vibrated through me where our bodies connected. Would it be strange to wish his hands could stay anchored to me longer?

"Maddie, you sang *my* song." Sam's voice sounded rougher than usual, and I wondered if it was due to him belting out lyrics two nights in a row or if my presence affected him with an intensity I'd never truly realized before.

"You…huh…you heard that?"

He bowed his head, now standing so close my lips could skim his if we just tilted our heads little to the right.

"I heard from the second verse. Goose bumps spread on my arms. I'll say it again, even though I already know it —you have a great voice, Madison."

He took his time pronouncing my name, rolling it on his tongue like a prayer.

My heart, my composure, my head, they all spun at a vertiginous speed.

We fixated on each other.

"Sam, what are you doing here? You said you were coming back tomorrow."

He cast a glance at his watch. "It's already tomorrow, isn't it?"

I dissolved at his proximity.

"Being alone in a hotel room sucks. I missed you guys. And there was something I kinda had to do."

Blood couldn't reach my brain anymore because I saw

stars. Now, I had no more doubt. This husky tone was Sam's turned-on voice.

"What?" I swallowed—or tried to—in vain.

"Thank you. For what you did. Also, I gotta tell you something else since I had a lot of time to think."

"You gotta? You had?"

He bobbed his head.

I swallowed my angst. "What about?"

"Us."

Like two poles attracted to each other, the space separating us shrank.

His smoldering gaze nailed me to the floor, and I got sucked into the vortex of everything that Sam Stevens was. He hadn't even touched me yet, and already he possessed me in the most intimate ways.

My jaw went slack as I watched him.

Mischief and hunger crossed his eyes, all directed at me.

Only one question echoed in my head. Would I survive the night?

# Chapter 10
### Sam

"I gotta say, that video, with the girls and me… Wow. Riley told me it was your idea. Maddie… It's the most amazing thing anyone has done for me in a very long time. It touched me…in a way I'll never be able to fully explain."

I wished nothing more than a chance to swim in the pool of her irises as Madison watched me with something akin to adoration. Was it? I watched her a little longer, taking in the trembling of her lips, the spark in her eyes, the quick, uneven breaths. Those signs didn't lie. Yeah, this girl was as gone for me as I was for her.

"It was nothing, I…I just thought you'd like it. Have a piece of them with you. Every night."

"Maddie, it was not nothing. It was everything." I paused, my eyelids heavy, the moment hanging between us. "Both nights I was away, I wished for one thing…and one thing only."

Her tongue teased the edge of her lip as she waited for me to go on. The small movement felt like a quiet invitation.

"*You.* I wished I could share those moments with *you.*"

She blinked twice. "You did?"

"For an instant, I tried to forget you. To convince myself I was too old, too damaged, and my life was too complicated for you."

The column of her throat rippled. "How did it turn out?"

"Bad. Super bad. I'm desperate. I wanna know if it's all in my head. The connection we share. The lust. The desire. The chemistry. The easiness. Tell me I'm wrong, and I'll never bother you ever again. Tell me it's all in my mind and that I'm an old man and you feel nothing for me. Tell me to leave you alone and to move on."

Her eyes darkened. Her pupils dilated, almost wiping out the color of her irises.

Desire flooded us, thick and unrelenting. It clung to our skin, saturating the air between us. I could feel it in every one of my cells, wrapping around me. Making me its prisoner.

Madison shook her head. "No, I won't. I-I shouldn't think about you like that, but I can't help myself. You're *always* on my mind. My days get better the second you look at me…or smile at me. Or when you enter a room. I'm sorry. That's not… That's not why you hired me. Every day, it gets harder to keep the longing that consumes me locked inside."

I exhaled my relief. "All I want is to kiss you, but I can't. God knows I crave it… I crave you. Every part of me aches to. But we can't cross that line. If we do, we'll never be able to work together afterward, and we're leaving for almost six months on a tour bus."

"I...I agree." Her low murmur only fed the inferno that burned between us.

Lust and craving—they were tearing at my sanity. Soon enough, I'd lose my mind.

Madison twisted a strand of her hair around her finger, and I was dying to do it myself. I wanted to touch her, to feel her heart beating against mine. Her heat all around me. Engulfing me. Possessing me.

I forced out the words that made the most sense. "I-I'm sorry. I need you... The girls need you. I can't...I can't risk everything. They've lost too much already. I can't be the one who chases you away from their lives if getting together messes everything up."

Instead of pulling back, we collided.

I cradled her face with both hands, and I lost myself in her eyes.

Her lips called me in.

Her breast molded to my chest as I pulled her closer, my fingertips digging into the crests of her hips.

"Sam, I—"

"I know, babe." I closed my eyes. "Just bear with me here." I couldn't look at her anymore. The temptation to eat her up staggered my being.

Madison's hand froze over the bulge in my pants, and I forgot how to breathe as fireworks exploded inside me.

How could just her caress feel so right?

The shackles of my constraints crumbled. I stopped overthinking the meaning of our magnetism and chose to be its willing participant—to surrender myself to the electrifying pull simmering between us. My reasons deserted me, and I ceded to the lure of her heart-shaped mouth. Backing her up against the wall, I dug my fingers into her plump ass and lifted her until she could lock her legs around me, her center rubbing against my painful erection.

Madison's tongue swept over mine. She stole every speck of air from my lungs.

I could die now, and I'd die a very happy man.

"Sam," she purred in a way that left me in pieces, then stitched me back together. "I never wanna stop."

I kneaded her breast over her top with one hand, and she deepened the kiss. "Me neither. Never. I'm so gone for you." Every trace of common sense I once had evaporate.

Flames licked my insides.

"Keep doing what you're doing because it feels too damn good," she muttered against my lips.

Her words acted like a magical spell, and my dick throbbed in my pants, desperate for the attention of the woman rocking my world. Every inch of her.

Her fingers traveled under the fabric of my shirt, and I tensed, every part of me alert and ready to be cherished. It'd been so long. How could I have spent all this time without this? Affection and sex. Someone to love. To share my life with.

My chest muscles tensed under the pads of her fingers, each touch bewitching.

A carnal thirst rose in me, and my lips found hers. I peeled her tank top over her head and cupped her naked breasts with my palms. I flew to heaven right there. I died and came back to life. "You're beautiful," I said, between pants. "So fucking beautiful."

"I'm all yours. I want you… All of you. Claim me."

Her words broke years of restraint. They brought me back to my essence. To me. The one person I had neglected over the last two years.

I pushed her hair away from her face as I lost myself in the depths of her eyes. Into the promises that shone right through them. In the simple but powerful gesture, Madison bared her soul to me, not hiding anything from me. All the answers I was looking for lay right there, ready for me to hold on to and never let go.

My heart vibrated against my ribcage.

The vision of her, exposed and vulnerable, but taking what could be rightfully hers stole my breath away.

My mouth returned to assault her with a passionate kiss. I couldn't breathe on my own. Madison possessed the only viable air my body required to survive.

We kissed until it shut all the voices in my head. Until only *us* mattered. Until I surrendered myself to the animalistic desire coursing through my bloodstream, and nothing could stop me anymore.

After she got rid of my shirt, she took my hand in hers and pushed it past the elastic waistband of her night shorts, her eyes pleading with me. As if it already had memorized the path before, my fingers followed the moisture trail leading to her wet heat. Her breath hissed out when I slid one finger inside, then a second. She bit her bottom lip as I glided my digits back and forth, yelps spilling from deep within her. A melody to my soul.

She rode my hand and looked both magnificent and incredible as she did.

Fucking mine.

Our hastened breaths mingled. My head spun, the oxygen molecules around us getting scarce. The temperature of the room reached dangerous heights as we combusted together.

We were humming the same chorus.

We were singing the same lyrics.

Madison Prescott was the music in my life. More real than any note on a sheet of paper could ever be. More than any chords from my guitar.

She rolled her hips over my hand, chasing a release. She dug her nails into my nape, anchoring herself to me. I slid my digits in and out faster and captured each of her whimpers with my lips. I tangled my fingers in her hair, guiding her head so I could steal every breath. She traced the seam of my mouth with her tongue. My balls tightened, and I clenched the muscles of my ass, doing all I could to prevent myself from shooting my load. Madison was my downfall. I had become a bomb, ticking and ready to explode.

Her moans filled the silence of the night.

My pace turned frantic. Goose bumps tickled my spine. A heady heat surged through me.

"Sam." She whispered my name like a prayer.

I played with her swollen bundle of nerves with the pad of my thumb and lowered my other hand, my fingertips digging into her soft ass cheek to lift her up and hold her closer to me.

Her head tilted back. I watched her, relishing the lust drawn on her features and the blush coloring her cheeks.

My mouth devoured hers, our tongues famished for each other. My teeth and lips feasted on her slender neck.

Her grip on me tightened, and she shut her eyes. I accelerated the rhythm of my fingers. Her body clenched around my digits as she surfed the first wave of pleasure. I fastened my arms around her, holding her against me, wishing she could decode the thrumming of my heart and grasp the depth of my feelings. I couldn't speak them aloud —not now, at least.

Not before the tour was over and we could give our relationship a real chance.

My fears lingered on the outskirts of my mind, ready to make a comeback and screw with my head.

I lowered Madison back to her feet, helping her with her balance. We fixated on each other. If I indulged us, there would be no going back.

"Sam, I need you. Inside me," she said with a trembling voice.

It brought me back to the present. To us. It killed the apprehension lurking at its source. Before I could react, she plunged her hand into my pants and boxer briefs and fisted my steeled length, shaping her hand around it. Taking ownership of the part of me that already belonged to her —no matter what lies I told to convince myself otherwise.

A relieved puff of air escaped her lips. A guttural growl rumbled from mine.

I had no more doubts.

Madison owned me. Body and soul. And I wished nothing more than to be hers. Here, now, and forever.

"Fuck, I don't have a condom," I said, breathless and barely able to speak coherent words as she worked my rock-hard manhood like nobody else had done in years. Like only she could. Scorching heat clung to my vertebrae. My breathing hitched. How could I be so stupid? I hadn't worn or bought a piece of rubber in almost ten years. That was a rookie mistake. A faux pas. I was in such a hurry to get here tonight that I'd convinced Riley to drive me straight home after my show, not thinking clearly. The adrenaline of giving a concert always got me horny. For the length of the entire show, Madison had been the only person I wished I could live that moment with. I pictured her standing on the side of the stage so often that I started believing she was there with me after the fifth song. In my head, I dedicated each one to her. Only her.

I raked my fingers through my locks. "Babe, I'm sorry."

"Sam, I never had sex without one, and it's been a long while since the last time."

I blinked. "I believed—" I didn't want to voice those

thoughts out loud. I didn't want the idea of her with another man to spoil the moment.

"No." She shook her head, pursing her lips. "I… couldn't." Two words. Two words that wrecked me and spread a wave of euphoria and something else I couldn't quite name through my being. We eye-fucked each other for far too long, air still rushing to get in and out of our lungs. "I'm on the pill." She studied my reaction. "I'm okay with it…with you. Unless you wanna stop." She looked vulnerable right now, offering herself to the greedy man in me without a second thought.

"You sure?" I smoothed the length of her bottom lip with my thumb.

"Only with you," she murmured, her eyes pulling me into a new trance.

My lips returned to hers. Hungry. I ate her mouth as if it were my last meal. Our tongues tangoed with each other. I cupped one naked breast, rolling the hard tip between my fingers. A scorching rampage stirred within me. How could kissing and touching her feel so damn right? The clouds of my conscience parted. Light came back into my life, brighter and more blinding than ever before.

Her hands returned to my crotch, pumping me until my knees weakened.

I leaned forward to lick her diamond-hard rosy nipples and played them with my teeth while Madison's hand worked me in long and tantalizing strokes.

"Only with you," she repeated, bewitching me with her hooded eyelids, flushed cheeks, and swollen lips. Looking perfect. All my doing.

With an exhale, I ordered, "Turn around."

This wasn't delicate. This was desperate. A yearning I couldn't contain anymore. One I knew I might regret later but couldn't stop. Couldn't deny myself any longer.

Yanking her tiny shorts and cotton panties down her legs, I held her arms over her head with one hand while positioning her pelvis with the other. With my knee, I pushed her legs further apart. Her face pressed against the wall, and the sparks that flashed my way when our gazes met over her shoulder got me harder—as if it could even be possible. My fingers returned to her folds, coating them with her arousal. Urging her down with a palm between her shoulder blades until her ass pointed up, I lined my dick with her opening. Chills ran along my back. My teeth dug into my tongue, forcing me to focus and not let go too soon. Inch by inch, I pushed into her tight channel. Madison welcomed all of me with one push, her ass flush with my lower abdomen.

"Ohmyfuckinggod," I mumbled. Bending my upper body to mold to her back, I caught a fistful of her hair, searching for her mouth.

We breathed out together. Embedded inside her walls, unable to move, too many overwhelming sensations coursing through me, I devoured her in a manner I couldn't prevent myself anymore.

My fingers tangled in her hair.

Slowly, I got into a rhythm. My hand holding her arms above her head grounded me to this instant.

I accelerated the movements, unable to go slow anymore. Too engrossed in this woman to deprive us of this. The connection. The ecstasy.

Thrusting into her, my hips moved with purpose.

Madison cried out my name, and I swallowed the whimpers tumbling from her lips.

"You're perfect. So perfect," I said, breathless, getting her hair away from her nape so I could feast on the flesh there.

My growls became her moans.

My body ended where hers began.

I pounded into Madison again and again. My brain blanked out, my body only driven by the sounds passing through her luscious lips.

I let go of her hair, withdrew from her warmth, and flipped her until her back hit the wall. We stared at each other, panting, no word strong enough to express the intensity of the moment.

"Oh, Sam," she moaned as I lifted her up, spearing her with my dick, and rammed into her with abandon. Her grip around my neck tightened. I sank into her, using my arms to glide her up and down my shaft.

We were catching fire together.

The chains I had fastened around my unavailable heart loosened.

Madison cried out my name again, and I hammered into her like it was my sole mission in life. The reason for my existence. My purpose.

My fingers wrapped around her neck of their own volition, and I pressed my forehead to hers as I caught my breath. Our lips reconnected. I'd never get enough.

One of my palms returned to her breast, and I kneaded it while my tongue cherished her other nipple.

My hand traced down her body, halting at the junction of her thighs. As I pushed into her deeper, my fingers rubbed her clit, eliciting muffled cries from her.

Madison moaned. Her back hit the wall with every roll of my hips.

A loud groan exited my mouth. I was combusting inside out.

I clasped her chin between my fingers, holding her in place, and lost myself in her eyes as she surfed her climax.

She vibrated against me, and we never broke eye contact.

My own release was held by a flimsy thread. I was so close, but I dreaded the instant it would all be over.

My movements were less precise as I fought with my orgasm.

I tried, I really did, but I couldn't prevent myself anymore.

When I lowered Madison to her feet, I pulled out. She wrapped her fist tight around me, milking my cock to the last drop.

Gravity left me.

I nibbled her bare shoulder with my teeth, grounding me to this world. She cried out, and I soothed the sting with my tongue and more kisses. I surrendered myself to her, my eyes closing, desperate to remember the bliss. More jolts traversed my body. Panting, I tried to suck in a breath. A million sensations filled me. Colored dots danced in my vision.

Once I came down from the high, I opened my eyes.

My release adorned Madison's bare stomach, and both our gazes landed there.

I rested my hand on the side of her face as I pressed my forehead against hers, the two of us panting for air.

I'd never experienced anything like this before. A sense of belonging, of being home. A perception I had found my place in this world. More than any concert could ever provide me.

My mouth descended on her reddened lips, and I took my time kissing her, aware it would be the last time. No way would I let myself go there ever again—for the time being—no matter how incredible it felt. Not before we finished touring together. Because if I messed up, it would affect my kids and everything we all had been working for.

"You know it can't happen again," Madison said as if

she could read my mind—and my worst fears. "Not for the next six months at least."

I bobbed my head.

"Then kiss me one last time."

Without another word, I molded my lips to the woman's who owned my heart a lot more each day. The one who was quickly becoming the center of my universe. And my dreams.

She grinned at me as I stepped back. The lightness in my chest was something new to me, and I relished the feeling and the freedom it provided.

I balled the fabric of my T-shirt and wiped all traces of me from her belly.

Madison watched me with eyes beaming with adoration. "Thanks," she said once I finished.

My forehead returned to hers, and our fingers intertwined. "Tell me to walk away," I asked.

She shook her head, a soft laugh breaking the wheezing of our breathing.

"I'm not strong enough to resist you, Maddie. I don't have it in me to stay away from you. You gotta be the bigger person here and order me to go. To leave you alone. It's been too long since the last time I've felt something for someone else. And right now, I'm feeling lots of things for you. And my mind is spinning with a whole lot more dirty things I wish I could do to you after what we've just done."

My eyes followed the length of her, lingering for a moment over her chest, her breasts rising and falling with every intake of air. I closed my eyes, doing my best not to touch them again, to remember how they fit into my hands. Not to let my dick rule my common sense and love her with infinite passion this time around. Sure, we got rid of the built-up tension that had been intoxicating our relationship since day one, but I wanted to cherish her with passion now. But if we continued what we'd started, I'd never be able to stop or be reasonable.

Her eyes glistened with bliss, and she chewed on her lips. I ran my thumb across their fullness, relishing the aftermath quakes of her body under my touch.

"You'll be the end of me. We must come up with rules on the road, or I'll get you naked every chance I get. And fair warning. The adrenaline coursing through my blood-stream after playing concerts makes me horny."

"I can stay in the crew bus. It's no big deal."

"No." I clutched her upper arms. My throat worked. Electricity darted between us. "I want you on *our* bus. On *my* bus. That's where you belong. I don't consider you staff, Maddie. You're much more than that. You're much more to me. You should know that by now. You're family. Whether we want it or not, we're tied together by some invisible thread neither of us can escape. And in all honesty, I could never envision going on this tour if you weren't there—beside me. Loving my daughters as your own. Sharing our lives... *My* life. I trust you. I need *you*. The girls do too. You'll stay with us. End of discussion."

Madison nodded, her irises drawing me in, threatening to swallow me whole and make me hers now and forever.

"What if it doesn't work?" Her voice had lost her previous amusement.

"Babe, we'll make it work. Don't worry. I'm just... We'll find a way to be around each other without compli-cating everything until we can be together for real. As I said, we'll set rules. Trust me, okay?"

"Yeah," she said, her voice low and tantalizing as it blanketed us with promises we had no idea how to keep. "Rules...right." Moisture clouded her eyes, and I almost threw all my own words out of the window right there and promised her everything she was silently begging for.

I couldn't look away. Madison's energy always captured me, and I liked every minute of it. I felt alive. I felt like a man again, not just a father, but a complex being with desire and a dick useful for more than just taking a leak.

"Walk away now," I urged. "Or I'll lock us in my room, and I'll never let you out. I'm a starving man, and you woke up the beast in me, babe. My blood boils, and my dick stirs when you're around."

"Sam, I'm not sure I can…"

I placed a finger against her lips. She kissed my digit, and the simple touch awoke new sensations inside me.

"Believe me, I'm dying to touch you, all of you, again. To savor your flesh. Every corner of it. To hold you in my arms while I sleep, to kiss you every second of every day." I shut my eyes. The smell of her washed over me, and I wondered if she could spray it over my pillow. Just for tonight. I shook my head again, flushing away my silly thoughts.

My mouth returned to hers, and our bodies blended together. Less desperate this time around, but our hands still in discovery mode.

"You smell divine." One kiss on her shoulder. "Your skin is velvet." A kiss on her collarbone. "I could eat you up for the rest of my life."

I sucked on a pebbled nipple while she massaged my scalp with her fingers. Her whimpers increased when I played her with my teeth. She ground her hips against mine, and I held her still. My entire self hated me as I leaned back. I noticed the gloss in her eyes. The love marks on her neck. The rosiness of her puckered peaks. Dropping to my knees, I laved her soaked center with one flick of my tongue.

Madison gasped.

"Now I can't wait for the tour to be over," I said.

"You'll think about me every time you touch yourself. And the taste of you will linger on my tongue."

"Leave now, or it'll be me who locks you up in my bedroom. You're not allowed to tease me this good. It's unfair that I'll have to wait half a year for the real thing." A contagious grin stretched across her face.

I kissed the apex of her thighs and made my way up to her sticky abdomen, the moist valley of her breasts, her scruff-marked jawline, and her cherry lips. All traces of me, I had branded onto her.

"Yes, it is unfair," I confirmed.

Madison crashed her lips on mine. My head spun at a dizzying pace. Her touch jolted my heart back to life. Fireworks, butterflies, sparks, all that shit filled my stomach. I clutched her waist, pulling her closer to me, wanting to feel every inch of her pressed against every inch of me one last time.

Before I could deepen the kiss, she leaned back. "Sam, be honest. Every time we touch, your heart rate picks up." She positioned a hand over my chest. "Don't go to bed thinking it was a mistake, okay? I feel it too." She grabbed my hand and splayed it over her left breast. "See?" We stared at each other for a few beats. After a minute, she pushed me away, using both hands. "Go. Now."

"Good night, Maddie," I said, kissing her one last time, branding my mouth to hers.

With my heart swelling in my chest, so full it could burst at any second, I turned on my heel, leaving her behind, and climbed the stairs leading to my room.

"Night, Sam," Madison whispered in the dark before turning the light off. Her bedroom door clicked as she closed it behind her, the sound sinking my spirit.

How would I ever be able to resist her now that I had tasted what should be mine?

# Chapter 11

## Madison

"Do we have everything ready for tonight?" Sam asked, listing the items he had noted on his phone. "Bouncing house. *Check.* Endless supply of hot dogs. *Check.* Ice cream. *Check.* Music. *Check.* Decorations. *Check.* Makeup for the kids. *Check.* Drinks for the adults. *Check.* We're good to go." He put his phone away, pushing the buggy toward the checkout counter, Justine and Mikaella standing at the far end, giggling.

He brushed his fingers along my lower back as I helped him place everything on the conveyor belt, and I shivered under his gentle touch. We were leaving in a week, and since the night we had sex, despite our best resolve, we couldn't keep our hands to ourselves for long periods. Not completely at least. A touch here. A caress there. A kiss on my temple. Grazing of our fingers. Those were insignificant details for any onlooker, but to me, they meant a lot.

Each time we faced each other, my body hummed,

begging to be abandoned to his expert hands. This dance had become our reality, and our nightmare, tied together with a giant bow of blazing lust.

Tonight, we were having that party Sam had talked about when I first started working at his house. The one to celebrate us going on tour. Friends of the girls were coming over. Some of Sam's friends and neighbors, Emily, my sister, and her friends too. People we loved and would miss while we were away.

Back home, I put excited little girls down for a nap before helping Sam to finish the last details. We had made plans to sleep on the bus tonight. For the second night in a row. Last night was a bit chaotic. The girls stayed awake past their bedtime, unable to calm down, and I barely slept in my bunk. Just the thought of Sam lying behind the wall had my body and mind going haywire. How many times had I pictured myself joining him in his room or woken up with a start, thinking the noise I'd heard belonged to him as he climbed into my bed?

As the party raged outside and the guys ran the grill, I retreated inside, making sure nobody missed anything.

Devon came to me after a moment. "I was wondering where you went. How are you doing?" she asked, bringing her drink to her mouth. "Is everything all right?"

I pasted a smile onto my lips. "Sure. I just felt like escaping the madness for a few minutes."

She leaned against the countertop next to me, her eyes following my line of sight through the window. "Have you talked about it?" she asked after a beat.

"About what?" I asked, unable to grasp where our conversation was heading.

"Those feelings you two have for each other."

I coughed behind my fist and sipped my drink, trying

hard to look unaffected. "Not sure what you're talking about."

With her eyes still trained outside, she continued, "It's easy to see, Maddie. Only fools wouldn't be able to grasp the intensity of your chemistry."

As if he sensed my eyes on him, Sam's gaze found mine through the glass, and he aimed that irresistible smile in my direction—the one I couldn't resist—and waved.

A lone tear leaked from my eye, and I wiped it off. "It doesn't matter. We won't be doing anything about it." I shrugged.

"Why not?" Devon asked, her attention now locked on me.

"Because… The girls. The tour. The risks. The complications. Nothing plays in our favor. We'll wait until after the tour and see. Anyway, I'm on his payroll. I'm just an employee, so it would be weird."

Devon gripped my upper arms and turned me so we faced each other. "You're not. You're the woman who stands beside him as he tries to give his dreams another shot. You're the woman his kids are head over heels in love with. And he is too, in case you were wondering. Sam can't stop talking about you when you're not around. Maddie this. Maddie that. He adores you. You changed him…for the better."

"It's the music."

"Nah. It is, in part, but it's mainly due to you. You put his heart back in his chest."

"Does Riley know?"

She shook her head. "I think he suspects something but has never said anything about it. Right now, he's so wrapped up in the tour that I'm not sure he grasps anything beyond it."

"Please don't tell him, okay? I'm not ready for the truth

to be revealed. Like I said, the tour is the priority. And the girls. Nothing should come between any of these."

"I'll never tell a soul. But promise me that when it gets too much and you need to vent, you'll come to me, okay? I'm having my first tour bus experience too, so we'll have each other to lean on. I wasn't sure at first when Riley proposed we join you guys for a few months, but I think the change of air will do us all some good. Life has been intense since we've met. We both need a breather in our daily lives. And I can work remotely, so why not?"

She squeezed my arm one last time before leaving me alone with our shared confessions.

Seconds later, Emily walked in. "There you are," my sister said. "That man of yours told me I'd find you here."

I pressed a hand over her mouth. "Shhh, Ems. He's not my man."

She burst out laughing. "Yeah, right. That's why he's not making conversation with anyone, too busy stalking you from his spot in the backyard. When Becks and I arrived, he made a joke about where my sexy baby sister was, and Sam almost jumped him. Told him to grant you the respect you deserve."

I blinked.

"See? I'm sure you two are banging. I'm just surprised you haven't said anything about it."

Warmth pooled in my cheeks at the way she studied my reaction. "We are not. It's complicated. We'll go on tour and discuss whatever this is afterward if there are still feelings involved. The timing sucks."

I downed most of my drink in one gulp. First Devon, now my sister.

"So, there are feelings involved?" she asked in her *big sister knows it all* tone.

"I didn't mean feelings, I meant attraction. Lots of it. It's distracting."

"Distracting. Nice choice of word." She smirked, and the urge to rip it off her face with my nails tickled my fingertips.

I offered her a pointed look instead. "Fine. I have feelings. Happy now? Nothing says he mirrored them, though." I sighed. "It was supposed to be a short-term crush, not a *full blown scorching head over heels* firework."

"Ha, I knew it." Her smirk vanished.

Our eyes drifted to Sam through the window. As if he could tell I was staring, his eyes found mine again, and we both froze, transported into a world where no one else mattered but us.

"See?" my sister whispered. "It's not just you. He's infatuated with you too. What's meant to be will be. Don't overthink it. Just see where it takes you."

I bowed my head and sighed. "That's the plan."

"Maddie, one thing, though. Whatever goes down between you two, just make sure you're not pushing your own dreams away in the process, okay?"

"I'm not. I'm exactly where I wanna be. This tour, the chance to go on a new adventure, has my blood pumping. That's what makes me feel alive."

"After that. If you two are together… How will you fit your lifestyle with being a mother? Because no matter what you tell yourself, that's ultimately what you'll become. A mama to those kids. Are you ready for what it implies?"

"To be honest, that's the part that scares me the least, Ems. We are already bound. I love them so much. But you're right… After the tour, I don't wanna work a nine-to-five job or get a permanent teaching position. Or be someone else's trophy wife. I guess we'll see how the next six months go, and I'll reevaluate my career choices from there. Lots of things can happen in half a year. I'm confident it will turn out okay."

My sister pulled me into her arms. "Now I'll have to serve Sam Stevens my big-sister *I'm watching you* and *don't mess with my little sister* warnings. I'm already excited." She rubbed her hands together, mischief flashing in her eyes. "You think Mika and Justine will one day be as close as we are? That their tragedy will bring them closer? Like it did to us?"

"Yep. They already are." I paused to drink a glass of water and cool down my conflicted emotions because the mere thought or talk about Sam got me unnerved.

"Have you told him? About our past?"

I shook my head. "Not yet. I opened up to Jacob. It was the first time I trusted someone enough to be honest about everything, and it didn't prevent him from walking away. Next time I'll tell someone I love about my history, I'll make sure we're meant to have a long-lasting relationship. I've learned my lesson. It hurts too much when someone I care about breaks my heart."

"Love. You deserve it. Never settle for anything less."

I looked away, the tumult inside me messing with my composure.

"Maddie, about our story… I understand. I have a hard time telling it too. It's okay. Don't rush anything. I'm not a relationship expert, but if Sam Stevens is the one, you'll know. Yeah, I believe he'll respect you enough to wait until you're ready to share. Don't stress over it."

"Thank you, Ems. For always having my back. Even when you were just a kid. I wasn't your responsibility, but you always made sure I was safe and sound and nobody could hurt me. That I had food to eat. You sacrificed a lot for me. And you saved my life."

"Anytime. I would do it all over again if we were faced

with the same situation. You're not only my little sister, Maddie, but also my best friend. I'll always have your back."

"We turned out pretty good, considering the shitty hand we were dealt with. It made us stronger. In retrospect, I'm not sure I'd change our past because we wouldn't be standing here today if our stories had been different."

"It feels like a lifetime ago. Are you happy?" she asked.

"I am. The reality of the tour gets me giddy, and along with that, all aspects of my life are finally clicking into place."

"Big sister's warning. Follow your heart, okay? It's usually pretty perceptive and rarely wrong."

I nodded, and my sister wrapped her arms around me.

"Everything will be fine, Maddie. I have a great feeling about this. I love you."

———

"I heard my girls have rehearsed a song, and they asked if they could sing it today," Sam announced in front of the people crowded in his backyard.

His eyes searched mine when he said *my girls*. Effervescent feelings soared inside me.

"Yeah, they're following in my footsteps. I had no idea, I swear. It was a surprise to me too." His proud grin illuminated his face. "Please give my daughters the applause they deserve."

Justine, Mikaella, and I took the stage, aka the back deck. Jitters worked inside me. How could Sam do this for a living? Entertain a crowd. The girls looked to be in their element, though. They inherited their father's performing genes, both of them confident and strong-headed, even at their young age.

"The girls and I have worked hard to be ready for tonight. Sam, this one is for you," I said, my voice quivering. I held my breath.

He watched me with sizzling intensity and tipped his head. I dissolved there, unable to look elsewhere. The connection we shared broke only when our gazes drifted to the girls, now standing in front of me.

Aisha Jones, whom I'd asked earlier if she could accompany the girls with her guitar, strummed the first chord of "Summer Night."

Justine and Mikaella started singing like we'd practiced, standing tall in the middle of the makeshift stage, holding each other's hands.

> **One Friday afternoon, that summer**
> **The wind was blowing my hair**
> **Convertible, country music, a picnic in a basket**
> **And the girls in the backseat**
> **The kids asked for waterfalls and sunshine**
> **I asked for fresh air and a sign everything would be all right**
> **We drove for hours, lost in our world...**

Sam's eyes darted to me, and he mouthed a *Wow* and a heartfelt *Thank you*.

I placed my hands on my chest and mirrored his elated expression. I'd never be able to lie to myself. Emily was right. I loved him—more than logic could explain. Even after all this time, the night we'd gotten drunk in that bar, lost in each other, still haunted my dreams. The dance we'd shared under the girls' watchful eyes still sent jitters through my heart when I let myself relive the moment. And the night when we'd finally given in to temptation still haunted my days at the mere thought of it. No matter however much I tried to block the memories, they came back with a vengeance, pulsing through me until I combusted.

Aisha stepped forward and joined the girls in the chorus, her voice low, making sure not to steal the spotlight.

> **…Sunset, laughter, memories
> in bulk
> This is how happiness should
> be (yeah, it should)
> As long as those smiles on
> their faces never falter
> As long as those magical
> summer nights never
> get old
> Just grab my hands, babies,
> and hold tight
> And together, let's forget about
> everything else for a little
> longer…**

Riley walked to me and nudged my arm. "Maddie, what you're doing for those kids is priceless. You are a blessing in their lives."

I squeezed my eyes shut to control the dampness forming behind my eyelids.

We returned our focus to the girls, so adorably dressed in matching ruffled denim dresses and teal cowboy boots.

The song ended, and Sam rushed to them, hugging his daughters and praising their performance.

From a safe distance, I melted at the scene, feelings of glee shooting through me.

Sam steered his face my way, and a spark I'd never noticed before flashed in his irises. A sparkle intended for me. Only me.

Right there, I had the certitude that if given a chance, we'd make it work because we were two parts of the same soul, always drawn together and finding comfort in each other's presence.

———

Sitting outside the bus hours later, around the portable fire pit he'd bought earlier, Sam and I enjoyed the silence of the night. The party had been a success, and the last guests had left over an hour ago. The girls were fast asleep in their beds inside, the day having drained all the energy from them.

"You rarely talk about your dreams," Sam said, uncapping a bottle of beer, his profile illuminated by the dancing flames. "Want one?"

I shook my head. I was satisfied with water at this late hour, my head still spinning from all the sangria I'd had earlier.

"What do you want?" he asked.

I frowned. "What do you mean?"

"In life. Career-wise. Family-wise. Passion-wise. In general."

I wiped the condensation off the glass in my hand. "It's

funny you ask. My sister told me today to never put my own dreams on the back burner for someone else."

Sam let out a throaty groan, and my gaze drifted to the rippling of his throat. "Are you? Putting your dreams on hold?"

I said *No* with a shake of my head, unable to stop smiling. "Nah. I'm exactly where I wanna be. The tour, this opportunity, it's what I like. I can't say it's what I'll always want, but for now, I'm perfectly happy where I am. Thank you for taking me with you. I've never said it. But I'm thankful. Every day."

His piercing eyes studied me. "What about the rest? Where do you see yourself five years from now? Still traveling the world or doing something else?"

"I will still work with children. That, I wouldn't trade for anything else. And I hope to be settled down. Maybe have kids of my own, a husband, be happy, and aim for new dreams. I know most people my age would cringe thinking about it and just wanna have fun, party, get high, and surf life, but I've never been like anyone else. I march to the rhythm of my own drums. Whatever it means."

"I think too many people in their twenties miss opportunities because they're trying to do it all without getting attached to anyone or anything. I'm not saying it's bad, but when I was your age, I had a plan. I stuck to it, and it worked out. So, I feel you."

I pinched my lips together, things I had meant to ask him burning the tip of my tongue. I breathed in a mix of air and courage and spoke. "Hypothetically, could you see yourself going the distance with me? I mean if it could work out between us, or are you always gonna see me as a kid? Someone not old enough to be with you… Someone too inexperienced to share your life…and your world."

He said nothing for a long while. I squirmed in my

chair after I put my glass down on the ground and hid my hands in the sleeves of the hoodie he had lent me earlier. The one that smelled of him. Woodsy aftershave and clean man. The moonlight shone on him, and it distracted me, as I couldn't detach my eyes from his angular face sporting a happy grin most of the time nowadays. A part of me believed I was the reason—or at least, a big part of it.

A wave of discomfort washed through me. The longer it took him to reply, the worse the scenarios my mind fabricated became.

"Maddie."

I held my breath and stayed silent.

"I tried. I really did. To come up with tons of reasons why you and I wouldn't work out in the long run. Age mattered at first. Or maybe it was just an excuse to find… well, an excuse to keep you at arm's length. And for the record, I don't see you as a kid. That's another thing I tried to convince myself of. It didn't work either. You're a kickass woman. All grown-up. You're smart, funny, distractingly beautiful, sassy, and you have me wrapped around your little finger." He let out a warm chuckle. "I can see the appeal because it seems to work great with the girls. Anyway, there's nothing I wouldn't do for you, and we're not even an item. So, conclude whatever you want and scratch the word hypothetically from your vocabulary. I don't do hypothetical stuff when it comes to you. To answer your question, yes, I can see myself going the distance with you. Have babies, share our lives, grow old together. If that's what you wish too."

Was the blood pooling in my cheeks visible in the inky night?

"You'd have more kids if I asked you to? Hypothetically. Sorry, not hypothetically…"

We exchanged smiles laden with heavy, unsaid promises.

"I would if it were something you envision too…with me. We never know how the future will turn out to be, but so far, you and I, we make a great team. We connect on a level I had no clue existed before we met. We understand each other without words, and there's the pull. It's hard to resist. Also, I can picture us in a couple of years. You with a huge belly. Someday. And a little Maddie running around. No pressure, though. I have my arms full right now."

We both snickered. And my frantic pulse found its rhythm back.

Sam cleared his throat. "Before she quit on us, Lisa suffered two miscarriages."

"I'm sorry. I had no idea." I paused, surprised by his confession. "Do you think it broke up your marriage?" I asked.

"No. Life has a way. As if it knew we weren't destined to be together much longer. So, somehow, it prevented more children from being hurt by their mother's abandonment." He laughed as he said, "Took me hours of family therapy to acknowledge the fact. And to accept it."

"I'm glad it worked out in the end. Do you think the girls are better off without her?"

"At first, I didn't. Now I know they are. No questions asked. I can see how wrong our relationship was and how it would have affected them in many other ways growing up if she had stayed. Looking back, I'm not sure we even loved each other. We came together very young and got lost in the excitement of my career. It was fun… Until it wasn't. She was toxic to our family because it was never about our kids and always about her. She would often use headaches as an excuse to avoid interacting with them. She was lethal with me too. When she would make unreason-able demands and get angry when I couldn't meet her unattainable standards. It took another dozen hours of therapy to grasp that piece of info."

We watched each other, both of us assessing the latest confessions we'd shared. Something potent simmered between us. It charged the air with more lust particles and a meaningful amount of trust and respect. For being able to open our hearts with no limitations. For being able to tell our truths as they were.

"Why did you walk out on me that day? At the agency?" I asked. The question had been nagging me since the day we had met, and the intimacy we shared right now felt like a good moment to clear the air once and for all.

"Because"—Sam rubbed his nape—"at first, I felt contradictory emotions toward you. And I had a fucking hard-on. You woke up something in me, something strong, and I panicked because I couldn't picture myself spending six months in close proximity to you. Some fifty-year-old woman wouldn't have threatened my sanity. And my libido. But you did. From the get-go. And it freaked me out."

I relaxed my stance. "What changed your mind?"

"Riley. He said to give you a chance. To dream again. And that in order to do so, I needed you by my side."

My skin heated up at his words.

"Let's just say he wasn't wrong. And not just on the nanny part of the deal."

Neither of us said anything else for a long time, every-thing we'd confessed becoming more pieces of string binding us together.

"Can I ask you something?" Sam asked, sipping his beer. "Why did Emily threaten to ruin me if I messed with her little sister, aka you? What did you tell her?" He arched a brow, and I could tell he wasn't mad I confided in my sister, but rather curious.

"She said you were acting like a possessive creep out there when Becks made a joke about me. And she came to the conclusion our relationship wasn't just..huh…business. Or platonic. I confirmed nothing, but she knows me. She's good at reading people. Don't worry…you're not special. She gives the same speech to any guy getting too close to me."

Sam arched his brow higher, amusement playing on his features now. "So, I'm not special?"

I snorted. "Just a teeny tiny bit," I said, bringing my thumb and forefinger together. My teasing faded. "We leave in a week. Does the reality of kicking off the tour make you anxious?"

He held his hand out, palm facing up. Without thinking, I slid mine into it and relished the way our fingers threaded.

"Truth?" he asked.

I nodded.

"Every tour. Every album. Every concert is stressful. You never know how it'll turn out. How the crowd will react. But it's also addictive. And this time, I have you… and the girls. So, I'm calmer than I've ever been. Even if I fail or it doesn't work out, I know I will have tried. Now I understand that my life doesn't begin or end on a stage. There are people counting on me. People I care about. In the equation, they are much more valuable than any song I'll ever write or any crowd I'll ever entertain."

My heart bloomed in my chest. Even without saying it in words, Sam had just declared me as an important part of his life.

"We should get some sleep because you look very hot right now with the moon shining on you. And that curve of your lips is hard to resist," he said with a glint in his eye.

I loved how we had come to terms with our attraction and could now talk about it openly, without having to keep everything under wraps anymore.

"Are you sure we'll be able to behave once we're on that bus seven days a week for months?"

Sam grinned, the tilt of his lips giving him a boyish, mischievous allure. "No. But we'll try."

"I should get to bed then because I've had a few drinks tonight. My control is flimsy right now, and I can't promise to be on my best behavior."

Never letting go of my hand, he turned the fire off and led me inside our home for the next six months.

His lips descended on the side of my face.

He kissed my cheek, and my knees buckled as his hand found my waist and held me in place. "Again, thank you for today. The song, the girls. It was amazing. I'm still at a loss for words, which says a lot. Now I'll have to watch them closely, or Riley will try to sign them."

"They were badass up there, right? It looked like they'd been doing this multiple times in the past. A natural talent they've inherited from you."

"Pride isn't strong enough to describe how I felt. For now, I'll stick to thank you. Thank you, Madison Prescott, for coaching my kids to sing one of the songs that means the most to me. And for making us ridiculously happy." His lips brushed mine in a featherlight kiss. "Night, Maddie."

I sucked in a breath imprinted with the scent of him. "Night, Sam."

Lying in bed, unable to catch some sleep, my mind raced as I thought about my day, my conversations with Devon, Emily, and Sam. Everything he had said. All he'd confessed. My pulse went ballistic as I replayed his words —all perfect to me.

The expression in his eyes when the girls had taken the stage. It would forever live within me. The exhilaration. The pride. Because I felt important to him. Cherished. Unique.

On my tiptoes, I escaped the confinement of my room and approached his bedroom. He had a queen-sized bed and a dresser, and a private bathroom, while the girls and I shared ours. Not that it mattered, though. A shower was just that, a shower. And fancy wasn't in my vocabulary. My living quarters, which were exclusively mine, were more than enough.

I inhaled a cleansing breath and knocked on his door.

"Come on in." His voice resonated from the other side of the panel.

I walked into the dark room, careful not to bump into anything.

"Hey you," Sam greeted me when I reached his bed after he turned the bedside lamp on. "Can't sleep?"

"Nope. You?"

"Same." He flipped the covers over and invited me in.

I hesitated for a moment, but he reached forward and tugged at my hand, and I surrendered.

"I was about to come get you."

"You were?" I turned to my side, and his arms pulled me closer to his chest.

"After everything we shared tonight, it felt wrong to put that much distance between us. And I wanted to make sure I didn't scare you with my honesty."

"Why?"

"Because I talked of babies. And the future. And I don't know... I feel it's best to know from the get-go we expect the same things from a relationship, but sometimes it can come out as a bit intense. Just so you now, I'll never put pressure on you, Maddie. I just wanted to clear the air. Make it obvious in case it wasn't before."

"Can I sleep here? For a few minutes? With you?"

My boldness impressed me, and my heart flipped in my chest as I waited for his answer.

Sam nuzzled my neck from behind, his unconcealed manhood pressing between my ass cheeks. "If it were just me, you'd sleep here forever. If it were just the two of us, there would be no questions asked, no self-denial, no walls to erect around us. I wouldn't waste another second being without you. Not being buried inside you. Kissing you and loving you."

A batch of happy tears lodged in my eyes. "What would you do to me if it were just us?"

His breathing quickened, and my body throbbed at the first words that passed the rim of his lips. "First, I would get rid of all these clothes between us. Then, I would take my sweet time, exploring each inch of your body. With my hands. With my teeth. With my tongue. With my cock. Once I'd know it so well I could draw it from just memory, I would taste you. All of you. Until you climaxed on my tongue and you saw nothing else but faraway galaxies when you closed your eyes. Until my name became the sole word in your vocabulary. Then I would kiss you. So you could taste yourself on my lips and see why you're driving me so crazy. Finally, I would push myself deep inside you. Until our bodies and souls bonded together and there was no telling us apart. I'd play your body the same way I play my guitar, with dedication and confidence and in perfect harmony. And then we'd come together in a bliss neither of us could escape from, our souls forever connected. Then I would start all over again because I would never be satiated."

I hadn't even realized Sam's hand had plunged between my thighs, too entranced by his words while he recited how he'd pleasure my body if given the chance.

He shoved my panties to the side, tracing the seam of my arousal with a rough finger.

I swallowed, new sensations surging through me. "I thought we said we'd wait?" I whispered, my body responding to his touch like he knew it inside and out already.

I rolled my hips over his hand.

Fireworks exploded in my belly.

I moaned, and Sam growled behind me, his lips busy sampling the skin of my shoulder, his teeth nibbling my flesh, and his tongue soothing the pain.

"I won't be able to sleep until I know you're fully taken care of."

"What about you?" I croaked out, breathless, whimpers exiting my mouth.

"I'll wait, babe. Let's say kissing and you coming apart in my arms aren't things I can forfeit anymore. These are both allowed. I've just changed the rules."

His fingers accelerated their pace, pressing inside me as the heel of his hand brushed my clit with every stroke.

"But…" I couldn't think clearly anymore. My vision blurred. "Y-you." I could barely keep it together. "I wanna please you too. Touch you." The sensations inside me exploded. With my hand blanketing his, I made sure he never went off rhythm as I chased the orgasm about to rip me apart. "Please."

Sam laughed behind me. "Are you begging me to end you or to make me come?"

"I…" I breathed faster. "You." Why was I unable to form a complete sentence? "Me. This." My toes curled. My head tilted back. "Both. Ohmygod, Sam." His fingers pinched one of my hard nipples over the fabric of my shirt, and I came undone, turning my head and crying my release into my pillow.

"Stay," he whispered against my skin.

With my hand still enveloping his, I kept them between my legs, not in a rush for him to withdraw his intoxicating fingers from my body. No doubt I'd feel empty without them inside me once we broke apart. "I don't wanna leave. What are we gonna do?" I asked, breathless.

"I'm done being afraid." Sam flipped me to my other side and tilted my head back to meet his eyes. "I was think-ing..." He rolled his jaw back and forth, and I was mesmerized by the action. "I'm done here."

A chill traced my spine, and I steeled against him.

His hands froze on my scalp. "I've thought about it. We have no idea what life will throw at us. Why should we wait to be together? I'm dying to do all those things I promised earlier. My bed feels empty each night you're not in it. We could make it a permanent thing... You sleeping here. What do you think?"

I blinked. My pulse kicked up. "You-you wanna make it official? Us? You and me?"

He shrugged, and his lips turned into the most bewitching smile, all aimed at me. "Not at first. Because we gotta ease the girls into the idea. Justine would be okay with it, but Mika... She'll react. And I can't prevent it or guess how it'll go. Thus, we better go slow and show her it's better for everybody. And that you're taking the place that is rightfully yours."

"You sure?"

"One hundred percent. And perhaps we could wait a bit to tell Riley. Until he knows it's serious and we're not trying to mess up the tour. He put a lot of work into this, and I don't want him stressing over the repercussions of our relationship."

"Sam? You really wanna be with me? No more restrictions?"

He shook his head. "Been thinking. A lot. Lying here in the dark. I'm done not living my life the way I intend it to be. If it goes south, let's promise each other, here and now, the girls will always be the priority."

"I swear." It was impossible to contain all the euphoria spreading inside me. The emotions I read in Sam's gaze—commitment, devotion, trust, and a whole lot of lust—played with every string of my heart. A dreadful thought arose in me, spoiling the moment. "Sam, there's something, though. I can't be paid to be your girlfriend. It's wrong. On all counts."

He smiled at me. "You're not. I'm paying you to care for my kids. I'm paying the nanny and teacher in you. It's just business. When you're not teaching them or watching over them, you're mine. And no one is paying you to be with me. Okay?"

Twinkles of mischief flashed in his eyes, appearing for the very first time. I relished how they were directed at me. As if he couldn't refrain from the dirty thoughts swimming in his head anymore.

"Wanna continue what we've started?" I asked.

"Nah. Tonight, I wanna hold you in my arms. And feel your heartbeat. We have our entire lives in front of us."

Time slowed down.

My pulse evened out.

His breathing steadied.

And before either of us realized it, we fell asleep in each other's arms. For the very first time.

Safe and content.

And closer than we'd ever been before.

# Chapter 12

### Sam

Waking up to an empty bed, I sighed and scanned my surroundings, wishing Madison could still be in my arms this morning. My bed felt oddly cold without her in it. My palm lingered on the pillow next to mine. The one she'd cried into when she'd come last night. Having her here, in my arms, felt so natural. It was like she'd been always sleeping beside me. For a second, I wondered if she had switched bedrooms in the middle of the night, fearing my kids would catch us, because I had no recollection of her leaving my side.

Refreshed, in a better mood than I'd been in a long time, and ready to kick off the tour, I showered and exited the silent bus on my tiptoes, not wanting to wake up the three girls still asleep inside, the ones who owned all of my heart. The rain outside did nothing to deter my cheerfulness as I sauntered to the house.

In the kitchen, I found a note Madison had left on the

counter, and it eased my mind to know she hadn't left my side out of fear or because she had second thoughts about us.

> *Gone to get donuts.*
> *Be back soon.*
> *Last night meant a lot.*
> *x*

A traitorous grin formed on my lips. After fighting my own desires for a long time and keeping Madison at a distance, I had no more fear where she was concerned. I meant everything I'd said to her yesterday. Every word. My life had a new meaning, a new direction, and I loved every minute of it. It had just taken me a moment to acknowledge the fact that she made me a better man and to stop the self-inflicted torture of keeping her at arm's length.

A wave of thrilling happiness I had never experienced before washed over me, and my heart soared at the realization I might have found my person—when I least expected it.

The doorbell disrupted my thoughts, and I welcomed Riley in.

"Hey, man." I glanced at my watch. "What are you doing here at this hour?"

"We have some last-minute details to go over. Sorry I didn't call ahead. I was in the neighborhood and decided to stop by. Is it a good time?" He surveyed the silent room around us. "Where's everyone? No morning greeting from the two little superstars?"

"They're still asleep. Enjoy the quiet while it lasts. Coffee?"

"Yes."

I was about to sit when the front door opened and shut. Seconds later, I got cornered by a cheerful Justine wearing a bright orange dress with blue butterfly wings strapped on her back and a plastic crown perched on the top of her head. I forgot Madison had helped them choose outfits yesterday.

"*Daddyyyy*." She sprinted into my arms and I lifted her up.

"What's up, Princess? Sleep well?"

She squeezed my face with her tiny hands. "*Yesss*. Love the big bus."

"Where's your sister?"

"Coming. Where's Maddie? I can't find her anywhere. *Maddddddie*?" she hollered.

"Out. She should be back soon."

"Breakfast?" I asked at the same time Mikaella walked in, her hair a curly mess. I fought a smile. "Morning, sweet pea. Hungry?"

She growled something I interpreted as a *yes*.

"Mika," Justine said, rushing to her sister and hugging her as if they hadn't seen each other in months, not just mere minutes ago.

My heart vibrated with a new layer of excitement at the journey we all were about to embark on together.

Once the girls were settled with waffles in front of the TV in the den, I focused my attention on my friend. "Sorry. Where were we? Oh yes, last-minute details. I'm all ears now."

"Where's Maddie?" he asked. "You never said. I thought she would attend our meetings because there's a thing or two we gotta figure out with her. Logistically speaking, it would be better if she were here."

My phone went off in my back pocket, and thinking it might be her, I brought it to my ear and raised a finger toward Riley, as if to say, *Just a sec.* "Hey, where are you? Everything all right?"

"Mr. Stevens? Mr. Sam Stevens?"

I made a throat-clearing noise and straightened at the sound of my name, spoken in a voice far too serious for this early hour. Just the caller's tone sent chills down my spine. I could already tell it wasn't a courtesy call. My blood iced in my veins. Goose bumps spread across my body.

My airways constricted, but I succeeded in letting a low "Speaking" cross my lips, bracing myself for whatever news this person would deliver.

My heart pounded in my skull. I tried to swallow, but my throat tightened, making it nearly impossible.

Riley's phone buzzed, and he frowned at the screen before bringing the device to his ear, a somber expression taking over his face.

The voice on the other end of the phone kept talking, but it sounded miles away. I could barely make out the words.

My heart felt like it had been punctured, and I feared I would bleed out on my kitchen floor.

# Chapter 13
## Madison

I can't see. I have gone blind. No, not blind. I can't open my eyes. My skull feels as if it has burst into two. Pain. So much pain. More than I can bear. I can't feel the rest of my body. Why is my pulse racing? What is happening to me? I can't breathe. Sam. I need Sam. Where is he?

Darkness pulled me under.

I pried my heavy eyelids open to a blur of light and shadow. I blinked, trying to dissipate the fog, but it wouldn't clear. How much time had passed? Had it been hours? Or days? The pounding of my heart reverberated against the walls of my skull. An iron taste lingered in my mouth. *Blood.* Why was I bleeding? Nausea swirled in my stomach at the stench permeating the air. I rubbed my temple, trying to soothe the pain all over my head and neck. Nothing worked. A tear flowed down my cheek. Dark spots appeared in front of my eyes.

*Where am I? Where is Sam? I want Sam.*

My eyelids weighed a ton. No matter how hard I tried, I couldn't keep them open. A curtain of darkness descended, swallowing me whole.

Another wave of nausea hit me. Stronger than before. The ringing in my ears wouldn't go away. Excruciating pain held me captive as if a dozen trucks were running over me. I couldn't seem to move my left leg. Panic crept in. I tried to wiggle my toes, but only the ones on my right foot responded to my silent command. Something held me in place. I tried to move my hand, to feel around me, but a sharp pain shot through my ribs and stopped me.

*I am feeling cold. So, so cold. Why am I freezing?*

Shivers started deep in my core and raced up and down my body in multiple ripples. Sweat drenched my clothes. Or was it blood?

*Sam, please save me.*

My stomach churned. My heart felt like it was going to burst out of me.

A scream built inside me. Why did my entire being hurt so bad? It was as if I were trapped in hell.

Shadows closed in around me. I wanted to sleep.

*Sam, are you there….? Can anyone hear me? Ems? I should call my sister. She would come get me.*

A sharp pain radiated through my body, and I wailed in agony.

I lost the battle against the exhaustion taking over me.

An alarm rang in the distance.

Then nothing.

Only darkness and silence.

# Chapter 14

Sam

"Accident."

"Madison Prescott."

"Surgery."

"Car crash."

I blinked. The words didn't register. I must have heard them wrong.

My entire body hurt.

What was going on?

My children, now standing beside me, tugged at my shirt.

"Daddy, why are you screaming?" Justine asked, her eyes full of questions, her brow creased with fear.

Was I screaming? In what parallel universe had I landed?

"Daddy?" Mikaella echoed, her voice quivering. "Daddy? Why are you crying? There are tears on your cheeks."

Tears? I brought a hand to my eyes. They were damp. What was going on with me? Was I going nuts? Was this how it felt to lose your mind?

With a step back to escape the little hands pulling at my clothes, I surveyed the space around me, not registering anything.

Riley tore the phone from my grasp and spoke to the stranger, whose name or role I didn't know.

The buzzing in my ear blocked all other sounds.

Tears burned at the back of my eyes, then spilled down my cheeks. I could feel them now. Shards of glass lined my throat.

After what appeared to be hours, Riley led me to the couch and forced me to sit down. "Stevens?" I watched him but couldn't see him.

I blinked. My focus refused to come back.

"STEVENS?" he repeated, louder this time.

That did the trick because I snapped out of it. "Wh… what?" My voice came out gravelly and weak.

"I called Devon. She's on her way. We'll go as soon as she gets here."

I blinked again. Nothing he said added up.

"Sam," he ordered, sternly this time. "Listen to me."

My friend wasn't the type to get angry, so when he spoke to me in that tone, I had no choice but to listen to him. "Madison had an accident. She's at the hospital. Her sister Emily called me. She'll meet us there. I won't lie to you. It…it sounds bad. They reached out to her, but she's in Atlanta for a medical conference. She needs you to go there until she gets back. Can you do that?"

I nodded, still unsure I was hearing him right.

"Wh...huh…what? How?"

Devon joined us and exchanged words with Riley, but nothing registered with me. She rested her hand on my shoulder in a comforting gesture before taking a seat opposite us.

"Okay," Riley continued, "I had June on the phone moments ago. You know, my assistant. Sam, are you even listening? She'll take over, so I can go with you. She's already made a few phone calls." He rubbed his eyebrows, averting his eyes for a second. He inhaled before bringing his attention back to me. "A guy ran a red light and crashed into the side of Maddie's car at full speed. She got stuck inside. They had to use the jaws of life to extricate her. We gotta go. Now."

He helped me to my feet.

"Is Maddie okay?" Mikaella asked nearing us, and I hated the idea she'd witnessed this. My daughter was seeing another moment of pain. She was growing up too soon. At first, it was her mother abandoning us. Now Madison was hurt, and her father was in shock. I needed to pull myself together. For her.

Before I could do that, Devon kneeled before her. "We don't know yet, sweetie. Your daddy and Uncle Riley will go find out. You and Justine will stay with me."

"Is she going to die?" Mikaella asked, despair swimming in her glossy eyes.

"Let's pray for her, okay? I'm sure she'll be able to hear us," Devon continued. She swallowed, and her eyes met mine for a fleeting second.

Mikaella turned to me, fat tears streaming down her cheeks. "Daddy, do something," she pleaded. "When I'm scared, Maddie always holds my hand. Hold her hand, okay, Daddy? Make her better. Bring her back."

I lifted my daughter in my arms. "I swear I'll do my best, sweet pea. Stay with Devon and your sister. Be a good girl."

I kissed the top of her head and hugged both my kids, reassuring them, before Riley led me away to his car.

For the entire ride, I watched the scenery pass by through the passenger window, unable to make sense of the turmoil raging inside my head. Riley spent the entire time on the phone, barking orders to one and all, discussing press releases and deadlines with June, and calling the hospital to have them ready to meet with us.

"Hang in there, Stevens." His words reached my ears, then dissipated into thin air.

He clapped my shoulder a few times and said something to me, but I couldn't hear it. In a state of numbness, I looked at him without computing any word he said. I had no emotions, no fears, no nothing. The whole scene felt like a dream. And none of it seemed real.

Riley stopped the car in front of a door in the basement where no one could spot me. For now, I required a little privacy, and I was grateful to my friend for having set this up. Brent, my head of security, met us there, and we followed him and a nurse through a series of corridors up to an elevator. On the sixth floor, we were brought to a room where the medical team was waiting for us. I registered only white walls and recessed lighting as we walked toward them. Frigid and cold.

A doctor wearing green scrubs held out his hand. "Mr. Stevens, Mr. Burns, I'm Doctor Bera, the head of surgery, and these are Doctor Connor, the head of orthopedics, and Doctor Patel, the head of plastic surgery."

The roaring of my heart rang in my ears.

*Plastic surgery?* My stomach churned. I felt lightheaded. Bile rose in my throat. With a step back in an attempt to capture some air to breathe on my own, I closed my eyes to avoid fainting. I joined my hands together in prayer over my mouth while I made every effort to stay in the moment, to silence the scenarios my mind wanted to conjure.

*Plastic surgery?* It crushed my heart just thinking about it. Fuck, how bad was it? Would Madison even survive? I licked my lips, inhaled, and raked my fingers through my hair, trying to keep my cool.

"How is Madison?" Riley asked, and I thanked him mentally for taking over, as all my words were locked in my throat.

"Ms. Prescott suffered injuries all over her abdomen and leg, with metal fragments lodged in the left side of her ribs, pelvis, and thighs. We managed to remove them. In the impact, she banged her head. There's no fracture of the skull or brain edema at the moment. We are monitoring her closely, but we're not overly concerned. Her brain activity is normal, and there is no active bleeding. What we're worried about is her left leg. The bones are crushed, and she's lost a lot of blood. She will be in surgery for some time as we are trying to salvage her limb. But it is touch and go. We are doing our best, but we cannot be certain yet whether she will need an amputation. With an injury this extensive, we also have to closely monitor for infection and sepsis."

My tongue untied, and words finally passed my lips. "Is she—? Will she—?" Even if I tried, I couldn't voice those possibilities.

"At this point, we have no way of knowing how it will turn out. She needs surgical debridement of her limb and stabilization of her multiple fractures with rods and screws. Her young age plays in her favor, though. Still, if she survives the rounds of surgeries, she'll have a difficult and painful recovery in front of her. Therapy will be an extensive and long process. Tough on her and on all of you."

A wave of shock nearly knocked me off my feet. I

clenched my fists at my sides and dug my heels into the linoleum, struggling not to crumble as pain coursed through my body.

"Can I…can I see her?" I asked.

"No. Not right now. Sorry."

"Just once. I need to see her once."

"Please let us do our job. I know how hard it must be for you, but you have to trust us. We're doing our best to save her. We'll keep you updated. Our staff set up this room for you, so you don't have to sit in the common waiting area. We're aware if the news leaks out, the media and some unwelcome fans may invade the hospital, and nobody wishes for that outcome. Again, if you need anything, let us know." The same nurse who was with us earlier entered the room. "Mr. Johnson will take over from here."

After the medical team left, silence filled the room as we tried to absorb the weight of their words. Seconds later, Riley was on the phone, slipping back into manager mode and informing June of the latest development in case she had to answer any questions. Then he asked her to be ready to cancel my shows and all engagements for the first two weeks of the tour. He called someone else, but by then, I had tuned out his voice.

Time idled.

My brain went blank.

Nothing else mattered anymore.

The arms on the clock, fixed on the opposite wall, moved at a sluggish speed. Seconds felt like hours. And hours like years.

All this time, I sat in a chair, leaning forward with my elbows resting on my knees and my face buried in my hands. I turned down every attempt my friend made to talk, and every cup of cheap hospital coffee Brent brought me.

The morning passed in a blur.

The sun wasn't at its zenith anymore when a familiar figure entered the small room.

"Sam."

Emily hurried into my arms when I moved to stand up. We hugged for the longest time. "Any development?" she asked when we broke apart. I took in her swollen eyes and reddened cheeks.

I shook my head. "The doctors said something about metal fragments in her body. Left leg being crushed. She's lost a lot of blood."

Riley jumped in. "She'd been in surgery for hours. I would have flown in another surgeon, but it turns out Dr. Bera and his team are the best in their field. Madison is lucky they're the ones in charge. We're still waiting for an update. When we talked earlier, they said they were trying to salvage her leg."

Emily spoke again. "Yes, Dr. Bera is indeed a very good surgeon. I've assisted him a few times, and I can vouch for him. I'll get updated on Maddie's situation. You all stay here. I'll be back as soon as I have more news for you." As she spoke, the concerned sister vanished, leaving only the doctor. I bet it helped her cope with the trauma. Maybe seeing it through the eyes of a doctor made this surreal reality easier to bear. She squared her shoulders and let out a long, deliberate breath before leaving us.

Without another word, Riley, Brent, and I all sat down, with our silence for company. Only the ordinary hum of the hospital and the rush of our breaths echoed through those bleak walls.

The wait became untenable. I watched my phone screen every couple of minutes as if Madison would text me any second to tell me it was all a prank. Unable to stay still any longer, I jumped to my feet and paced the room. With my fingers laced behind my neck, I inhaled through my nose, praying for the coils tightening my stomach to loosen.

After what felt like forever, Emily walked in, followed by Dr. Bera and his team.

Riley joined me in the middle of the room. I held my breath, balling my hands into fists, bracing myself for the updates about Madison's condition.

Emily stood next to me, clasping my hand in hers. I was grateful because at this moment, I needed every bit of support I could get.

"So?" I asked, in a breathless voice.

# Chapter 15



Seated in an armchair, I held the hand of a heavily sedated Madison, just as Mikaella advised me to. Since I couldn't pull her into my arms, it was the only thing I could do, other than speak to her, that would let her know I was here by her side and would never go away.

"Hey, it's me," I said.

Her visage was bruised and swollen. She had stitches on her cheek, a bandage over her forehead, IV lines attached to her arms, a neck line for life-saving drugs, and a tracheal tube down her throat connected to a ventilator. The rest of her body was wrapped in dressings under the hospital covers. She looked nothing like the woman I'd kissed goodnight almost twenty-four hours ago. Since she was placed in isolation to prevent infection, I had to be suited up—gown, cap, mask, gloves—before I could meet her.

The constant beeping sounds of the machines regulating all her vitals reverberated through the room.

A tear trailed down my face. "I'm…I'm so sorry…for everything. You shouldn't be lying here." I used my sleeve to rub my watery eyes. "The doctors said the next few days are critical. They can't tell me your prognosis until then. I am shaken up, Maddie. I need you. You-you have to fight this. Do you hear me? You gotta come back to me." I raked my fingers through my hair. "I don't wanna lie to you. It is…it is bad…huh…pretty bad. You have been banged up inside out. Don't worry about your head, okay? It is fine. Your left leg suffered the brunt of the injury. Nobody knows the outcome yet. You were in surgery for almost sixteen hours." I paused, collecting fragments of courage within me, steeling myself to continue speaking. "The surgeon said there were some moments when the blood loss was massive, but you did good. I swear. You didn't allow yourself to be sucked in. I'm so proud of you. You are strength and courage, Maddie, and right now, I am learning so much from you."

My voice stuttered to a stop as I tried to swallow the giant lump in my throat.

"Maddie, I gotta tell you something. I…I am done hiding my feelings from myself and from you. You see… I love you. I've been afraid to voice them out loud for the longest time. Afraid if I did, my happiness could be stolen from me. I realize now it never mattered." I snorted. "I-I didn't even say the L-word out loud, and you still got hurt. My heart almost got ripped out of my chest no matter what. I should have told you when I had…when I had the chance… I'm so sorry you never heard those words from me before now." I tightened my squeeze on her fingers and took a deep breath in to calm the storm raging in me. "Madison Prescott, I love you. I'll tell you that every day for the rest of my life if you come back to me…to us. I will make your happiness my life's mission."

I leaned forward, hoping my words carried to her ears.

"You gotta be strong, okay?" I stared at her as if the intensity of it could reach a place deep inside her, and I addressed the flame, I knew she possessed, to fight for her life. "You better fight this and win. I know you'll get through this because you're strong and stubborn, and you never back down when you know you can do something. I won't let you give up. You have my word on that." I huffed. "You're not alone. You have me. Just get better, okay?" A soft laugh left my pinched lips. "If you could see how badass you look right now. Like you got knocked out in the ring. Don't worry, your face…it'll all heal."

I pressed my forehead to our joined hands, hoping I could send all the healing power I could muster through this small contact. I closed my eyes, trying to quiet the wild beating of my heart, and prayed like never before.

Then I opened my eyes. "Emily has been taking care of you. We're all waiting for you to get well. I'm right here. I'm not going anywhere."

The automatic doors of the ICU slid open, startling me. I straightened in my chair, wiping away the tears that soaked my face.

"How are you holding on, Mr. Stevens?" Mara, the nurse in charge of Madison asked, wearing an isolation gown identical to mine, observing the data displayed on the monitors and noting them on a tablet.

"Same."

"Let's talk outside, okay?"

I nodded and followed her after I whispered one last *I love you* to Madison.

Mara and I both removed our masks, and I let the

heaviness of the situation register. Away from Madison, I didn't have to pretend to be stronger than I really was.

"Any updates?" I asked, pushing my hands into my pockets, not knowing what to do with them.

"Ms. Prescott's vitals are stable. The next forty-eight to seventy-two hours are critical. She's not out of the woods yet, but she's in good hands. She's strong. We're hopeful."

I bowed my head.

Emily joined us and moved to stand up beside me, gripping my arm fiercely. "How is she holding up?" she asked the nurse.

"Your sister is a fighter." Mara addressed both of us. "We'll continue to monitor Ms. Prescott closely. Don't hesitate if you have questions. I'll give you two some time before I come back to check on her in a little while."

The door closed behind her, and Emily pivoted to face me.

"Sam, you look like hell," she said, the corner of her lips lifting up. The expression in her eyes betrayed her worries.

"Yeah, well, I have no idea what I'm doing. Beside her, I can't seem to stop talking. Filling the silence and masking the beeping of the machines. I'm a mess."

"Even if she can't speak, Maddie knows you're here. I know how hard it must be for you," she said, squeezing my arm. "Hold on, okay? Keep talking to her."

I inhaled, averted my eyes for a beat, and returned my attention to her. "Last night...after everyone left...we made the choice...we've decided to be together. To give our relationship a try. Not to hide from our feelings any longer." I let the words settle in. "Ems, I love her, and I never told her. For the longest time, I was being a chicken-shit, keeping her at a distance, convincing myself she was better off without me. And now I'm afraid I'll never get a chance to tell her how much she means to me."

The tears I swallowed felt like tiny needles when they ran down the fragile, raw lining of my throat.

Emily wrapped her arms around my shoulders this time, and I held her there. In the simple gesture, we brought each other comfort. Strength to go through the reality that was hitting us. In that instant, she reminded me so much of her younger sister, her heart bleeding for those she loved. Like Madison, I could recognize the strength emanating from her, and for a moment, I wished it would rub off on me. One thing was clear, though. The Prescott sisters were angels on this Earth, and I was thankful for their presence in my life.

"And you, how are you holding up?" I asked once we broke apart.

She sighed. "Inside, I'm freaking out. But the doctor in me is trying to see the situation from a medical perspective. I've never faced this kind of challenge before." We both remained silent for a long while, watching Madison through the glass door. "I spoke to my parents. They're arriving tomorrow."

"Ask Riley for June's contact. If you need anything, she'll take care of it. She always does."

Emily returned her attention to me. "Sam, you're one of the good ones. Maddie is lucky to have you in her life. For the longest time, I feared she wouldn't find her place in this world. She never had a lot of friends growing up, always preferring to be on her own... Unable to let people fully in. Then she started traveling, looking for something she thought she couldn't find here. A purpose. She's the best person I know, and my gut tells me everything she's been searching for was right under her nose the entire time."

I dragged my hand through my hair, unable to avert my eyes from the pallid figure on the bed.

"Thanks to you and your children, she's thriving. I haven't seen her this happy in…forever. She has never seemed as at ease anywhere than around you guys. I'm thankful to you for all of it. We've been through a lot together, and I'm happy she's loved the way she should be. Even more with the current turn of events."

A fresh batch of tears welled up in my eyes. "Ems, be honest with me. I know how strong she is, but do you think she will fight back? Or if she makes it through, do you think this," I pointed to the monitors, "will change her forever?"

"Maddie went through some hard times when we were little. If she survived those years, I have no doubt she can survive this ordeal. She's a fighter…always has been…or else, she wouldn't be here."

My attention drifted back to her, and I tried to read between the lines to grasp the words she didn't speak out loud. "What do you mean?"

Her eyes dimmed, and an expression I could not decipher filled her eyes. "If she hasn't told you yet, it means she's not ready. The time will come. I have no doubt. And, to be honest with you, I would rather she tell you herself."

I nodded. "Should I worry? She once said she'd been neglected when she was a little girl."

"Sam, give her some time. It's hard for her to open up about her struggles. She'll do so when she's ready. But don't worry. The past will never come back to mess with her."

I cast my eyes on Madison's figure and watched each wave on the ECG to make sure she was still alive and with me.

My eyes burned. The tears and exhaustion had taken their toll on my body and mind in the last few hours.

"Sam, you should get some sleep," Emily said after her while. "I can take over. I'm used to staying alert and awake all night. And Mara is a good friend of mine. I'll be the first to know if anything changes. I won't leave her side, I promise."

"What if she wakes up while I'm gone?"

She shook her head. "She won't. The medication will keep her sedated and on the ventilator until she shows signs of healing. If there's any change, I'll call you. Your kids need you. Your little girls must be scared. They need their daddy."

"Yeah… I talked to them earlier. Explained as much as I could." My voice cracked. "I have no idea how to face them without being able to answer all their questions because I lack the answers."

"Be honest. That's what matters. Right now, all we can do is pray. And hope for the best."

I hung my head low and stepped forward to hug her one last time. "I'll be here first thing in the morning," I said.

"Just rest for now. Want me to write you a prescription to help you sleep?"

"No. I refuse to numb myself. Thanks, though."

After I followed protocol and put on another set of sanitized clothes, I returned to Madison's side. Bending over the bed, I grazed the small patch of skin with no bandage on her forehead with my fingertip. "Get better. I love you and will be back in the morning. Emily will stay with you tonight." My lips curled into a tentative smile. "Don't give her trouble, okay? Good night."

———

I crashed on my bed as soon as my feet landed on my bedroom floor without even undressing. Devon had called earlier to tell me she'd keep the girls overnight. She'd taken them home after dinner. The gears of my brain worked at a dizzying speed. How did I go from hopeful to this version of despair within a day? I had no clue how to stay positive while facing this type of tragedy. Madison, my heart, the tour, my children. They had formed one big chaotic mess I wasn't ready to analyze. My insecurities clung to me like a second skin.

Madison must have been terrified, even if she couldn't show it. In the state she was in, how much could she understand about her situation? Could she tell that her life was hanging by a flimsy thread?

My stomach churned at the idea she was aware of the reality that had hit her.

I wondered if she could tell or if the medication prevented her brain from forming thoughts. There were so many questions swirling in my head for which I had no answer.

Then it hit me. That the next few hours could change the course of her life. Forever.

My eyes stung, and I squeezed them shut, pressing my fists against them to ease the pain. The one reminding me I was alive—and that I had to stand up for those I loved.

Unable to sort out my own thoughts, I abandoned myself to sleep, praying I would wake up and this shit show would turn out to be a very horrible dream.

The subdued voices of my daughters woke me up the next day.

"Justine, walk on your tiptoes," Mikaella whispered. "Don't wake Daddy up."

"Okay," my baby whisper-shouted. "Can I kiss him good morning?"

My eldest daughter sighed. "Sure. Uncle Riley said not to wake him up. That he didn't sleep for long and needed his rest. Hurry."

"Do you think he's still sad?" Justine asked.

"Yes, Justine. Devon explained it to us. Maddie got hurt, and Daddy is taking care of her."

"Will she go to heaven?"

I heard Mikaella's loud swallow. "I don't know."

Their conversation roused me from my sleep. I blinked, trying to make sense of everything that had happened the previous day. A stone was crushing my chest, preventing air from fully reaching my lungs. According to my daughter's discussion, none of it was a dream.

Trying to evade my gloomy thoughts and needing some love, I sprang to a ninety-degree position, and my girls came running into my arms.

"Daddy," they screamed.

This morning, I hugged them a little tighter than usual. "I love you," I said in a gruff voice that betrayed all the tears I had cried in the last twenty-four hours. "I missed you two."

"Where's Maddie?" Mikaella asked.

"Is she okay?" Justine asked next. "Can we see her?"

I sat them on my bed and inhaled through my mouth to dissipate the wave of nausea swirling in my empty stomach. "Let's see. Maddie had an accident yesterday morning. She got hurt a lot. The doctors did their best to repair her broken bones and heal her wounds. Now she's asleep because it will help her get better. She gotta rest a lot."

"Is she going to wear a *clast* like Mika?" Justine asked.

"Cast. And yes, I think she will."

"When will she come back home?" Mikaella asked next.

I rolled my shoulders back, trying to project a bit of

confidence, even though my tone betrayed my agitation. "I don't know. Her sister is with her. And her parents will get here later today. I may have to spend a little time there too later."

"Can we see her?" Justine asked. "We drew butterflies and kittens yesterday. And made a card. For her."

"Not today. She's in a special room at the hospital, and people can't really visit her for now. Once she gets better, I think she would very much like to see you two. Even if she's still asleep." I paused and reached for my babies' hands. "Maddie will need all of us to be strong for her. She will need us to air blow kisses her way because kisses make everything better, right?"

"Like when you kiss my booboos?" Justine asked.

"Same." I mirrored her tentative smile. "Okay, you two. Hug me once more." We stayed in one another's arms for a long beat. "Hey, how did you get here on your own? Last I heard, you were sleeping over at Uncle Riley and Devon's."

Mikaella pushed back. "Uncle Riley is on the phone downstairs. He drove us here to get clean clothes, because last night we forgot to take any, while he's dealing with someone named June. Devon had to work, so he's watching us. He said you two gotta talk while we play outside. And if we're nice, he'll order pizza and slushies for lunch. We wanted to see you first. Are you mad?"

"Me? Never. I missed you too much. I'll never be mad at you two for wanting to see me."

"Can we eat bunny pancakes?" Justine asked.

"Sure. I'll walk you back downstairs, shower, call Emily, and get to it afterward. Do we have a deal?"

"Yes," they both cheered.

Once I locked my bedroom door to make sure the girls

wouldn't enter and eavesdrop on my conversation, I called Madison's sister.

I firmed my back, trying to inject some courage into myself.

"Sam," Emily greeted me. "Did you get any sleep?"

How could she worry about me when her sister was confined to a hospital bed?

"Yeah, I think I did. How is she? Any development?"

"Same. Which isn't bad news per se. As I told you yesterday, it means she's holding on, and right now that's what we wish for."

"You should get some sleep," I said. "You've been up all night. I'll take over."

"I was waiting for you to be back. I have a few of my own patients to see this morning, so don't stress over it."

I sucked in a breath. "Listen, I promised my kids we'd make pancakes. I'll try to swing by right after."

"Sam, you're already doing a lot. Don't blame yourself for being a father first. I'm aware of how much you love my sister. I could tell two days ago. She argued there was nothing going on between you two, but I knew better. And I know her. Which means, your daughters should always come first. That's what she'd want."

I blew out a long breath. "You're probably right. Thank you. For everything."

We hung up, and I squeezed my eyelids shut, trying to keep the fresh tears at bay.

———

It was almost eleven o'clock that morning when I finally made it to the hospital. After breakfast, I'd met up with Riley while the girls busied themselves in their castle. We had agreed he'd ask Janice to send help. Someone to watch over the girls while I found my bearings in this new reality. The idea of trusting someone else with my daughters was a big stretch for me, but what other choice did I have? I had to compromise to make it all work.

Riley and Devon were already doing much more than they should, but last night, I'd come to the conclusion that I couldn't do everything on my own. I would exhaust myself, and my children and Madison both required the best of me.

After much consideration, I refused to postpone the tour. We all had worked so hard to get here. Canceling shows would mean failing all those people. The girls, Madison, and me included. Pacing my house for hours every day wouldn't help the situation. It wouldn't heal the woman I love faster, nor would it make me keep the promises I had made to my daughters. On my drive to the hospital, I'd called June, trying to work out a flight schedule in between engagements so I'd be in Nashville as often as possible. She was mainly Carter's assistant, but she had agreed to be mine too until I found my own. My trust in strangers wasn't fully back yet, but I was getting there.

The hallways of the intensive care unit were silent as I sauntered toward room fifteen-zero-three. With every step, I could feel the fragility of life clinging to the walls. Dr. Bera was already in the room when I entered, dressed in a disposable gown to reduce the risk of infection for vulnerable patients such as Madison.

I held my breath at his sight. "Any good news?" I asked.

"Mr. Stevens. Hi. Right now, we're monitoring Ms. Prescott closely for any sign of infection. As we told you, with the extensive repair we did to her leg, post-operative sepsis is a real threat. We've started her on broad-spectrum antibiotics. Her vitals are good. Her blood pressure is a bit high, which is not surprising after what she has gone through. Nothing to worry about for now, but we're keeping an eye on it just in case."

I nodded and secured my hands in my pockets because I had no idea what to do with myself. "Will she—?" A new lump formed in my throat. "When will we know she's out of the woods?"

"It's a bit too early to tell. So far, she's hanging in there. The next few days will let us know more. We can't assess the damage to her leg. We'll have to wait and see. The scar across her pelvic bone might become puckered and not very pleasant to look at. The other scars down her leg may lighten over time but won't completely go away. Plastic surgery can be an option later on. She's lucky to be alive, so in the bigger scheme of things, the scars aren't what concern us the most. As long as the wounds don't get infected."

"What about her spine?"

"Her spine is fine, not damaged in the accident. Her leg is still our major concern since we had to repair bones, muscles, nerves, and restore blood supply."

I nodded and couldn't think of any other questions to ask, my brain going blank.

Dr. Bera checked Madison's pupils with a penlight. I hated the idea I had to stand on the sidelines, but there was nothing I could do to make her situation better.

"If you have any questions, ring me. Try not to worry."

It was almost one in the afternoon when I finally found myself alone with Madison in her hospital room.

"Hey, it's just the two of us now. You can't wake up just yet… Listen, it's best if you stay sedated for a little longer. The girls asked questions this morning. I had no idea what to tell them because I don't know a lot myself. They miss you. We all do. They wanted to come visit. When you are out of the ICU, I'll bring them over. I know you'd enjoy having them around."

The beeping of the monitors filled the thick silence.

"I did something. I-I asked for help…to take care of Mika and Justine while you're here so you can heal without stressing about anything. Devon has work. And your sister too. I can't be with them while being by your side or onstage. Janice will send another nanny. I'm not replacing you, I swear. It's just for now. Until we figure it all out and you get back on your feet. It's a big step for me, asking people to help me out. I thought you'd be proud of me." I exhaled. "The girls were kinda excited at the idea you'd wear a cast too. They're already planning on adding glitter to it. I also packed you a bag with some of your stuff for when you get your own room. That fluffy blanket you always wrapped around yourself and a stuffed koala the girls asked me to bring for you. I have no idea if you can hear me. I…I hope you can. That you can tell you're not alone." I pushed a tendril of her hair back, trying to busy myself with something. "You're beautiful. And strong. In a day or two, we should know more. I promise to keep you updated on everything going on."

A nurse walked in, drew some blood, and left after noting data on her tablet.

"I'm still here," I said. "I made bunny pancakes this morning at Justine's request. They weren't as fabulous as yours, but for once, she didn't seem too concerned. I'll try my hands at brownies later. The recipe you always bake. When the hospital called me, I thought you were gone…"

With my thumbs, I massaged her palm.

"I've decided something else. I'll continue with the tour. It was a hard decision to make. I could hear your voice in my head, pleading me to go. It's not the same knowing you won't be there with us, though, and that I have to do this without you by my side. I was really looking forward to sharing this experience together—" My voice cracked, and I paused, trying to regain some control. "We're working on a schedule so I can be here as much as possible. I'm not leaving you, okay?"

I drew patterns on her palm with my fingertips.

"I wish things were different... The plan wasn't to watch you fight for your life." I tipped my head back and closed my eyes, struggling with the emotional overload about to crash through me. "The plan was to do this together. All those silly rules about staying apart... We're both aware it would have failed. Big time. I don't know about you, but when you asked me the other night if I could see myself going the distance with you, it lit up a spark inside me. I never want it to die. I have no idea how you did it, Maddie, but you stole my heart—every piece of it. This journey we're on... I'm done pretending we shouldn't give it everything we've got."

I watched her, once again wondering if she could hear my words.

Her face missed the usual curl of her lips and the glint in her irises.

It missed the look she would give me when she thought I wasn't looking and the cheerful grin she always displayed when she was with the girls.

The automatic doors slid open, drawing my attention. Emily walked in followed by a middle-aged couple I assumed to be her parents. A mask of distress painted the woman's gaze. She blinked her red-rimmed eyes as she neared her youngest daughter. On my feet, I went to meet her husband.

"Sam, these are my parents, Evangeline and Rupert." The woman joined us. "Mom, Dad, this is Sam Stevens."

She hesitated for a split second, and I offered her a tiny nod. "Maddie's boyfriend."

"Mr. and Mrs. Prescott, it's nice to finally meet you. I wish it was under better circumstances, though. Maddie speaks about you two all the time."

The woman patted her eyes with a tissue before pulling me into her arms. "Mr. Stevens, we heard so much about you too."

"Please call me Sam."

"Sam," she continued. "You and your precious daughters make my little girl happy. And I'll forever be grateful you were put on her road."

I swallowed around the rock-hard lump in my throat. "I'm the one who should thank you. Your daughter is one of the best things that has happened to me in a long time. She's the most loving and generous person I know. You should be proud."

Madison's mother hugged me once again. "Thank you for loving our precious child."

When she pulled back, Mr. Prescott wrapped his arms around me. "Thank you for making sure she gets the best care. It means a lot to us."

"It's the least I can do," I said. I spun to face Emily. "Ems, I'll give you some space and go back to my babies. Call me if anything changes, okay?"

"Yes. And Sam, thank you for spending the day. I'm aware you're dealing with a tight schedule."

"There's no place else I'd rather be."

I walked to Madison and leaned in to whisper, "Heal my love. I'll be here tomorrow."

As I made my exit, I called out, "Night," waving my hand over my shoulder.

# Chapter 16
## Sam

"**W**anna hear the song I came up with on my way here? It's not done, but it sounds good. I'm sure you'll enjoy it. I wrote it for you," I said as I sat in the chair next to the bed.

It'd been three days since the accident. Madison was still hooked up to the ventilator because she had to undergo another round of surgery on her leg—less extensive this time—later today. Her doctor had explained the nerve damage would be mind-numbing for quite some time and they preferred to keep her asleep for as long as possible to avoid her suffering because, once awake, the painkillers wouldn't do a good job of masking the pain. After the full repair her leg had undergone, they were hopeful for her recovery. Madison's life wasn't in danger anymore, and I held onto this piece of information to get through my days. Late last night, they'd moved her from the isolation ICU to a regular ICU room, one with a large window spread on one wall because I knew that was what she'd wish for. To see the daylight when she'd wake up. Because the sky always dazzled her.

Nights and days.

I sang the melody to a song I'd only rehearsed in my head so far.

Once I got to the chorus and last verse, I took a deep inhale to be able to deliver the words that meant so much to me, and I hoped she could hear, even in her sleep.

> **...Come back to me, come**
> **back to me**
> **I'm half the man I should be**
> **When you're not here**
> **The sky is darker**
> **The colors faded**
> **And my heart is lost**
> **Come back to me, come back**
> **to me**
> **Here and now, I don't wanna**
> **live without you**
>
> **There's something I gotta tell**
> **you (yes, there's something**
> **I gotta tell you)**
> **There's something I can't keep**
> **to myself anymore (no,**
> **baby, I gotta tell you)**
> **I'm in love with you.**

I cleared my throat and breathed out. "What do you think? I won't perform it on tour. I'll record it, but it'll be yours. I called it 'Maddie.' It's yours," I repeated, about to break down. "And so is my heart."

Tears rushed to my eyes. For the longest time, I let them flow. Once I regained enough composure, I sang to the woman my heart belonged to. All the songs she loved. Including the one we danced to, that time in my kitchen. I had no clue if she could hear my love through the lyrics, but I hoped she did. Because it prevented darkness from enveloping me and my brain from going crazy.

"Nurses should be here soon," I told her. "To prep you for surgery. I'll be here waiting for you when you get back. I know we're asking a lot from you these days. The girls are making you *Get Well* cards every day. I swear you'll have the biggest collection when you get out of here. Justine demanded we find you a prince who could kiss you to help you wake up." I smiled at the memory of my baby girl speaking the words. "I told her I'll see what I can do. I wish I could heal you with just one kiss, Maddie."

Madison's parents joined me, cutting short my confessions.

"Mr. Stevens," her father greeted me.

I moved to my feet. "Please, call me Sam."

Mrs. Prescott neared her daughter and whispered words of love to her.

"When are they coming to get her?" Mr. Prescott asked.

"They should be here any minute. The doctor said it would last two hours if everything goes as planned. Just a few more repairs they hadn't tackled after the accident. Nothing major." I paused, my eyebrows knitting together in confusion. "Huh, have you seen Emily? She hasn't been here at all today."

"She's in surgery. She'll try to come by later."

I nodded. "Gimme a minute, and I'm out of here. You deserve some time with your daughter."

I neared Madison and kissed her forehead. "I'll leave

you with your parents for now. I'll see you later. Be strong out there. I love you."

I started to walk to the door when Mrs. Prescott stopped me. "Sam, our daughter is lucky to have you in her life."

I darted my tongue out to moisten my lips. "I'm the lucky one. She makes everything better. Even my music."

"Did you sing to her?"

"Yes. Thought she'd like it. When I'm here, I ramble all the time. I'm sure she prefers music."

"She does enjoy it. I can tell. Call it a mother's instinct. My daughter is a big fan of yours."

———

I woke up with a strained neck and a hand shaking me out of my slumber. "Stevens, we gotta get going. Did you spend the night here?"

I forced my eyelids open and used my sleeve to rub the sleep away from my features.

"What time is it?" I said, stretching my neck from side to side to relieve the tension there.

"Eight. We said we'd get going at seven-thirty. We drove to your place, but Doris said you hadn't come home last night."

Today was day one of the tour. And day seven since the accident. The excitement from yesterday, when the girls couldn't stay still for more than ten seconds, died the moment I stepped into the frigid hospital room. It drained all the cheer from me, leaving my heart heavy and cold.

For most of the night, I'd sung to Madison, hoping she could hear me again, and that it would make up for the days I wouldn't be able to visit her. I sang until my voice quivered. Until my insides clenched so tight, it hurt to even breathe.

"You look like a mess, man. I'm glad we hired drivers. No way would I let you drive yourself."

My grip around Madison's hand tightened.

"Have you told her you love her yet?" my friend asked.

My eyes snapped in his direction. "What are you talking about?" I asked, doing my best to prevent my face from betraying my feelings.

He snickered. "Did you forget I was there the day you two met at the nanny agency? Sparks ignited between you guys the moment you stared at each other for the first time. I'm not stupid. I knew back then that's why you panicked and ran away. It had nothing to do with Madison's age."

I offered him a sharp look.

"Okay, maybe you freaked out because you realized she was younger than you. Or that she was younger than you expected her to be. But I witnessed it. The attraction. The magnetism. You can fight it all you want, but it's there. It's all around you two when you're in the same room. It's dazzling. No wonder Jacob let her go after the barbecue on your birthday." He paused. "The other night, while the girls sang at that party, I thought you'd eat her up every time you glanced in her direction. I felt like a voyeur, watching two people making love, and you were both dressed and standing thirty feet apart."

"You're talking shit," I blurted out.

The smirk on Riley's face turned devilish. "You wish."

"Whatever. We were supposed to keep it low-key. We failed. I've been alone for so long... She's the one, man. I'm fucking gone for her. Now I can't imagine walking away from her when she needs me the most."

"I gotta say you're much happier when Madison is around than when she's not. It's obvious to everyone already. You're a grumpy asshole when you're by yourself. Now I understand so many things. *So many things*," he repeated, stretching each word. "Eye-fucking each other is almost a full-time job for both of you."

"And I thought I was being subtle." I rolled my eyes and sighed.

"Think again."

He shook his head, and I punched his arm unable to hide the waves of joy filling me whenever the topic of Madison was evoked. "I'm just trying to do the right thing the right way. And now, I'm torn about leaving her. It's hard, man."

"Madison would want you to go on with the tour. I don't even have doubts about it. I talked to her sister, and she confirmed it too. She'll be proud of you, Stevens. For not walking away when things got tough. It's a great love lesson. And for what it's worth, I'm proud of you too. Music will do you good. It always does. Trust me, we'll make it work."

"You really believe it?"

"I'm convinced. And when have I ever been wrong?" He winked, and I winced at his confident poise.

Riley exited the room, and my heart banged in my chest when I returned my focus to the person I couldn't leave behind without pieces of me staying with her.

"As you might have heard, today is the day. The one you circled on that calendar you and the girls fixed to the kitchen wall at the beginning of the summer. For a long time, it appeared so far away in time, but now that it's here, I can't seem to find the courage in me to leave. The girls are beyond thrilled. In a way, I am too. But I'm also sad. It's a weird combination." I molded our hands together. "It's so fucking hard, you know. I'm excited to go back there, but it feels wrong since you lie silent here."

For a long beat, I watched her chest rising and falling, the soft lines of her profile, the shape of her lips, her smooth eyelids. I wish they would open right about now so I could lose myself in the sea-green pool of her eyes.

"I love you, Maddie. I'll come back between my shows. I'm not leaving you behind. You have family around. You're not alone. And I'll come visit. Just get better, okay? That's all I'm asking."

Whatever lesson life was trying to teach me right now, I could really do without it. I already had my share of lessons. I could skip a few.

A knock on the door cut short my drowning thoughts.

"Hey, Sam," Emily said as she entered the room. "I saw Riley in the hallway. It's time for you to go."

I nodded, my throat so tight no word could pass the rim of my lips.

As she did every time she was around, Emily checked all vitals and the readings on the monitors. "Go. She is in good hands. I'll never let anything bad happen to her. I'll call you every day to keep you updated like we've discussed. I promise."

I bent over a still Madison and kissed her forehead. "I love you. I'll be back in three days."

Without looking back, I walked away. Because if I did, I would never go on with this tour.

———

It had been thirteen days since Madison's accident. And as much as I could, I split my time between my music, my children, and the women I loved. Doris, the new nanny, was the antipode of Madison—stricter, more somber, and less energetic—but so far, she got along with my girls. That was all I could ask for right now.

Armed with my guitar case, I followed Brent through the basement-level maze toward the elevator. I knew the route by heart by now, but he still made sure, every time, I wasn't hunted down whenever I visited Madison.

Her parents had gone back home two nights ago. The day before I left on tour, we had lunch together. They formed a quick bond with whom I hoped one day they'd consider to be their own granddaughters. The girls couldn't stop bragging about Madison the entire time. Justine sat on Mrs. Prescott's lap all through dinner after showing her around the house and parading in every princess gown she owned. I could tell the woman relished the distraction. Just like her daughters, she had love in buckets pouring out from her.

"How is it going today, Mr. Stevens?" Mara, the nurse caring for Madison, welcomed me as I passed before the nurse station, carrying my guitar case. "We missed you around here."

"As best as I can in the circumstances." I placed a box of pastry in her hands. "For you guys. As a thank you for watching over her."

"Thank you," she called after me. "Your lady is lucky to have private concerts every time you're in town. I know a lot of staff members who are jealous they missed the one you gave here the other night. It was very generous of you and your team to organize this little gathering. We're all grateful." I mirrored her smile. "Go ahead, I'll come see you in fifteen minutes."

"Hey, Maddie. How are you?" I asked after I kissed her forehead and sat in the chair by the bed. "The girls are asking about you twenty times a day. We miss you so much. Our new home on wheels feels empty without you. I played a concert in Arkansas last night and flew back as soon as I could. I boarded a jet at eight this morning, once the girls and Doris were set for the day. I'm flying back later this afternoon because I have a show tonight in Dallas at seven. Somehow, I'm glad I refused Riley's offer to cancel the tour. Honestly, I didn't think I had it in me to go back up there without you around, but I did it. I faced my fears. And I have faith it will all work out in the end. I'm doing what I know you'd want me to do if you were awake. To keep living. And thriving. Until you're ready to join us."

If music left my life too right now, I'd go nuts. Yeah, I'd been there before. A guy angry at the world. I wished to never be that version of me ever again.

"Ready for your stop on the Sam Stevens's US tour? You get all the free spots on my schedule."

Just like every time I was by her side, I played Madison her song as an opening act.

> **...There's something I gotta**
> **tell you (yes, there's some-**
> **thing I gotta tell you)**
> **There's something I can't keep**
> **to myself anymore (no,**
> **baby, I gotta tell you)**
> **I'm in love with you.**

I was about to continue with "Snowed In" when Doctor Bera walked in.

"Mr. Stevens." I rose to my feet to shake his hand. "As we discussed yesterday on the phone, we've been tapering the medication since this morning. You should expect her to wake up soon."

"Oh, it's that fast?"

"Yes. Patients usually wake up within three to four hours after being taken off the ventilator."

I rubbed the column of my throat to erase the dryness there. "Will she be okay?"

"We're watching her closely and monitoring her vitals all through the process. She's in good hands."

He checked her reflexes and wrote something down before promising to come back later.

I grabbed Madison's hand and squeezed it between mine. "Babe, you're going to wake up. Listen, I need you to be brave when you do. Your life is safe now. You might hurt some." I kissed her knuckles. "I wish I could take away your pain. No matter what, I'll be by your side. Emily says you're a fighter, and it is so true. I have seen it these past few days. I just want you to know I miss you. And I love you. We'll get through this, you hear me? Whatever challenge life throws at us, we've proved we are a great team so far, you and I, so make sure you remember this."

Playing my guitar, I sang for the woman who held my heart.

"If I grab something to eat real quick, will you wait for me? To wake up?" I asked when I took a break around one in the afternoon. "I don't want you to open your eyes and be all alone. Emily is in surgery all day, so it's just you and me now."

I skimmed the back of her hand when I felt a barely perceptible twitch of her fingers. I blinked, certain I had conjured the movement. Just in case it wasn't my imagination playing tricks on me, I rested my gaze on her hand for a tad longer.

It took about a minute for Madison's fingers to spasm again, and only about twenty seconds for a third spasm.

Springing to my feet, but never releasing her hand, I pressed the emergency button attached to the railing of the bed. My pulse went haywire. A new form of energy arose in me. I hesitated between jumping around, pumping my fist, and screaming my excitement at the top of my lungs. Then I remembered just in time that this was the ICU, not the place to be loud.

Within seconds, Mara walked into the room. "Mr. Stevens, how can I help you?"

I sucked a cleansing breath in to calm the jitters filling my stomach. "She moved. Her fingers. I think she's waking up," I said, the words tumbling out of my mouth. I zoomed in on Madison's face. The bruises were mostly faded, and the bandage on her forehead had been removed days ago. Even the laceration on her cheek looked better. "Maddie, do it again. Please. Move. Do it for me." I lifted her hand and kissed her knuckles one by one. This time, her eyelids fluttered. Like the wings of a butterfly. "See?" I asked the nurse. "I told you. Did you see it? Please tell me I'm not going crazy. Is she waking up?"

"Yes. She is." She pushed a button, commanding a blood pressure reading and checking other waveforms on the machine, before saying, "I'll get the medical team. Wait here. We'll be right back."

"Okay." I talked to Madison, my voice strained with new emotions, hope and fear mixing together in nerve-wracking anticipation. "Babe, you gotta do it again. Moving, I mean. Your fingers. Or your eyelids. Even your toes." I leaned over the bed, waiting for another sign.

Madison's eyelids fluttered faster this time, until they finally opened and locked onto me.

My voice got stuck down my throat.

My eyes filled with hot tears.

My heart flipped in my chest.

I stood there, barely able to take a full breath in, readying myself for her next action.

We stared at each other, taking in our expressions, as if we were seeing the other for the first time.

At the sight of her, awake, a million different feelings surged through me.

Dr. Bera and his team entered the room, and I was asked to step back while they examined her. I let go of her hand reluctantly. It broke my heart to sever the only connection we shared.

Standing in one corner of the room, I was transfixed by all the commotion surrounding me. Buttons were pressed, and orders were given. The beeping sounds of the machines stuffed the silence in-between the chatter. The doctor nodded, and the nurse asked Madison to take a deep breath, then removed the tracheal tube, a harsh cough escaping her lips.

Her eyes perused the room, and when they landed on mine again, they stole my breath away. *Sam*, she mouthed this time.

"I'm here. I'm right here," I said, unable to hide the turmoil invading me. My feet brought me next to her of their own volition. My fingers laced through hers before I could even comprehend what I was doing, and my lips connected with her forehead. "You're awake. I'm not going anywhere."

Her glossy eyes stayed glued to mine. The doctor asked her questions, and the entire time, Madison watched me watching her, and it slid the bruised part of my heart that belonged to her to its rightful position.

The doctor touched my shoulder to catch my attention. "She'll be in and out of it for a few hours. Don't worry. It's normal. We'll come down later to get her to perform some tests. So far, everything looks promising."

"Even her leg?"

"Even her leg. Don't hesitate to call us."

They all exited the room.

Madison had fallen back asleep. For the next hour, I

watched her, counting her breaths and staring at the monitor to make sure her heart was still strong and her oxygen levels were high enough. Just in case the doctors had missed something.

"I love you," I repeated over and over. "I can't believe you're awake. God, I've missed you so much."

She squeezed my hand back, and for the first time in almost two weeks, hope fully returned to my heart.

"What do you mean she should stay in Nashville?" I asked Riley when he joined me later that day, fury bleeding from me as I spoke the words. "She just fucking woke up. What is it supposed to mean? Why would I leave her behind?"

He rested his hand on my shoulder, forcing me to take a full breath in and calm down.

Madison was out of it. She'd been all day. That was the only reason I had agreed to leave her room, and I couldn't wait to get back to her side.

"I'm about to break at the seams here, and you wanna remove me from the only person keeping me sane. Tell me how being away from her is logical, especially when she is awake now. I'm listening."

I sat down in a chair, trying to give him the benefit of the doubt. My friend had never screwed me over, and I couldn't believe he'd do it this time. He knew what was at stake. Not only the tour, but also my heart. And my fucking sanity.

Restless, I fisted my hands and rested them on my thighs. "Talk."

"If you wanna help Maddie, you gotta be at the top of your game. In every area of your life. Right now, you're exhausting yourself. The doctors said her recovery would be long and painful. You can't bring her on the bus. She requires constant medical care, along with daily physiotherapy, to relearn how to walk. And above all, she needs stability. And to keep her stress levels as low as possible. How do you picture the next few weeks? Tell me. Because I've been trying to come up with a plan, but I can't. Nothing makes sense except for keeping her here, where she has all she needs. And before you tell me, flying in and out every day or two is also not realistic, Sam. You've been doing it for two weeks, and already you look drained. How can you keep doing that for eight, ten, or fifteen additional weeks without collapsing?"

I stayed silent, doing my best not to bark at him. His words weren't farfetched. It didn't mean I had to agree, though.

"Mika and Justine need you too. Right now, they are spending more time with Doris than with their own father. When you agreed to this tour, it was the one thing you were adamant about. To make them the priority."

Riley pulled a chair and sat before me, elbows propped up on his knees, leaning forward.

"I know it will break your heart, but Madison won't be on her own. Emily, her parents, and friends can visit her if she stays in Nashville. If we move her around, she'll be alone when you're busy. It's not good for her recovery to feel like a burden. How will she be able to move around the bus in a wheelchair? Before you argue, I'm not saying you're not doing all you can to make it easy on her, but she'll be better here. In Tennessee. You can fly in once a week to visit."

"Ry, I wanna watch over her myself. To make sure nothing bad happens ever again. How can I make sure she's safe if she's not around me?"

"Stevens, if you had been in that car with her, would you have been able to prevent that jerk from running the red light?"

"No."

"And she would have been under your watch the entire time. It just took a split second for her accident to occur. Whether she's with you or not, you don't possess the power to prevent destiny."

I ran a hand over my short stubble.

I hated the fact that everything my friend said sounded accurate. In my head, I had pictured Madison coming back with us, with medical professionals caring for her when I couldn't. This scenario would appease me the most. But would it be what was best for her?

"Ry, what you're asking from me is hard. It goes against everything I wish for." I paused, casting a glance down while I rubbed the sole of my shoe against the tiled floor. "I'll talk to her. See what she thinks."

"I already made all the arrangements. If she agrees, she could be moved to your home in about a week. Her doctor said she'll be discharged by then. Emily is on board already. It's for the best."

I got to my feet and kicked the chair next to mine. "Nothing goes as planned. It's all a big giant fuck-up."

Riley pulled me into a hug. "Life happens. It wasn't part of the plan, but we're all doing our best to accommodate you and your family. Trust me, okay?"

I nodded as we broke apart and shoved my hands into my pockets.

Without another word, I spun around, got the hell out of the room, and exited the building, desperate for some fresh air to settle my mind.

And assess my options.

———

"Hey you," I whispered when I walked back into the hospital room an hour later.

Madison's breathing was soft and steady, and I listened to it for a while before taking a seat beside her bed.

When I touched her hand, her eyes wavered open, and she offered me a weak curl of her lips.

"Sam," she whispered.

I leaned forward, my lips connecting with her cheek.

"What's going on?" she asked. "Why am I here?"

Tears filled her eyes, and I used the pad of my finger to dry them.

"Two weeks ago, you got into an accident. It was bad. The doctors weren't sure you'd make it."

"Two weeks?" She winced. "You sure?"

"Yeah. I'm sorry. You were put under sedation."

She swallowed a sob. "How bad? No rainbows. Be honest with me." Her voice had lost all her usual spirit and sounded so slurred I had to make an extra effort to understand her words.

"Your left leg. It got crushed. They did extensive reconstruction work to fix the damage, but it will be a long recovery. You could have lost your limb. There're scars across your pelvic bone and down your left thigh and leg. They might require plastic surgery in the future. We gotta wait and see."

Madison lifted her arm, her hand seeking mine. I knitted our fingers and brought our joined hands by her side, squeezing hers a little more than usual.

"Will I—?" More tears escaped from her eyes. "Will I ever walk again?"

I bobbed my head. "Yes. Your spine is fine. With time and physical therapy, your leg should be fully functioning again."

A heart-wrenching sob punctured the silence.

I let her cry. My own eyes were watery at the sight of her distress. I combed her hair back with my free hand, resting my head on her shoulder while we navigated this new reality together.

"And the girls? Who's watching them?"

I swallowed the bile rising at the back of my throat. "A woman Janice sent over. Her name is Doris."

She bowed her head. "Is she…is she nice?"

"Yeah. She doesn't teach math while baking and doesn't throw dance parties, or know the steps to a line-dance, but other than that, the kids like her. They miss you, though. They ask about you all the time."

"When can I see them? I need a hug. Or two hugs." A little smile peeked through her sadness.

"Soon." I gathered some courage from deep within me to speak the next few words. "We gotta talk about something," I began. "I'm touring Texas right now. I fly here every couple of days, but I talked to Riley. And he talked to Emily. And we think it would be better if you stay in Nashville. For now. Here, you have your sister, who happens to be a surgeon, and your parents live a few hours' drive away. Bringing you on a bus right now doesn't make sense. We have to discuss logistics."

"You want me to stay here?"

I looked away, putting order into my messy thoughts. "It

would be for the best. If it were realistic, you'd be on the bus with me, and I would hire a nurse to care for you when I'm unavailable. But the truth is, you need physical therapy and a schedule. A wheelchair. And lots of rest. And I can't provide that. Not short-term at least. Not until you are a bit stronger. If you agree you'd be better here, Emily could move in with you at home. You wouldn't have to leave the house."

She nodded, not saying anything.

I tightened my grip on her hand. "I'm sorry. If you don't wanna go ahead with this plan, we'll figure something out. I might just require a little more time to make it happen."

Madison swallowed and looked away, and a tidal wave of sadness and guilt enveloped me.

"I love you, Maddie. I love you so fucking much. And the thought of losing you almost killed me. You came this close. I…I was so helpless."

"You love me?" Her glossy gaze locked on mine.

"Like crazy. I'm sorry I didn't tell you sooner. I thought I would never get to tell you… That you were gone. I decided it was time to be honest with myself. And with you. About us."

"Sam, I love you so much. Before meeting you, I had no idea I could love someone this much."

I pressed my forehead against hers, and we stayed immobile for a long time.

"My home is you and Mikaella and Justine. That's the only place I wanna be. Where I belong." She paused. "Since I can't wait to be with you and I need to heal for it to happen, I-I'll stay in Nashville. It's not like I have a lot of options…"

A part of me wished she had disagreed, that she had gotten mad and forced me to bring her along with me.

I buried my face in the crook of my elbow, calming the conflicted storm raging in my core. I couldn't let her see how much the idea troubled me.

I firmed my back, trying to project confidence. "Fine. I'll tell Riley to set it all up."

"Can I ask you a question, though?" The vulnerability in her voice rattled every cell in me.

I nodded.

"Did my parents visit since the accident, or is my brain playing tricks on me?"

"You remember?"

"It's like I dreamed of it. It's hard to explain."

"They did. Do you recall anything else?" I asked, holding my breath for whatever she was about to say.

"A song. It's not one of yours even though it sounded like it. I heard it all the time. It spoke about the sky and colors and love. It was beautiful."

My breathing hitched. "Babe, it was…me. I sang to you every day I was here after you were moved out of isolation and into a single-patient ICU room. Your song. It's called 'Maddie.' I can't believe you heard it." I leaned in to drop a kiss on her cheek. "Wanna hear it?"

Her eyes shone, bringing some color to her face. For a fleeting second, Madison looked like herself, glee radiating from her.

With my guitar in my hands, I sang the melody, watching the array of emotions painting her features. From elation to joy to pride. And love.

**…There's something I gotta
tell you (yes, there's something I gotta tell you)
There's something I can't keep**

### to myself anymore (no,
### baby, I gotta tell you)
### I'm in love with you

"Sam… It's beautiful. That's the one. The one I held on to. When everything was dark. When I had no idea how to find my way back."

Sobs shook her body. Her shoulders heaved. She hid her face with her hands.

The high-pitched sound escaping Madison's lips shattered my heart.

Balancing myself beside her on the bed, I wrapped my arms around the love of my life. She relaxed against me, accepting the comfort I brought her. Never loosening my grip around her body, I rocked her until sleep claimed her once again, my lips lingering on the top of her head.

At some point, I must have fallen asleep because a nurse touched my arm, and my eyes sprang open. Confused by her sudden appearance, I blinked to reboot my sluggish brain.

"Mr. Stevens. We need to perform some tests and change her dressing. Can you be back in thirty minutes?"

I untangled myself from a still-sleepy Madison and kissed her cheek. "I'll be right back. I love you. Don't go anywhere."

A soft tilt of her lips told me she'd heard my words. "I love you too," she murmured.

I found Riley still seated in the office the hospital had let him use and informed him Madison had agreed to stay in Nashville. For the time being.

For the rest of the day, I remained by her side while she drifted in and out of sleep.

Around six, I gathered my stuff. I was supposed to fly back two hours ago, but I had rescheduled my flight after

Madison woke up. Now I would need to get to the venue right after I landed. I had missed sound check and hoped I could still be able to deliver a great performance, even though my heart was stuck in a hospital room in Tennessee.

"Maddie, I gotta go, or I'll be late," I whispered in her ear. "I'll be back in four days because I have three back-to-back shows."

She cracked her eyelids open, and her sea-green irises swallowed me whole. Her throat worked. "Sam, don't come back." Her voice sounded so weak.

My hair stood on end on my arms. "Why?"

"The girls. They need their daddy. You can't spend all your free time here. They'll resent us. They will want to be with you. That was the plan…for the tour. To make them a priority."

"But—"

"No buts. We agreed on this. Listen to me. I want this. For you to thrive. And be a father. I'm not going anywhere anyway. Please don't come back. Not for the next week at least."

I pulled her into a hug. "I'm not sure I can stay away that long."

"You must. It's a dare. Don't deceive me."

"Will you call me if you feel down? Or change your mind? Or if you just wanna hear my voice or your song?"

"Yes. Now go. I'm glad you didn't cancel the tour. I would have been very angry if you had."

I locked my emotions inside. "I know."

After I kissed her one last time, I neared the door, my heart sinking to my heels as I padded away.

"Hey, Sam?"

I pivoted to face her.

"Don't fall in love with the nanny, okay?" She winked, and I burst into a mix of giggles and tears.

With the back of my hand, I wiped my damp cheeks and returned to her side. "Never." I closed my eyes and kissed her lips. "I love you. Only you."

"I love you. Thank you for everything you are doing for me." Her voice trembled. "I'm sorry I can't be there to cheer you on."

With her hand hooked around my nape, as if she feared I'd disappear before she was ready to say goodbye, Madison held me against her, returning the kiss. Together, we let the sadness wash away, bringing each other the comfort we both needed so badly.

# Chapter 18
## Madison

It had been six days since I'd moved back into Sam's house, and into my old room. I was wearing one of his sweaters while lying on my side. My entire body hurt. Radiating pain crippled my left half. Every time I shifted position by myself, my eyes watered, and I had to grit my teeth until the wave of agony subsided. Even my arm muscles had weakened since the accident. June, Riley's assistant, had come over to set up the house so I would have everything I needed. Sam had hired a nurse to live here with me full-time, and Emily had taken over the third bedroom upstairs.

I wasn't alone, but in a sense, it felt as if I was.

Unable to bathe or go to the bathroom by myself, I was dependent on so many people. For someone who wasn't used to having people hovering over her, it was a tough pill to swallow. The permanent state of pain I was in added to the embarrassment. I felt like I was losing my mind. Anger simmered just below the surface, and every time things didn't go my way, I wanted to hit something—or someone.

Since waking up after the accident, I had spent most nights crying in agony. The doctors weren't kidding when they said the painkillers would only partially work. The rest of my atrophied leg would demand grueling physiotherapy. Muscle spasms ran down my leg, paralyzing me and making it hard to breathe.

Due to the cast covering my flesh, I could not massage my thigh, the half that had required the most work, and had to ride the excruciating pain. Not knowing what the scars looked like got me anxious. And being unable to comfort my own leg was hard enough.

A part of me wished Sam would be by my side, reassuring me and murmuring in my ear I'd get through this. That his strong arms would wrap around me in a tight hug, his love soothing every ache.

The rest of me thanked the tour for his absence. I didn't relish the idea of him seeing me like this: a victim of circumstances, glued to a bed all day with no choice but to wait it out.

With every passing hour, my positivity drained away bit by bit. Each time I woke with a start and screamed in agony, I felt myself slipping further and further from who I once was.

A new bout of excruciating pain coursed through my body, and I had to clutch my pillow with a death grip to ride it out. I lashed every curse into the soft cotton until it released me. Scorching tears prickled the back of my eyes. My pulse hastened, and I could barely suck in any oxygen through my clenched teeth while I waited for the tremors to subside, aware they'd be back soon, ready to haunt my days. This happened every few hours, a relentless, vicious cycle.

Yesterday, Sam came to visit me and left within a few hours. He had spent every minute by my side, lying beside me and shielding my body from the outside world as he held me against his heart the entire time. I fought with myself the entire time to pretend his presence didn't affect me. Now that he was gone, I struggled not to miss him. I still hadn't seen the girls. When I told Sam, I had changed my mind and wasn't ready to face them yet, hurt flashed in his eyes. He said nothing, just nodded with quiet resolve.

Deep down, I knew that if they made the trip to see me, I would be heartbroken once they left. Even my soul would have a hard time letting them go. For now, I'd chosen to keep them at a distance. We video chatted twice, and it was about all I could manage for the time being.

Jeremiah, the nurse on duty, peeked his head through the ajar door. "Madison, dear, there's someone to see you."

I wiped my runny eyes with my sleeve.

Before I could refuse, the door opened, and Jacob stood there.

I gulped a big intake of air. "You? No. *No, no, no.* You can't be here. Why are you even here? You…you should go. I'm not in the mood to see you right now."

Images of our last time together flashed through my mind.

"Maddie—"

"Jake, what do you…what do you want?" I tried to push myself up to roll onto my side and winced.

Soon, Jacob had his hands around me, helping me shift position. "Hold on to me. Let me help you," he said. Just the sound of his voice created a tsunami inside me.

"Thank you," I mumbled. "Why are you here? Who told you?"

He glanced away for a second, discomfort written all across his face. "I ran into Becks two days ago. He…he thought I knew. I called Emily, and she told me what happened. I'm sorry, Maddie. I know how much this tour meant to you. It hurts me to see you in pain." He took a seat in the chair next to the bed. "Wanna tell me what's going on in that head of yours?"

Averting my eyes, I refused to talk for the longest time.

"Maddie. Don't keep it all inside."

"Why should I tell you shit? You flushed me from your life, remember? You kicked me out of your car in the middle of the night."

"That's not how it went down," he argued.

"You didn't want me there. Same result. You pushed me out of your life."

"Maddie—"

"Don't Maddie me. We haven't talked in months unless you count that phone call where you asked me to drop everything and run back to you. You were my best friend, Jake. My closest friend. I confided secrets in you I've never told anyone else. I thought you had my back. And because I couldn't return your feelings, you acted like I never mattered to you. You broke my heart. Big time. And now that I'm confined to a bed, you swish back into my life and act like we're fine. News flash, we're not." I paused. "Nothing goes the way it should. It's all a big clusterfuck."

He hung his head low and said nothing. After a moment, he hunched forward, and I could tell I'd hurt his feelings.

"I don't want to be angry with you." My voice had lost its previous edge. "But I'm not sure how to be friends with you anymore… Or if we can salvage what we once were." A yawn escaped me as I shifted on my pillow, my eyelids feeling like they weighed tons.

Jacob stood to pull a blanket over me—the same one

Sam had brought to the hospital, noticing it was my favorite. Without a word, he sat back.

"Sam and I, we-we're together," I said, unable to keep my eyes open, the painkillers finally doing their job.

"I figured. We'll talk later. Don't worry. Now sleep, okay? Rest will help you heal faster. I'm staying right here. I promise. I'll watch over you. Let me do this. I need to do this. Please."

I sighed. "Fine."

I heard the distinct sound of Jacob swallowing, but he said nothing as I surrendered myself to sleep.

Hours later, I woke up to find him reading beside me.

I blinked, trying to make sense of the scene.

"You're real?" I asked. "I thought it was all a dream. What are you reading?"

He shrugged. "Something I picked up on my way over here. Thought I could read to you, and you might…huh… like it. Change your mind and stuff."

I said nothing for a while.

"Unless you want me to go," he finally said.

Was the silence stretching between us as uncomfortable for him as it was for me?

"You can stay. Only if you get me tacos."

"Tacos?"

"Yep. I want fun food. And chocolate chip cookies. If you can make it happen, you don't have to leave just yet. Chocolate is—"

"Good for the soul," he continued. "I know." A large grin illuminated his face. For an instant, my best friend was back. Gone was the tension in his demeanor. He jumped to his feet. "Mission accepted. Be right back."

Once he exited the room, I bit my tongue as debilitating pain spread through my lower self. I clung to the mattress with all my strength, praying it would recede quickly.

"How am I supposed to live like this?" I asked through my tears, to everyone and no one. "It doesn't get better." The excruciating agony seemed to worsen every day—or was it my tolerance for pain that was waning?

Once the bone-deep ache released me from its claws, I grabbed the empty glass of water I kept on the nightstand and hurled it at the wall with all my might. I fixed my gaze on the shattered glass shards scattered across the wooden floor, and they reminded me of my body. For a moment, I wondered if I would ever feel whole again, or if, like the slivers of glass, I would remain forever broken—pieces of me lost for eternity.

Jacob came back twenty minutes later. I could hear his footsteps approaching on the other side of my bedroom door. I straightened my posture, wiping away all traces of sadness from my face with a corner of the blanket. Seeing the smile tugging at his lips, I knew Jeremiah hadn't exposed my earlier meltdown to the guy who used to be my best friend.

He insisted that we ate in the kitchen, so after helping me sit in the wheelchair I kept by my bed, Jacob and I settled ourselves in front of a Mexican buffet. For the first time in weeks, my mouth watered at the sight of food, and some of my appetite returned.

For the next two weeks, Jacob visited me every day after work. Slowly, we were learning how to be in each other's lives again. I doubted we'd ever be best friends in the long run, but for the time being, I cherished our moments together and his company. It felt like it could heal the wound we never had a chance to fix.

Tonight, we were in the den, admiring the fireplace as I sat in my favorite chair, a blanket tight around my legs while Jacob read me chapters of the novel we'd begun three days ago. After a few days, I'd come to enjoy our daily reading sessions, a simple pleasure I had not enough energy to indulge in by myself.

A loud yawn escaped my mouth, and without missing a beat, he helped me to my bed. Knowing my routine by heart, he handed me two painkiller pills and a glass of water from the bedside table.

"Do you need anything else before I go?"

"Nope. All good."

With a heavy gaze, he scanned my bedroom, searching for his next words. "Maddie, I gotta tell you something… We've always been honest with each other. The truth is… I'm still not over you, and I don't know if I'll ever be," he whispered. "The time we've been spending together, it means something more to me."

"I know. But you gotta move on," I whispered back.

He bowed his head, his eyes slowly drifting to my face. "Do you regret it? I mean…huh…choosing him?"

"No." Tremolos shook my voice as anguish clouded his face.

"I was hoping you'd say yes." He offered me a sad smile.

"You've been coming here every day. Perhaps we should take a break. Not that I won't miss you, but I don't want you to expect something from me that won't happen. The last thing I desire is to break your heart all over again. I can't be anything else than your friend."

"You'll get back on your feet. I know you'll thrive. I'm just sad I won't be by your side when it happens." He squeezed my hand with his, injecting me with tiny doses of courage.

"Again…I'm sorry. For everything," I murmured.

Jacob let go of me. "Our moments together are always

too short. We always run out of time." Hurt filled his words, and it bled on me. "You should call him. He misses you. How can he not? If I were him and you were keeping me at a distance, I'd go nuts. It's been almost ten days since you last answered his call."

I looked away. Over the past two weeks, I'd refused every attempt Sam made to visit me and always pretended to be too tired whenever he called. He had to focus on his daughters and the tour. Not me. I had become the unforeseen variable, throwing off the careful balance of his life.

The well of darkness surrounding me was tightening its grip, and I refused to let Sam become one of its collateral victims.

"Maddie, I know you. I'm aware you've been pushing him away, thinking you're doing the right thing. What if it's not what you both need? What if it makes the two of you miserable instead? Have you thought about it?"

We both stayed silent for a while.

"You should rest," Jacob said, breaking the awkward silence. "I'll make sure the pantry is stuffed with cookies and brownies before I leave."

I returned my attention to him. "You don't have to."

He shrugged. "That's what friends are for."

"If I go to sleep, will you be there when I wake up?"

"It's better if I'm not," he said after a stretch of silence.

Tears pooled in my eyes. "Jake, you're going to be okay. I swear. You'll find the one. You're a special kind of someone. Any girl would be lucky to call you hers."

"Anyone but you…" A smile appeared at the corners of his mouth. "Sorry. I know you mean well. You own the biggest heart in the world, Maddie. Now rest. You need that sleep. Whatever happens between us, I meant everything I said. I want nothing more than for you to get better and to go back out there and catch up with the tour."

"Jacob… Thank you for being my friend. I'm sorry you had to put your life on hold to be by my side. I'll never be able to tell you how much your taking care of me has meant." Hot tears rolled down my cheeks, and I covered his hand with mine—the only comfort I could offer after he'd lifted my spirits and cared for me in the most selfless way, making me his priority over what his heart truly desired.

He drew in a shaky breath. "Today is the last day I see you, right? It's goodbye." He could still read me after all this time.

"Yes. It's for the best. I'll miss you." My emotions swallowed my words. "I'll forever cherish the memories of us."

"You really love him?"

I wiped my teary face with my free hand. "I do. I'm happy. For a long time, you were my entire world. I would never lie to you."

"Goodbye, Maddie. And for the record, you were the best friend I've ever had too."

He moved to kiss my forehead, and I let sleep claim me so I wouldn't have to witness him leaving and breaking my heart all over again.

rustration poured out from every inch of me as I exited the stage. I almost threw my guitar after the third song, unable to get in the mood to perform and belt my heart out to the screaming crowd. Usually, I could slip into my performer mindset even when my personal life was a mess or I just wasn't feeling it. But tonight? Impossible. Too many things weighed on me, and made it hard for my mind to rest.

Every conversation I'd had with Madison lately left me seething. She was pushing me away, thinking it was what was best for me. And the tour. And the whole fucking world. Breaking news, it wasn't.

She was slipping away, I could tell. The realization had shattered the last shreds of hope left in me.

Before walking onstage tonight, I'd called her, and she refused to talk to me. Again. The last time we had a real conversation, she made me promise not to visit her for at least a month. A whole fucking month. I was going insane. Her sister kept updating me every day, but it wasn't the same as being there and seeing for myself how she was really doing. Being there to kiss it better on the days she felt like there'd never be light at the end of the dark tunnel she was trapped in.

Yesterday, Emily had confided that her sister's mood swings were getting harder to handle. They'd started around the same time she began distancing herself from me. I knew Jacob had been visiting her for a while, reading to her after dinner. Then, one day, he stopped coming over, and that too coincided with Madison's new bout of fussiness. And here I was, playing music instead of being there to comfort her. What a joke.

In about three weeks, I'd have a stretch of four days off, and I'd planned to fly to Nashville with the girls to spend a couple of days at home…with her. I was done being on the sidelines, feeling helpless, and watching my heart crash and burn without doing anything about it.

If we were in the same room, Madison would have no choice but to hear me out. I'd given her enough time and space. It was time to face the music—and everything that came with being in a relationship with me. I took care of the people I loved. No exceptions.

Enough was enough.

My own temper agreed with me. And my daughters probably did too. Mikaella told me this morning I was back to being *grinchy* and that she missed her cheery daddy.

Justine had called me a *mad, mad, mad daddy* last week after I'd broken a glass and was tempted to storm out.

When I got home, I would take Madison on a date and shower her with love, hoping she'd reconsider keeping me at a distance. That she would open her heart to me. She was struggling, bottling everything up, and being angry at everyone wouldn't fix a thing. I knew, I had been that guy. She had saved me, and now it was my turn to save her from her demons, and, in the process, reclaim my own inner peace. I didn't like the angry version of myself. Nah, I much preferred my in-love persona.

When I'd confided in Riley, he told me to be patient. Well, my patience came with an expiration date. The more space Madison put between us, the more restless I became.

That had to stop. Right about now.

Storming off the stage, I handed my guitar to a technician, chugged down a bottle of water, and wiped my forehead with a towel. People came to shake my hands and congratulated me, but I blocked the noise. I didn't deserve the recognition. Or the accolades. I didn't deliver what the crowd expected of me tonight. I was haunted. Angry. And sad. And it showed. The critics would agree. They would call me a fucking mess, and I wouldn't be able to get mad at them because it was the truth. I hadn't only failed my fans tonight, I had failed myself too.

"What was that?" Riley asked, cornering me as I stalked toward the green room, ripping my shirt open, my flesh on fire and my throat dry.

His presence cut short my spiraling train of thought, keeping me from blowing a gasket out loud.

I waved my hand, dismissing him. "Not now." My tone was clipped and my words rugged.

"Stevens. Stop." It wasn't a demand but an order.

I kept walking.

"Right now, it's not your manager talking, but your friend. Even though the manager in me should have a talk with his artist right the fuck now."

I swiveled around. "What? You wanna tell me I was a mess up there? I'm aware. No need to remind me."

He placed a hand on my shoulder, and I jerked away. "Talk to me."

"No." I clenched and unclenched my hands at my sides. "What's the point?" Fury blurred my vision. Black dots danced before my eyes. "She's too far away. It weighs on me, man. I'm trying here. Real fucking hard. She refuses to let me fly down to see her. The kids are asking for her too. What if she has changed her mind? What if she has no intention of ever letting me in again? What if the accident fucked us up?"

"Stevens." Riley's annoyance had decreased a notch. "It's just a minor setback. You two will be fine. Give her more time to heal. The accident didn't just crush her leg, it crushed her spirits too."

"I sound like a jerk. I know I do, but I can't help it," I said. "I'm back to my broody ways. My kids are sad too. We're all missing her. She makes us better. She makes *me* better. She makes the entire fucking world better."

"Sam, you don't have a show tomorrow. Let's go out."

"Not in the mood," I barked.

"It wasn't a request." Those words shut me up.

We went back to the buses, and after I showered and drowned some of my rage away, my friend joined me. His feet hadn't even touched the floor before Riley slid a whiskey bottle into my hand. "Nick's private label. He and Dahlia gifted it to me on my birthday. Great stuff. The girls are asleep on my bus. Let's drink this, then go out and get shitfaced. Like old times. It's been a while, and I could use the stress release too."

I nodded. What else could I do? I had run out of options. "Devon is okay with that?"

"Yes," my friend said. "She's happy to have the girls over. She's the one who spoke to Doris this morning and offered to take over for the entire day. They had a spa day, did the school stuff Maddie had put on the schedule, and made their own pizzas for dinner. They're more than fine."

"You two should be parents. It suits you both."

He snickered. "Yeah. Maybe. We've talked about it. Your kids are growing on us, man. We'll see. I want to propose first. If I'm doing this, I'm doing it right."

"You're lucky. Dev is perfect for you."

I didn't miss the irony of my own words as I spoke them out loud. My eyes took in the label. "Whiskey and Country? I sense a pattern here," I teased.

Riley shrugged. "It fits them. You gotta meet Nick one day. He's a nice man. Reminds me of you. A lot. Minus the grumpiness."

I gave him a sharp look. "Thanks… I guess."

Bringing the bottle to my lips, I let the liquid slide down my throat, relishing the burn. It made me feel alive. I had no idea when I'd last been drunk. Yeah, it was measured in years, not days.

I drained more of the whiskey in one gulp, ready to visit Drunktown.

"Hey, leave some for me, would you?"

"I need it more than you do, man. And you were right, it's pretty good stuff. I had no idea Dahlia and Nick were in the whiskey business. You should sell it at Wild and Country. Exclusively."

Riley stole the bottle from my grip. "Yeah. Well, for now, it's just a small production. If they wanna expand, I'll be more than happy to talk business with them. Anyway, Tucker has already set his mind on convincing them to turn their hobby into something bigger. The guy is relentless, and Nick is his childhood best friend. We'll see how it goes. About the bottle… I brought it, and it was *my* gift, so I'm entitled to at least half of it."

I shook my head. "Don't come crying tomorrow when you have a massive hangover."

"Don't be a pussy. Just drink. The sooner you get wasted, the sooner I might be able to drill some sense into your stubborn brain."

I scrunched up my face and took the bottle back, nursing it as if it were a newborn. "I'll be too drunk later to tell you this, but thank you, man. Again, thanks for getting me out of my stalled life. I'm thankful for all this," I said, using the bottle to point around me. "And for always having my back. And caring for my girls."

"You're worth it, Stevens. You're a good man. And a good father. Just a shitty lover," he added with a wink.

"Yeah. Stop talking. Let's get drunk."

———

I woke up to the sound of chatter. Little girls' chatter. When had they come back here? Who was watching them?

Then Devon's laughter filled the silence. My head thundered. I hid my head under my pillow, trying to muffle the sound. In vain. Once I regained consciousness, the voices of my little ones warmed my heart.

"Girls, be quiet. Your daddy and Riley had a rough night. They need their beauty sleep. I'm sorry we can't go play outside. It's raining. Let's hope freshly brewed coffee and bacon, eggs, and grit will wake them up from their slumber."

"Can we make hot *crotchcolate* too?" Justine asked.

"With marshmallows," Mikaella chimed in.

Devon chuckled. "Sure. Let's get to work."

I alternated between consciousness and sleep for what seemed like ten seconds when Devon's voice resonated through my skull again. "Girls, it's time. Let's wake up the beasts."

Seconds later, prickly fingers pried my eyelids open. "Daddy." I pretended to be deep asleep and snored. "Do you think he's dead?" Justine asked, strands of her hair sweeping my face and tickling my nostrils.

"No," Mikaella replied. "I think he's *grinchy*."

"*Grinchily?*"

"*Grinch-y*. Like in the Christmas movie."

"His skin isn't green," Justine remarked.

"Mm-hmm. It doesn't matter. He's still *grinchy*. It's because he misses Maddie."

My heart pinched in my chest.

"You think?"

"Yes. She's away and hurt, and now he's not happy. Let's bring her back," Mikaella suggested.

"How?" Justine asked.

"Let's get his phone like we did last time. We call her and tell her Daddy is sick…or dead. She'll freak out and run back here. I miss her too. Do you miss her?"

"Yes. She always plays with us and bakes the *most* better bunny pancakes." Justine paused. "Do you think she'll come back?"

"Yes. She loves us too much."

"I want a hug."

"Me too," Mikaella agreed.

"And a dance *partly*."

"We're calling her," Mikaella concluded.

I could picture my baby girl bobbing her head, quickly.

Listening to their thinking process and their plotting fascinated me.

"Do you know where his phone is?" Justine whisper-shout.

"Let's check his pants pockets."

Perhaps I should let my daughters call Madison and use their charm to persuade her to let us come see her.

Before they could empty my pockets, I wrapped my arms around their bodies and unleashed the tickle monster. The happy melodies of their laughter eased all my worries. No matter what, we'd be okay because we had one another.

"*Daddddyyy*, stop," Mikaella giggled.

Justine hiccupped, unable to get a word out.

"*Grinchy* bear is up now, little creatures. I wonder what he'll have for breakfast. Little girls sound like a fancy meal I could indulge in." I rested my back against the head-board and released them. "Run before I catch you. Run."

Once they gave Riley, who was deep asleep in Madison's bunk room, the same treatment, the five of us had breakfast, the girls talking a mile a minute, as if they could feel I enjoyed their conversation filling the silence and preventing my brain from going rogue.

One of my conditions to go on this tour was to take days off from driving around and just be with my children.

All these little moments—like having breakfast together without being rushed—mattered the most, because one day they would be the memories we'd look back on from this adventure. The concerts were mine, but our family time was ours.

The food and the painkillers I'd swallowed after I'd woken up helped to dissolve the rest of my hangover. Letting the hot stream of water from the shower loosen the tension in my back, I prayed it would chase my leftover grogginess away.

With red-rimmed eyes and dark circles around them, I grimaced when I saw my reflection in the mirror.

My last memory of the previous night was of Riley falling face first on the couch, snoring like an old pickup truck in desperate need of a new muffler. But between the moment we started drinking and then, I couldn't remember much. After I'd convinced him to use the bunk bed nobody used anymore, I had sauntered to my bedroom, my brain turned off, swimming in gallons of amber liquor.

"Ready?" I asked, my voice still croaky as I joined the girls and my friends in the small living room section of our bus after I dropped a kiss on my daughters' foreheads. "What are you guys doing?"

"Arts. We're making a *trapbook*," Justine said. "For Maddie. Because she misses all the cities we visit. And we did the numbers caterpillar with Devon after we woke up. It's Maddie who made them."

"You mean a scrapbook," I corrected my daughter. "It's a wonderful idea. Are you gonna put pictures of me in there?"

"Only if you're not *grinchily* anymore," Justine exclaimed.

"*Grinch-y*," Mikaella replied. "And only if you smile."

"I'll think about it then," I said with a wink that made both of them laugh.

My daughters, as usual, pushed my gloomy thoughts away.

Devon and Riley left to enjoy their day off, and I lifted Justine up when she raised her arms. Today, it'd be just the three of us.

"When is Maddie going to come back?" Mikaella asked.

I shrugged. "No idea. But I have a plan. Let me just put it into motion to see if it could work. Do you trust me?"

She bobbed her head.

"Are you ready to go to the fair?" I asked them. "I've heard they're only in town for the weekend."

"*Yesss.*" Their screams of joy sent a warm feeling through my chest.

"Daddy, can we eat *colton* candy at the fair?" my baby girl asked. "Lots of *colton* candy."

"You want lots of cotton candy? What about your teeth?"

She bobbed her head fast, her eyes sparkling. "Yes. I want a big, big *colton* candy. Pink. Maddie says it's okay if we brush our teeth after."

Her genuine delight healed a part of my heart, while the remembrance of the woman I loved cracked a layer.

Justine's tiny hands wrapped around my neck, then she wriggled until I put her down on her feet. "Come on, Daddy. Don't make us late."

# Chapter 20


"Ems, I'm not wearing that," I said, pushing away the knitted dress she was handing me. "No way. I'm perfectly fine in my PJs."

"No, you're not. We're going to get that cast removed, and then we're celebrating, you and I."

I shook my head a couple of times. "All good here. Not going anywhere. Forget it. There's nothing to celebrate, anyway."

"You need to get out of this house at some point."

I folded my arms over my chest. "I don't. I'm good. Just leave me alone, Ems."

I clamped my teeth together as the lightning of agony spread through my left leg. A stabbing sensation so strong a wave of nausea hit me. Using both hands, I pressed hard against my cast, aching to tear it off.

Emily sat beside me. "Breathe."

My jaw tightened, and tears filled my eyes. "It's like it's getting worse each day."

"Post-surgical neuropathic pain is real. But it's a good sign. It can take a few months to resolve." She touched my toes one by one, asking me questions. "I'm not worried. Given the repair your leg has undergone, this is all normal. With the supplements you're taking and the daily physical therapy sessions you are doing to strengthen your muscles, especially of the other leg, it'll help with the healing. And to relieve some of the nerve pain. You're lucky Sam arranged twenty-four-seven in-house care for you. It makes the whole appointment thing so much easier since you don't have to leave the place." Her voice softened. "But I hear you, okay? Give it more time."

"Time? Time?" I repeated. "It's been over two months. My heart almost jumps out of my chest every time the pain hits. I wish they had cut my leg when given the choice. At least I wouldn't have to endure the distress that comes with it being patched up."

My sister's eyes snapped to mine. "Maddie, you don't mean it. You're just hurting. Anyone in your situation would be."

"Easy for you to say. It's not *your* leg. *Your* body. *Your* life."

"No, it's not," she said. "But I've seen enough cases similar to yours to know what it implies."

I huffed, ire swirling inside me at a dizzying speed. "Again, it's not you who's glued to a bed all day."

She pointed to the discarded wheelchair in the corner of the room. The one I refused to use. "Maddie, you *are* choosing to stay in your room. You *are* choosing to forget you have options. I agree they're not the ones you'd normally aim for, but lashing out at the world won't help. You can do better than that. Where's the girl who survived neglect growing up? Where's the one who's always chasing her dreams?"

"She's dead. All I'm reduced to is a cripple, unsure if I'll ever get full use of my leg again, all because some idiot ran a red light. Why do I have to be the victim of *his* bad judgment?"

Emily shook her head. "Again, you're the girl choosing to position herself as a victim. It's so out of character for you."

I looked away, refusing to acknowledge her words.

After a long beat, I spoke up. "Maybe I'm just exhausted. Maybe it's all asking too much of me. What if I'm tired of always fighting for my life?"

My sister wound her arms around me. I steeled against her, but she didn't let go, and I relaxed after a full minute.

She caressed my hair and leaned back. "Maddie, you're doing a lot better. What angers you, aside from being injured, can be boiled down to two things."

"What?"

"Missing your man and the tour. You two were just beginning to acknowledge what you were to each other. Those first moments got lost in the chaos of the accident. They'll return…when the timing is right. You should call him."

I whipped my head around to look at her. "I was about to go on a once-in-a-lifetime experience, and it got stolen from me. I'm missing it all. I thought my life was finally making sense and *pouf!* All gone. I've missed two months, Ems. Two months I'll never get back."

"Why won't you allow them to visit you? You're both miserable. Sam loves you, Maddie. He's really trying to give you your space like you've begged him to and to just focus on the girls, but it's been hard on him too. Every time I call to update him, he sounds a little angrier."

"He can't fly here every time he has a day off. I'm not the priority here. The girls are. And that's what matters."

"Maddie, you matter too. To all of us, you do. Stop convincing yourself otherwise. Stop putting yourself last. It's okay to wanna be a priority too. Nothing wrong with that."

I cocked my head to avoid her piercing gaze. "There's so much rage boiling inside me. I'm restless. All I wish for is to regain full use of my legs…and my independence. To do what pleases me without having to ask others for help. It's heavy, feeling incapacitated." I paused. Some of my wrath melted away as I spoke the words that were poisoning me. "Ems, I'm tired of being angry, you know? I want my life back. I want it all back. The same exact way it was."

"The girls called this morning…while you were asleep. You should at least video chat with them. And let them visit, Maddie. It would be beneficial to all of you. They don't understand why they can't see you or why you keep them at arm's length."

I parted my lips to argue, but my sister kept going.

"I understand your point of view. But try to understand theirs. They are just little kids. It's stressful for them. When you got injured, their lives changed overnight too. What they had known for months was taken away from them without any explanation or heads-up."

Her hand reached for mine.

"All those years ago, when I got you out of that hell, you asked for *them*. Even though deep down you knew *their* actions were hurting you, the kid in you couldn't imagine a life without *them*. You told me once you would have a hard time walking away from Mikaella and Justine after the tour because they had already been deceived before by an adult who was supposed to love them before. And now, you got taken away from them too. The least you can do is not break that bond you guys share and reassure them you're still part of their lives. If that's what you wish too… Deep down, I'm pretty sure it is. You guys are all hurting. Why not rely on one another to go through this episode instead of doing it all on your own?"

"But—"

"No buts, Maddie. I'm trying here. I really am. At one point you'll have to snap out of it and just take the control of your life back."

"I've been on bed rest for weeks. I don't want to suck them into my darkness. Some days, I feel like I'm stuck under piles of bricks. My entire body hurts. I wake up at night in sweat because the pain paralyzes me. How am I supposed to feel like myself? And as if that's not bad enough, I'm scarred all over my lower half. I know it will look like I've been cut open. Oh wait, I was."

My sister didn't let go of me as she watched me while delivering the next few words. "You could be stuck in a wheelchair for the rest of your life. Or missing both legs. Would you rather be unable to walk ever again?"

"Yeah, okay, I sound ungrateful. Sorry to be a pain in your life."

"You're not. I love you, but enough is enough. Let's eat out tonight. Trust me, it will uplift your mood."

I remained silent.

"Let's get you changed first."

"Ems, I'm not going," I said with a pout. "I'm entitled to one more day of self-loathing."

"Guess you'll wear that cast until you turn fifty then. Or maybe it will disintegrate in a few years if we're lucky."

I poked my tongue out at her, and she just shrugged.

"I'm not supposed to celebrate being handicapped," I said after a long pause. "It's wrong."

"We're celebrating your cast being removed. Come on. Help me out here, Maddie. Getting rid of this smelly thing"—she pointed to the cast on my leg—"is one more step toward healing. You should be proud. Not see red."

"I-I'm just not ready… To see…to see how bad it looks underneath," I finally admitted.

She signed. "There will be scars, sure, but perhaps you imagine it worse than it is in reality. I'm not saying it will be all pretty and perfectly healed, but I'm sure you'd be surprised at how much better it looks than what you've pictured in your mind."

"Sliced flesh is a sight I can't miss. You're right. Go, me."

"Keep going. Be dramatic, Maddie," my sister added. "Let me know when that dress is on, and I'll do your hair and makeup. You'll see. It'll make you feel beautiful. It's good for the spirits."

She exited the room without another glance at me.

Once she closed the door behind her, I exhaled, letting go of my annoyance. "Fine," I hollered after a minute.

Emily opened the door, grinning like a fool. "I knew you wouldn't be able to resist. I'll get my makeup bag and be back." She tossed a cookie onto the bed. "Get your chocolate fix."

———

I exhaled. Fishing my phone out, I watched the screen for a long time before I gathered enough courage to make the call.

"Maddie," he exclaimed when he answered after the second ring. "Everything all right?"

"Riley, I want back in. I need to get on that tour bus. Can you make that happen? I'm going nuts being stuck here. I'm driving my sister insane. My mood is all over the place. I know I need physical therapy, so maybe not this week…but as soon as it's physically possible, take me back, okay? I'll lose my mind if I spend too much time away. I miss them. I miss him. I can't heal if my heart is broken."

"Maddie, I'll see what I can do. Have you talked to him lately?"

"Last week. It was tense. He doesn't agree with me about not wanting him to visit. It's…it's for the best… I'm doing it for him."

"He loves you. You gotta let him help you," he said. "He worries a lot and feels helpless right now."

"He's already done more than enough. All the care… It's more than I could have ever expected. Every time he leaves, I end up crying myself to sleep for days afterward. How is it beneficial for anyone? We're all suffering."

"I hear you. Can we talk later? I have a meeting in five. I'll call you after dinner, okay? We'll figure something out."

"Yeah, I gotta go too. Bye."

———

"That splint looks badass on you," my sister said after we exited the doctor's office. "The X-rays look better than I expected. I'm impressed by the healing so far. It's all promising."

She pushed the wheelchair while I scrutinized the new apparatus around my leg. All I could see were the scars decorating my flesh that I would have to learn to accept. I still had a hard time with the one on my left hip. The leg ones were longer, but at least they were not as awful in appearance.

"Ems, I'm not feeling good enough to go out. My head spins. I wanna go to bed—"

Pain radiated down my limb, stealing my thoughts in the process. My entire body became taut as I prayed for the blades of fire shredding my muscles to dissipate.

Cold shivers lined my back, and I nipped at my bottom lip to refrain from crying.

"Ems. Raincheck, okay? Can you drive me home?"

My sister engaged the brake of the wheelchair, circled it, then gave me a pointed glance. "How bad? On a scale of one to ten?"

A moan escaped my lips as I squirmed in my seat. "A hundred."

"Fuck."

She loosened the straps of the splint and pressed firmly on the muscles in spasm. Each movement of her fingertips sent a lightning bolt of agony through me. She kept the rhythm going, massaging the flesh in circular movements until they slowly relaxed, one fiber at a time. A sigh left me as my whole body collapsed and I sank into the chair. I could breathe at last. I wiped the moisture building in my eyes with my fingertips. "I seem to be wrecking all our plans."

"Hey, it's okay. You come first. We can go out some other time."

"I acted like a brat earlier. I really wanted us to have dinner somewhere. We dressed up. Sorry, Ems."

Emily cupped my cheek, wiping my tears away. "We can still have fun. Let's grab takeout on our way back. Then we can watch a movie. I really wanna spend my night with you. Just us sisters. Okay?"

"O…kay. Thank you."

# Chapter 21



I adjusted the crutches under my arms for the umpteenth time, my flesh raw where they dug into my ribcage. I maneuvered as best I could, pinching my lips together, as if that could stop me from falling flat on my face. Claudia, the physical therapist who'd started coming over ten days ago, stayed close but didn't intervene. I cursed under my breath as I lost my balance and had to grip the rail.

My foot pressed into the ground, and a sharp pain shot through me. The orthopedist, who had removed the cast, had instructed me to start putting a little weight on my leg and walk short distances every day. Easier said than done since it freaking hurt to do so. After the surgery I'd undergone, he confirmed it would take a while before I could walk on my own two feet again.

Being on bed rest had been hard on me. Even though the nurse, who'd been by my side since I came to live at

Sam's, made sure I exercised every day so my other limbs wouldn't atrophy, I still had lost some muscle mass. And most of my patience, and whatever faith I had left that things would turn out okay.

My eyes brimmed with tears at the intensity of the pain, and I cursed some more before capitulating and sitting on a chair, ready to throw a fit. Sure, I could walk around just fine with crutches. But using them while putting weight on my bad leg wasn't as easy as it looked.

"It's not getting better," I spoke through clenched teeth. "I've been practicing for days, and I'm still unable to walk more than half a dozen steps without nausea hitting me because it hurts. Stupid accident. Stupid leg. Stupid crutches."

"Are you done complaining?" Claudia asked with a raised brow as she neared me. "You can go back to the wheelchair if you prefer. Would you? But I don't see it helping you get back on that tour bus if you do."

I offered her a pointed look before murdering her with my gaze. Yeah, she had teamed up with my sister to make my life an even bigger living hell than it already was.

"Claudia, you're supposed to root for me," I said with a deep exhale. "Not turn into a boot camp instructor."

"Maddie, I am rooting for you. If I don't push you, who will? You seem to have lost faith in yourself. Good news, I haven't. So, get up. The break is over. Show me what you can do. No excuses this time. We're not done for the day until you walk across the house in one go."

I grumbled something under my breath, got up, and executed myself. It took me four attempts to succeed.

Once I did, pride sizzled inside me. Pearls of sweat lined my forehead. The temperature in the room felt ten degrees warmer.

After the third try, I almost announced I was done, but now I was glad I had persevered.

Claudia high-fived me. "See? I knew you had it in you. Now you gotta walk back there. I'm not gonna carry you around." She sauntered toward the kitchen, leaving me behind in the den.

With the crutches under my arms to help with the balance and remove some weight from my leg when it got too much, I gathered what little energy I had left and joined her where she rewarded me with a cupcake and a glass of lemonade. Yep, my sister was behind the bribing for sure.

"See? It wasn't too hard, was it? I knew you could do it. Practice till the next session. I'll be able to tell if you slack off."

Once Claudia left, I took a nap.

I woke up when my phone went off. I looked at the screen, and sighed, wishing it was Riley. Since we talked ten days ago, I hadn't heard back from him, and I wondered what was taking him so long to reach out.

Many times a day, I was tempted to call him, but I was choosing to exert some patience and give him more time. Maybe my request was not an easy one, and he needed longer to figure things out.

Emily picked me up at five. I had agreed to a redo of the dinner date I'd bailed on the day my cast was removed.

"Where are you taking me?" I asked as I hauled myself into her car without any help, panting as if I had run two miles, while she stowed the crutches on the backseat. "After what Claudia put me through today, I could use a drink. If Dr. Prescott agrees."

"One, since you're still taking meds. And we're having Thai tonight. That place we haven't been to in forever. Speaking of Claudia, how did your physical therapy session go?" she asked after I buckled my seatbelt and relaxed against the seat.

"Why did you recommend her to me? She's a sadist. I'm telling you. She gets high on the idea of putting people through the wringer. There's nothing sweet or gentle about her."

I caught the grin forming on my sister's lips. "I knew you two would get along just fine. You may hate her, but look at you, you're done feeling sorry for yourself."

I quirked one eyebrow.

"Okay, not done, but you're getting there. Hate is a form of passion, Maddie. And being passionate is good. It's getting you somewhere."

I shook my head. "I guess. Anyway, thanks to your barbarian of a friend, I can maneuver around the house with the crutches. And walk a short distance using both legs. I'm getting stronger." I sighed. "One day at a time."

"That's the spirit."

We were finishing our plates when Riley Burns walked in and sat across the table, propping his elbows on the table and watching me with his I-mean-business stare.

I blinked and wiped my mouth with a napkin. "Huh, hi. What are you doing here?"

"Taking you back home, Maddie. "Isn't that why you called me the other day?"

I swallowed hard. My pulse went ballistic. "Is this a joke, or is it for real? Because if it's a prank, I'm not sure I'm mentally strong enough to deal with it."

Emily reached for my hands across the table and gave them a squeeze. "If it's what you still desire, it's now a viable option. We've been working together"—she motioned to herself and Riley with her fingers—"on a plan to get you there since you left the hospital after the accident. We were just waiting to see what the orthopedist would say and get Claudia's insight about your physical therapy needs."

"Are you two serious? The last time I talked to Sam, he said nothing."

The two people opposite me exchanged a glance. "It's because we haven't told him yet."

"What? Why?"

"Let's just say, if your doctor or physical therapist hadn't agreed, or if you hadn't shown such progress, this wouldn't be possible. We just wanted to make sure you two wouldn't have to live on false hopes," my sister said.

"When?" That was the only thing I could ask right now as excitement bubbled up inside me and chased away any other thoughts.

"Tonight. If you're ready to go."

"But—"

"Your suitcase is in the trunk of my car," Riley said. "I picked it up as soon as Emily texted me after you left the house earlier."

"I'm going home?" I asked, just to make sure it wasn't all a dream.

Moving to stand, I used the table to support some of my weight and reached the opposite side to pull my sister into a hug.

A surge of emotion filled me, and I could barely get a word out. "Thank…thank you," I croaked through the thickness of my throat. "I love you."

She tightened her grip around me. "Go get him back, Maddie. You deserve your happily-ever-after. And you're doing so much better. I'm proud of you. I know it'll be tough for quite some time, but you're getting there. I have faith in you. I've always had."

I leaned back, drying my tears, then hugged Riley.

"We missed you, Maddie. I'm glad you're healing. I know a few people who can't wait to have you back."

I let out a teary giggle. "Is this a dream?"

He shook his head. "It's all real."

For the first time in weeks, I could contemplate letting the ones I loved back into my life. I still had a long recovery ahead of me, but with Sam, Mikaella, and Justine around, every challenge appeared easier—and possible.

———

"What's the plan?" I asked Riley once the private jet reached its full altitude.

"Wait a sec. I almost forgot." He fished his phone from his pocket, tapped the screen a few times, and handed me the device.

My eyes stayed glued to the screen.

My grip on the phone tightened.

I pressed play on the video.

It had been filmed from the side of the stage.

Sam filled the screen, bent over a piano—I had no idea he could play—and the first note of a song I'd never heard before reached my ears, tearing my heart apart. It wasn't just the lyrics. It was the melody. The melancholy in his voice. The raw emotions etched in his eyes. His stance, more fragile and less assured than usual.

A hot tear escaped my eye and trailed down my chin. I caught it with the back of my hand.

Goose bumps spread all over my arms and the nape of my neck.

My throat constricted, affecting my breathing, as my emotions lodged there.

"Is it—?" I asked, unable to complete the question.

The song wasn't the same one he'd sung to me at the hospital. I'd never heard it before.

"It's yours. I had no idea he had written it, and I bet he has written a few. It's his way of coping with the hardships of life. He played it last night…out of the blue. As an encore. Said he felt closer to you… That he wished his words could reach you somehow. To help him hold on to the specks of hope that you'd let him back into your life."

"It's beautiful. Listen… I-I didn't mean to push him away. I just wanted to ease things for him…"

"I'm aware."

I couldn't move my focus away from the screen, immersed in Sam's performance. In who he was. In the man hurting and pouring his heart to me into a song.

The song ended, and I was a sobbing mess.

Riley made a box of tissues and a glass of water appear, and I thanked him.

His lips stretched into a smile while he tapped something on his phone before bringing his attention back to me. "I was thinking. Only if you're up to it… You could surprise him at his show tonight. We'll miss the beginning, but we should be there for at least the second half. It's just an idea."

Warmth swirled inside me at the thought of seeing the man I loved again, knowing I would never have to leave his side afterward.

"I love it. Let's do this."

"Welcome back, Madison."

———

From where I stood, away from the stage, I let out a long breath, waiting for Riley's direction. A few feet away, Sam was belting his heart out to the crowd, and I could hear him, even though I couldn't see him. Just the sound of his voice was powerful enough to stir flutters in me and warm my skin.

Sadness laced his voice. His tone didn't carry the same potency, the same mesmerizing pull as the night he'd sung in that bar.

He sounded…lonesome. That was the only adjective I thought was fitting to describe Sam Stevens at this moment.

His performance lacked the contagious joy and energy he usually carried onstage. Sure, he was still an incredible artist and musician, but I knew him well enough to notice the difference.

A vise closed around my heart at the realization he was hurting because of me. Because he thought I was abandoning him too. Because the moment we chose to be together, everything went sideways.

Even though his vocals were filled with heartache, steeped in every word leaving his mouth, my love for him only deepened because he was himself—the one who never shied away from his emotions. That was what made his music so unique. So relatable. So intoxicating. And right then, I understood why he had been named *The Legend* of country music years ago. Yes, Sam Stevens was truly a legend in his own way. But right now, he was a lonesome heart alone on a stage, trying to mend the broken pieces of himself through his art.

I was staring at my phone for the umpteenth time when Riley's text message came through.

RILEY

A guy named Rocky will come get you. Stay
on the side where he directs you. There will
be a stool so you don't fatigue yourself. I
made sure he'll play your song again as the
encore. That's your cue. Like you asked. I'll
be cheering you on from offstage.

ME

Thank you. You're like our fairy love
godmother.

Or godfather, I guess.

RILEY

Not sure Sam would agree with this term of
endearment.

ME

It fits. What can I say?

RILEY

Go surprise your man. We're babysitting
tonight. Devon's orders.

ME

I'll owe you one the day you have kids of
your own.

RILEY

We have a deal.


I followed Rocky, maneuvering my crutches the best I
could, and took my place next to the stage, just behind the
thick black velvet curtain, out of Sam's sight. For the first
time, I was grateful for Claudia's tough love in getting me
ready for this day. Without her, I would probably still be in
bed, alone with my dark thoughts and sinking hopes.

Sam sang four more songs, and the crowd exploded in
cheers and applauded, begging for an extended
performance.

My heart jackhammered in my chest. All my senses were attuned to the man singing his heart out. Just being in his vicinity again was enough to make me forget about the pain numbing the left side of my body. Why had I kept him at arm's length for so long? I needed him as much as he needed me. We were two halves of the same whole. Two souls needing each other to reach our full potential. Two hearts carved from the same flesh.

I loved him beneath the broodiness and all the walls he'd built around himself when I first got to know him. I fell for him the moment I discovered how generous and beautiful the heart he hid inside truly was. Even when I tried to convince myself my feelings weren't reciprocated, I still loved him. Simple as that. What I felt for him could only be defined as a *one of a kind, I possess no words to describe it* kind of love. One that lived under your skin. That rattled your soul. That called to you in the middle of the night, waking you with a start because you thought you'd lost it. One that left you breathless. The intensity of my feelings for him was still disconcerting and foreign. Being here right now forced me to face the truth: how much I'd missed him, and how much of a fool I'd been for thinking he was better off without me.

I froze when Sam walked offstage, watching him through the crack between the curtains. He handed his guitar to Rocky, uncapped a bottle of water, and drank it in one gulp. After wiping the sweat from his face with a towel, he took his place behind the piano. He glanced around, as if searching for something he couldn't find. Could he feel my presence just mere feet away?

Riveted by the sight of him, I couldn't look away. I was bewildered, entranced, unable to tear my eyes from him.

Now that I could watch him—really watch him—I couldn't hide away or pretend anymore. The hurt radiating from him hit me straight in the chest, heavy as a boulder, pressing on my ribs, suffocating my breath.

Sam cleared his throat, and I blinked.

A force, strong and electric, pushed me forward. Toward him.

He scanned the stage, a frown creasing his forehead, as if he could sense my presence but couldn't bring himself to believe I was here.

With a roll of his shoulders, he shook his head and scratched his temple.

I linked my hands together under my chin.

Every second I waited felt like a lifetime.

The butterflies in my belly whirled at a dizzying speed.

The lights turned off, replaced by a single spotlight aimed at him.

Placing his fingers over the keys, Sam took a big inhale while I held my breath not to miss a word.

> **I've been turned to stone**
> **long ago**
> **I can't feel the sun warming**
> **my skin**
> **I can't feel the raindrops on**
> **my face**
> **I'm numb. So numb.**
> **My heart is locked up in**
> **a cage**
> **No one is allowed inside…**

On my crutches, I stood and followed the sound of his voice. The pull he possessed on me. The galvanic lure I had no idea how to escape.

Sam had written me another song. One he had agreed to share with the world. An emotional ballad that appealed to every particle of my being. To both my heart and my soul.

He launched the chorus, and I melted some more. Exiting the dark corner where I'd been hiding, I faced him, my lungs shaky with the air I was still holding in.

> **...The sight of you jolts my**
> **heart back to life**
> **Your smile thaws every layer**
> **of ice I hide behind**
> **Your touch soothes my sorrows**
> **It heals my pain**
> **Your lips taste like freedom**
> **Your skin feels like passion...**

Our eyes connected.

My breath itched on its way in.

Halting by the side of the stage and supporting my weight on the crutches under my armpits, I pressed my hands over my chest to calm my overzealous heart.

Sam blinked. And blinked again. His fingers played the keys with renewed determination, as if they were in control. His shoulders relaxed, and fire returned to his gaze. The one burning for me. The one directed at me.

A lazy curl grazed the lips I couldn't wait to kiss.

His eyes stayed locked on mine as he poured his heart out in front of a roaring stadium full of fans. Cell phone lights brightened the dark amphitheater. Shiny stars, the witnesses to our love story unfolding before them.

> **...Let me shine in your light**
> **Let me breathe in your air**
> **With you, I'm alive again**
> **With you, I'm myself again...**

With careful movements, I neared the center of the stage, unable to stay put. Sam's magnetism couldn't be avoided anymore.

He mouthed, *You're back?*

I bobbed my head , my lips stretched so big, they would stay fixed into a grin for the rest of my life.

A hint of a smile lifted the corner of his mouth. *For good?*

I bobbed my head faster.

With a jerk of his head, he gestured for me to join him.

I frowned, not sure if I understood right.

I perused the area around me and caught Riley's eyes. He nodded, letting me know it was fine.

My gaze returned to Sam, waiting for me, scooting to the left on the bench, engrossed in his music—and me—all at the same time.

Rolling my lips over my teeth, to prevent them from trembling, I tried to ignore the fact that tens of thousands of eyes were fixed on me. I blocked the wolf-whistles and "Oohs" and "Aahs" as I took the spot next to my man. While he sang the last verse, my love for him blossomed to a whole new level.

**...And kiss me**
**I crave the kiss of an angel**
**Of an angel**
**A kiss from my angel**

His band took over. Sam, abandoning his instrument, turned toward me and crashed his lips on mine, not giving me a second to catch my breath.

"I love you, Maddie," he whispered against my mouth. "I'm fucking gone for you. I'm not letting you go. Never again."

"I never meant to hurt your feelings. I just knew what this tour meant to you and your team and didn't want to interfere with it. I was wrong because I hurt you in the process. And I also hurt myself. I love you so much. And I missed you. Being away from you has been one of the hardest things I've ever done."

"I was a fucking mess without you."

I kissed him back, desperate for his love.

He detached his mouth from mine, faced the microphone, and hollered to his screaming fans, "My woman is back."

A nervous laugh escaped me, and I placed my hand over my mouth. "Ohmygod, you didn't just do that," I said. Laughter, shyness, and elation all blended inside me.

"Oh, babe, I'll shout it out to anyone who's willing to listen for the rest of my life. I can't believe you're here."

I straightened and circled my arms around his neck, molding my body to his and claiming his lips.

"Get a room," someone yelled from the crowd.

"We will," Sam muttered against my mouth. "And nobody is allowed to disturb us for the next twenty-four hours."

"Thank you, all y'all. Good night, Denver," he said to his fans, crushing me gently against him, the rhythm of his heart syncing with mine.

The curtains closed, and Sam lifted me in his arms, honeymoon style, our mouths hungry, and our hands busy.

"My crutches," I said, breathless.

"Someone will get them." A smirk formed on his lips. "God, how I wish I could fuck you in my dressing room right now."

"I don't know how we'll manage that," I said, my voice husky, casting a glance down at my left leg. "Though, I love the aftershow horny side of you."

"Maddie, I love you so much. I wanna make love to you. I never got a chance to show you just how much. We'll find a way."

Palpitations stirred within me, and my lips found their way back to his. "You and me." Kiss. "Riley is babysitting." Kiss. "Let's get out of here." Kiss.

"You won't sleep alone tonight," Sam said, shielding me with his body as he carried me offstage. Once we distanced ourselves enough from everyone else, he stopped, searched my eyes, and asked, "How are you doing? Be honest with me." His serious tone killed some of the sexual tension bouncing between us.

"I'm a work in progress. The pain is unbearable at times. And I'm still not accustomed to it. Not sure I ever will be. It's paralyzing when it diffuses through my leg. I can walk a few steps on my own with the crutches now. Also, my mood fluctuates…a lot. I get mad easily when it becomes too much, and the pain doesn't fade away. Fair warning."

His lips reached for mine. "I can't take your pain away, but I'll do my best to do everything in my power to make things easy for you. Let's say my mood has been shifting a lot too lately." He breathed out. "I'm so relieved you're here. You have no idea."

"I wouldn't wish to be anywhere else."

"Welcome home, Maddie."

# Chapter 22
### Sam

Holding Madison high in my arms, her mouth attached to mine, we maneuvered to shut the bus door after climbing inside. "I've missed you so much," I said, feasting on her lips. "I can't believe it's been over a month since I last saw you and held you in my arms."

Blistering desire unleashed inside me, and I believed I'd combust.

Madison unbuttoned my shirt with her small fingers, but unable to be patient, I sat her on the bed and ripped it open, buttons flying. Her eyes traveled over my blazing skin, her throat rippling and her face illuminating.

"Loving what you see?" I asked, unable to resist, relishing the blush on her cheeks.

"A lot. It's better than in my dreams."

"You dreamed about me?" I asked, arousal tinting my words.

"All the time," she admitted. "I was about to go crazy. Countless times, I woke up with a start in the middle of the night, thinking you were asleep beside me, only to realize none of it was real. I wore your clothes, trying to have a piece of you with me. When I couldn't sleep, I imagined your arms around me, rocking me until I found some comfort."

"Do you think…we…huh…can go ahead?" I asked, not sure how to bury myself deep inside her without hurting her injured leg in the process.

She worried her lip, studying me. "I want to. As long as the pain isn't too intense, I think we can manage. I'll tell you if we gotta stop."

Sitting down beside her, I peeled her sweater over her head in a slow, tantalizing movement that sent shivers through her.

We'd never made love before, and the realization got me both excited and nervous. The good kind of nervous.

Holding my face still between her palms, she sucked in a deep breath before talking. "The scar across my hip…it-it's ugly." She pinched her lips together. "It's not…I'm no… Let's just say I'm glad my left leg is covered right now."

"Maddie, everything about you is beautiful and endearing. The scar is just that, a scar. It's not a testament to who you are as a person. It doesn't define you."

Never detaching my eyes from her, I unclasped her bra and let the lacy fabric fall next to us. Trying to lengthen the pleasure when all I craved was to bury myself inside her, I leaned forward, my mouth finding her erect nipples. Madison let out a sharp yelp that vibrated through me and got me harder for her. I shaped my palm to one of her breasts and kneaded the softness of her flesh.

With the pad of my thumb, I traced the red line

marking her abdomen. "All I see when I look at it is strength. And vulnerability. And life. Because you could have died. This is proof you survived an experience that could have ended in tragedy. It shows me how brave you are… How resilient…"

"You mean it?" she asked in a low voice.

"Yes. Every word."

She tugged at my hair with her fingers, their tips digging into my scalp and sending tingles down my spine.

With my hand locked around her nape, I kissed her senseless. Our tongues tangled in a choreography of a dance we hadn't rehearsed often enough. Madison pulled my lower lip between her teeth, and I groaned, deepening the kiss when she released it. Our hands ventured all over each other, desperate to touch every inch of bare skin.

"Can I taste you?" I asked as we broke apart to catch some fresh air.

"I never…Nobody ever…"

"Relax, I'll make you feel good. I promise." I helped her to her back and kneeled on the floor.

"Sam?" I twisted my neck to meet her eyes. "Don't get repelled by my choice of underwear. Emily ordered those." She grimaced while I peppered kisses around her navel and along the scar across her hipbone. She tensed for a second before letting go as my tongue drew patterns over her bare skin.

"Maddie, you should know by now nothing that you say or do can turn me off. Much less a pair of… God, how does this thing work?"

She stifled her laughter with a hand pressed against her mouth. "Way to kill the mood, huh?"

I watched her laughing, and it eased the wounds of my heart her absence had caused.

"There's a Velcro on the left side. Sorry, it's anti-climactic."

I slid them off delicately. "No, I think it's clever. It serves its purpose." I threw the piece of white cotton behind me. "No need to worry. They'll not be needed anytime soon."

Now that I got rid of the last piece of clothing shielding her, I returned to my exploration. Still on my knees, I kissed my way down her stomach.

The air charged around us, and my pulse kicked up.

Madison trembled underneath my touch when my lips brushed the soft flesh of her clit. Using my tongue, I licked the seam between her thighs, and her hips lifted off the bed. "Oh, Sam."

I stopped, making sure her cries were from pleasure and not from pain.

"Why did you stop?" she asked, lifting her head from the mattress and searching my gaze.

That was all it took to unlock the side of me I'd been restraining for two years. I devoured Madison with my teeth, my tongue, and my lips. I sucked on the mound between her legs until a series of moans tumbled out of her mouth and she begged me for more. Sliding one finger, then another in, I glided them back and forth, spreading her arousal over her folds and bringing her closer to the edge. My tongue toyed with her at the same time, until an orgasm built inside her, and she clenched around my digits, surrendering her pleasure to my greedy self.

Still not satisfied, I stood at the foot of the bed and hovered over her, caging her naked body between my arms.

We had sex before, but this…this felt like the first time. The one that mattered the most. The beginning of something erotic. Beautiful and exciting. The beginning of us.

"Can we keep going?" I asked.

She nodded.

My dick stood tall between us, and with steady movements, she unbuttoned my jeans and freed it from the confinement of my boxer briefs.

She worked my length, and shivers spread through me. With half-masted eyelids, pleasure ignited deep inside me at the sight of her hand around the hardest part of me.

Taking my wallet out of my back pocket, she picked up one of the condoms, ripped the foil, and sheathed me with dedicated gentleness.

Our eyes fused together. Hers sparked with a lust I'd never witnessed before that cast a spell on me.

Careful to avoid touching her splinted leg, I eased inside her, inch by inch, watching the elation displayed on her visage the entire time I pushed my engorged self inside her walls. Madison gasped as I filled her to the brim, and we connected deeper than ever before.

Every cell in me shook with anticipation, as if I were floating, about to rip at the seams.

The sensations swirling inside me stole my breath away.

Madison shifted on the bed, as if adjusting to the feel of us. Nothing had ever felt this good. Nothing compared to the feel of her flesh against mine.

A string of whimpers passed her quivering lips as I thrust into her. She closed her eyes and tilted her head back, breathing out. Perfection. It was a privilege only I possessed to capture the essence of her in that moment.

Her hips rolled against mine in an enticing wave, sending high-voltage electricity up my spine.

I slowed down, making sure nothing I did could cause her any pain.

Madison's eyes snapped open and fixated on me. Her

pupils were dilated, her cheeks a light shade of pink, and her lips parted on a half-cry. She looked at me with a mix of adoration and reverence.

Right then, I had the certitude we belonged together. That she was the one for me—the only one.

With one hand, she gripped my hipbone, pulling me to her and encouraging me to keep going.

Our bodies fused in a primal way that shattered all my inhibitions—and all my doubts—as I rammed into her, unable to prevent myself, now that I'd experienced how perfect we could be.

"I missed you," Madison whispered as I kissed along the length of her collarbone before moving to her jaw and her lips.

I pushed a wild strand of her hair away from her forehead when she stilled underneath me. A soft gasp passed her lips.

I propped myself up, using my arms. "What's wrong? Are you okay?"

She closed her eyes for the longest second, her teeth pressed into her bottom lip, trying to mask the pain. "A spasm. They come and go."

"We'll stop," I said, about to withdraw from the depths of her.

She held on to me, preventing me from sliding out. "Don't. Stay there. Gimme a moment."

"I can—"

She silenced me with one finger. "I've been waiting for months for this. Don't you dare stop now."

I blinked, at a loss for words, seeing the determination and strength painting her features.

"Kiss me," she pleaded.

I obliged. Nothing tasted as good and looked as incredible as Madison Prescott naked with my dick embedded inside her.

Her right leg closed around me, erasing the space between us, and giving me permission to resume my pounding. We found our rhythm back. Pleasure built deep in my core, ready to be unleashed, unable to be contained anymore.

"Fuck, I won't last long," I mumbled. "Oh God, you feel great."

Madison's hand flattened on my chest while I increased the tempo. My hands rested on her hips while I tried not to explode and to savor every second. Watching me through hooded eyelids, she abandoned herself to the passion pulsing between us.

Her whimpers, our rushed panting, and the smacking of our flesh filled the silence.

I molded my hands to her waist and traced the scar on her hip with my fingertip. She shuddered under me, and the sensation rippled through my soul. I couldn't *not* touch her, fearing if I broke the connection, she would vanish.

"Sam, I love you."

I got lost in the woman who owned every bit of my heart, admiring her beauty. The devotion in her eyes. The curve of her lips. The halo of her hair. Everything that made her, *her*.

"Sam—" The plea in her voice, the sound of my name spoken in a breathless murmur, sent a discharge through me.

"I'm right here, babe. I'm right here with you."

I pounded into her with abandon. I bent over to suck on her nipples, to nibble the skin of her breasts, to lick the column of her throat. To cherish every inch of her and then surrender myself to her entirely, with all that I had left.

Madison wound her hands around my neck, keeping me close to her. Her eyes never left mine. She was mine. All mine. And right now, I had the assurance.

The clouds above us parted.

My thrusts accelerated. I had to brand her. To soak into her.

We moved in unison, enraptured and insatiable.

Her breaths quickened. Every inch of her took me hostage.

Her lips quivered. "Sam——"

When her body clenched around mine, I pounded faster, not missing a beat.

She held me against her, never breaking eye contact.

She cupped my cheek with her hand, and I locked my teeth around her thumb. She gasped. And I lost all sense of gravity.

I plunged into her with a rhythmic jerk of my hips. My fingers would leave bruises on her porcelain skin.

Madison purred. She cried out my name. She reached her high and surfed the waves. The entire time, my eyes were trained on her. She was magnificent. A gem I found when I wasn't searching. A precious gift who had driven away the darkness of my life. The part of my soul I'd been desperate to find. To reunite with.

The sight of her, spread naked on the bed, putting all her trust in me, unraveling me from the inside out, was my undoing.

I resumed my thrusts, my sole mission to go over the edge and take her with me. I pushed into her. Again. And again.

"Oh, Sam. Yes."

Madison's walls strangled my erection, and I surrendered. I committed everything I was to this woman. Drunk on her, I shot my load in powerful jolts, anchored where I was born to be.

Our fingers intertwined, and I guided our joined hands above her head, pressing them into the mattress.

My mouth descended on her, tasting her lips, my tongue sweeping hers with reverence. Only then did I relax, knowing I hadn't dreamed the last few hours of my life. My muse, my love, was back. She'd rocked my world in a way only she could, taking what we already had to a whole new level—and cementing what we'd forever be.

———

Madison and I fed each other French fries we had ordered in, still naked, lying on our sides on the bed. She had propped her injured leg on a pillow, gently massaging the top of her thigh every few minutes. We were waiting for the painkillers to kick in. After tonight's concert, Riley had made it back to the buses before us and had dropped Madison's luggage, crutches, and medication before we arrived. I was thankful he always had my back—and best interests—at heart.

My fingers left shivers in their wake, trailing up and down her arm. "You sure you're okay?" I asked, unable to mask the worry lacing my voice.

Madison smiled at me and nodded, but I could tell her limb was bothering her.

"I'm ordering you to rest. This was enough exercise for the day."

She watched me but added nothing for a beat. "It's just... I-I didn't wanna miss another opportunity with you. The accident made me think… Well, that's all I could do when stuck to that bed. Life is unpredictable. Not missing out is something I'll value more from now on." She reached for my hand. "Sam, I'm sorry…for pushing you away. You've been nothing but amazing to me. It was inconsiderate of me."

I swallowed. "I thought I'd lose my mind. It just… It felt like I was being left behind again… I hate fighting with you."

We remained silent, lost in each other for a long minute.

I traced the length of the scar across her hip with the tip of my finger. "Does it hurt?"

"It's not as sharp as the pain in my leg. It's more of a tingling sensation that comes and goes. If my leg wasn't hurting so much, maybe I'd consider this pain worse. Does it make sense?"

"Yeah. About your leg… I know the recovery is going to be long, but we'll get you the best specialists and physical therapists to look after you on the road. This is not a topic open for discussion, so don't try to get out of it."

"Sam, Riley and Ems took care of everything. They're the masterminds behind my being here. They have set up appointments all over the country to fit your schedule. Doris will stay for a while until I can get back to my feet and follow the girls around. If it weren't for your friend and my sister, I would still be miserable in Nashville while you're here. We'd *still* be apart."

I blinked. "They are? Wait, Ry said nothing about bringing you back. He never even mentioned anything."

"Emily neither. I learned coming to you was an option one hour before getting on that plane." Madison watched me, sucking in a breath. "Are…are we okay?"

"We are. Or we will be."

"How are the girls?"

"They miss you. But I missed you more." I couldn't hide the smile in my words.

"Whoa, that's a big claim to make," she said, a grin anchored to her face.

"My kids love you, but I'm *in love* with you. It means a whole lot fucking more."

"I love you too."

"You have no idea the impact of those four words on me right now. When I got that call… I…I thought I'd lost you."

"Never. And Sam?"

"Yes, babe?"

"I'm relieved to be home. You're my home. The three of you are."

"That's all I'm asking for. Your love. And to build something together," I confessed.

Tears glistened in her eyes, and a comfortable silence settled between us.

I brushed her cheek with a knuckle, smoothed the length of her lips, and pushed her hair back.

A quick shower later, I returned to bed. Sleep claimed Madison as we held onto each other under the covers, never breaking apart. I shaped my front to her back, and wrapped my arms around her waist, where her hands rested on mine. The sound of her breathing acted like a balm to my heart.

I listened to the steady rhythm, fearing if I joined her in sleep, I'd miss out on something. Her words from earlier replayed in my head.

*Life is unpredictable. Not missing out is something I'll value more from now on.*

I agreed.

My lips found her nape, and I kissed the soft skin there. Madison pushed herself against me and muttered something. I cherished the bare skin of her shoulder and the side of her neck with my lips.

A muffled purr escaped her, and I wished I could record the sound.

Lyrics that mirrored my feelings played in my head.

> **There's no more clouds shad-**
> **owing us from above**
> **Nothing stands in our way**
> **anymore**
> **I'm a country boy**
> **And you're an angel**
> **Please shower me with your**
> **light**
> **Please let me love you tonight**

Softly, I recited part of the chorus of the song I'd written for her months ago—the night she returned to my house after forgetting her purse. The song I never thought I would perform because I believed an *us* wasn't possible back then.

Life proved me wrong.

The past few months had taught me some invaluable lessons. Never again would I take anything for granted. We had both been hurt, but now I truly understood how precious our love was.

Sleep claimed me too, and for the first time in weeks, I wasn't afraid anymore.

# Chapter 23

## Madison

My eyelids opened, and I blinked to adjust to the semi-darkness around me. For a beat, I wondered I was lying. Sam muttered in his sleep, and his arms fastened around my waist, pulling me closer. I smiled, relieved my being here with him wasn't a dream but a reality.

I tilted my head to kiss his lips.

In the last twenty-four hours, I'd gone from despising my physical therapist to going back into the arms of the man I loved.

Sam splayed a palm across my stomach, preventing me from escaping his embrace.

"I need to use the bathroom," I whispered against his lips. "You gotta let me go."

Before I could register his movements, he was standing up and turning on the light on his side of the bed. After he put a pair of boxer briefs on, he held out his hand for me to grab. "Come on. Let me help you."

Pushing with my hands, I moved into a seating position. Sam slipped one of his T-shirts over my head, steadying me as I stood, his other hand anchored to my hipbone.

I tucked the crutches under my armpits and made my way to the en-suite bathroom. The bus's open layout made it easy to navigate with the crutches without bumping into everything each time I moved. At the front, a small living area with two couches and a TV mounted on the wall opened into a combined kitchen and dining space with a four-seat table. A narrow hallway led to the back, where two cozy bunk rooms were located—one of which had been my old living quarter—and a compact two-piece bathroom. Beyond them was the master bedroom, modestly decorated with a queen-size bed squeezed between two small nightstands and a dresser beneath a square window. The en-suite wasn't large by any means, but it had a decent-sized shower and a vanity with counter space. Our room at the back gave us the privacy we needed, and its small size meant I could always rely on the walls or furniture for balance if necessary.

Sam turned on the light and stood close behind me.

"I can do this on my own," I said. "While we're both up, I might give the shower a try if you don't mind."

"I can help," he offered.

I sighed, trying to refuse while not offending him. He just stood too close for comfort. I dropped a crutch, the narrow space making it hard to maneuver both of them, and a curse slipped from my lips.

Sam's hands steadied me rom behind.

I flinched and pulled away from his touch. "I said, I

can do this," I repeated with a tone harsh enough to surprise even me.

He backed up a step, his arms lifted in surrender. "Fine."

I shut my eyes to calm down and opened them again. "I-I'm sorry. I didn't mean to say it like that. Let me… Just let me do this. For now I can manage, but I'll need your help to shower, though."

He turned around and pressed a shoulder against the doorframe to give me a little privacy.

Clean and wearing his shirt, I returned to bed. I searched his eyes. "Earlier…I didn't mean to snap at you. I know you're trying to be there for me. It'll take a few days for us to adapt to this," I said, pointing to my leg. "Don't give up on me, okay? Ems said I was hard to live with. Don't lose hope. I'll try to be better."

Sam pulled me against him. "We'll find our normal. It's a lot of changes for both of us. A relationship, your accident, living in cramped quarters, being apart for so long, the girls. I don't wanna rush things, but I'm not waiting anymore. You're too important to me. I almost missed my chance once. Never again."

I claimed his lips—slow and torturous—unable to resist him when he spoke with that kind of honesty.

Pushing myself up, I removed the shirt covering my bare skin. Sam's irises darkened when they roamed all over my blazing flesh.

"You sure you're up to it?" he asked in his husky voice that always melted every cell in me.

I nodded. "Yes. I want you. I've missed you too much. We have two months to make up for." I dived my hand into his boxer briefs, and I pumped his hardening erection, relishing every groan his lips couldn't contain.

"Maddie—"

"I love you. And you know how much I love dessert. And treats." I wriggled my eyebrows. "The thing is... I can't reach down on my own. Would you feed me *your* treat?" I batted my eyelashes. "Please."

Sam's fingers lowered between my thighs and coated with my arousal, they played with my clit. I dug my nails into his biceps, pleasure clinging to me in waves as I rocked my hips over his greedy fingers.

"Oh, it feels good," I cried, barely holding it together.

He leaned back to remove the last piece of clothing between us and balanced over me, feasting on my mouth as if he feared I could disappear. Sliding down the bed and pressing hot kisses in his wake, my man licked a trail down to my throbbing center. "Sam," I pleaded, "I said *I* wanted dessert."

"I'm hungry too." Our eyes connected, his so dark I could barely make out the color in the early morning light.

"Feed me first. I *dare* you."

His gaze lit up at the challenge. I loved this playful side of him, knowing he would never back down from a dare I threw his way.

Kneeling beside my head, he leaned forward and returned his fingers between my thighs as whimpers of pleasure tumbled out. I enveloped his hand with mine to set the pace. My lips parted on a cry, and Sam used it as an invitation to guide his erection inside my mouth. I blinked and relaxed my jaw when he slipped himself further in. I secured one hand behind his ass cheek and steered the movements of his hips as he fucked my mouth. With hollow cheeks, I sucked him harder. He continued his assault on my sex with his fingers. Stars blinded me. I hesitated between closing my eyes and letting the pleasure consume me or keeping my gaze locked on him, watching him unravel—because of me.

Hushed gasps left me.

"Do you like being fed my dick, Maddie?" he asked.

I nodded, molding my lips to him.

Unable to resist giving in to the tension building in him any longer, Sam moved his hips with controlled urgency, and I relished the throaty growls he let out.

"Are you satiated yet?" he asked, his voice laced with repressed desire.

I shook my head.

Sam pulled away, and I tried to draw him back into my mouth.

"What do you want, Maddie?"

"You," I cried out as he dragged a first orgasm out of me with his fingers. I screamed my release, my walls engulfing his digits deeper and holding them there. I tried to fist the hard part of him, but Sam backed further away from my grip.

The flames rising in his eyes ignited my core. Plunging forward, he sucked on my lower lip, his teeth tugging, and his tongue licking every corner of my mouth.

Hovering over me, he lowered onto the bed until he could nestle himself between my legs, laving my center and tasting my arousal. I purred as he accelerated the pace of his tongue, the sweet torture of my demise.

His fingers returned to between my legs, moving in and out at a quick tempo. Before I could come undone, he kneeled, and pushed inside me. We trembled together when he thrust deeper, taking my breath away.

"You good?" I nodded. "Don't worry, I'll pull out."

He grabbed my shoulder with one of his hands, keeping me in place, and covered my mouth with the other, shoving a finger between my lips.

"Suck it, Maddie. While I fuck you."

He pounded into me faster at a slight angle—making

sure to avoid brushing my left leg—while fingering my mouth.

I moaned louder and pushed myself against him, increasing the contact of our bodies. Wrapping one arm around my waist, Sam rocked his hips in quick succession. Every cell in me quaked and vibrated with bliss.

His tongue circled one of my puckered nipples, and he teased the flesh with his teeth, forcing me to arch my back when addictive sensations invaded me.

When he lifted his head, our eyes met. The vision of him, covered in sweat and loving every inch of my body— even the parts I could barely look at myself—intensified my feelings for him.

Sam moved his free hand to my other breast, massaging the flesh and twisting the tip between his fingers. I yelped, the flimsy line between pain and pleasure highly addictive. He leaned over me, one arm hooked around my neck to kiss me. "I'm done punishing you for keeping me at arm's length, Maddie." His breath was warm against my skin, sending a shiver through me. "I'm done marking you. Now I wanna make love to you."

Sliding out of me, he kept his weight on his arms as he looked into my eyes. And my soul. The glint in his eyes brightened the room.

Panting, we eye-fucked each other, neither of us breaking the contact.

"I love you," I whispered, hoping he could read the honesty in my words.

My heart did a complete rotation in my chest when he replied, "I love you, Madison Prescott."

"Show me."

"If you let me, I'll show you for the rest of our lives," he said.

Sam pulled me to him, and we combusted together.

There was no more urgency. Just two people, devoted to each other, coming together. Fusing together.

My mouth devoured his. His tongue flicked around mine. I caressed the side of his face, wanting to immerse myself in his love until my heart only belonged to him.

Forever.

While we lost ourselves in an Earth-shattering kiss, he removed the elastic band from my hair, letting the wavy strands fall around my face.

Leaning back, he admired me, a twinkle in his eyes. "You're beautiful. Everything about you is." His mouth returned to mine.

My lips teased his, molding them as I savored their taste.

I glided my fingers over his arm. The contours of his ribcage.

He skimmed the dips of my waist. The bone of my hips.

Hoisting my good leg around his middle and clamping my thigh, Sam entered me, neither of us in a hurry for this moment to end.

We kissed, our hands insatiable in their mission to touch each other everywhere.

Sam plunged in and out of me at a slow, riveting pace. He combed a strand of hair away from my forehead, and I got mesmerized by his gaze. By the depth of his soul.

I had the certitude, right there, that Sam Stevens didn't appear in my life by mistake. We were destined to meet. To fall together.

His mouth descended to my neck, nibbling and licking my salty flesh.

My hand curled around his biceps, keeping him as close to me as possible.

We rocked in sync, about to go over the edge, to reach a new high together.

Our movements hastened. They became more urgent. Less delicate.

When I went rigid in his embrace, my back arching, and my moans intensifying, Sam leaned back, looking at me with reverence. Then he pounded into me with no more restraint.

Once I came, he tried to move out, but I held him in place. "Come with me," I said.

"Are you sure?"

I nodded. "Let go. I want you to."

Grinding against him, I rolled my hips until his words failed him.

My teeth left indents in the bare skin of his shoulder when he collapsed over me at the same time he went over the edge, still buried inside me.

Tremors shook my being. Heat spread through me, followed by a calming sensation I could easily get addicted to. I had found my other half. The missing part of my soul.

"Maddie." Sam spoke my name between harsh breaths. His full lips seduced mine in a lazy kiss. "I… We…"

"Whatever we just did, you've branded yourself to me, Sam Stevens, and now I'll never be the same. Only you can fill me the way you do. You're stuck with me now."

"Maddie. I don't have any intention of ever letting you go. Never again. I was miserable. Cranky and a whole lot fucking sad."

For a long time, neither of us dared to break the spell, lost in our love bubble.

"We'll have to tell the girls," I murmured against his chest once we climbed down from the rush and cuddled after cleaning up.

He held me against him, his heart rate reverberating through me. "Yes, but for a little bit longer, you're mine. Only mine. I'm not sharing you with anybody else. Once we return to the real world, I'll have to share you with them, and I'm not ready. Let's be selfish for a few more hours."

I felt his smile against the skin of my nape.

"Sam, I love being yours."

With a finger under my chin, he tilted my head in his direction. "I love being yours too. You belong with the three of us. Never doubt it, okay? Even if Mika—or even Justine—says something or they act out, you're mine. Even if I sometimes act like a grumpy old man, promise me you'll stick with me….with us. No matter what. I need you in my corner, Maddie. I won't survive another heartbreak. It may take the girls a little time to adjust, but they'll come around. They'll see how happier I am now that you're back in my life."

I traced the lines of his face with a feather touch. "We're in this together. I'm up for the challenge."

Sam shifted position, and an expression I'd never seen before painted his face. "Maddie, we'll be a family. The four of us. Don't you think playing mommy to my girls will make you run for your life someday? I know it's not fair, but I come as a package of three. I'll have to split my time between all of you guys. You're the only woman who's been in their lives since Lisa left. Sometimes, it won't be easy. Aren't you scared it's gonna be too much at some point?"

I placed a finger over his lips. "Sam, I've been around you guys for months. I know exactly what I'm getting into. I'm not only in love with you. I'm in love with them too. With all of you. The only thing I fear is that Justine and Mika think I'm overstepping into their lives and stealing their daddy from them. I don't want them to resent me. Ever. For the rest, I've never been so sure about anything else in my entire life."

"We'll talk to them today. Together. Okay?"

I nodded, and he tucked a tendril of my hair behind my ear.

"And I'll ask Riley to add babysitting hours to my contract. He's the one who pushed us together—not once, but twice—so it's only fair he volunteers some of his time to make sure our relationship starts on strong foundations."

My chuckle reverberated across the room. "I agree. We can't let your daughters walk in on us when I give you head in the shower or late at night. And they can't be there when you fuck me on the couch or against the wall…" I paused as I registered what I'd just said. "Not now…one day. When…huh…when it's possible."

"You dirty girl. I love you. Let's get some sleep because soon we'll have a lot of questions to answer and a lot of explanations to give."

---

I woke up to muscle spasms in my left thigh. Shedding tears in my pillow and gritting my teeth, I rode the waves of pain for a few minutes, praying the entire time it wouldn't wake up Sam. After how perfect our reunion had been, I wasn't ready for him to see me like this. Broken. And hurting. I anticipated the look of helplessness in his eyes and could do without it for a bit longer. When the pain released its death grip on me, I sat on the side of the mattress, stretched my legs, and checked my phone. Almost ten o'clock. Our love session in the early morning felt like a lifetime ago. My gaze lingered on the man snoring beside me, and I fought with myself, struggling not to touch his skin or kiss his lips.

Hopping on my good leg and fetching my crutches, I made my way to our small kitchen after I slid on the T-shirt Sam had lent me earlier.

My stomach grumbled, and I decided to surprise him with breakfast in bed. Maneuvering the crutches and the egg carton didn't go as planned when I lost my footing and dropped half of it on the floor. A new zing of pain traversed my left side. Silencing the curses teetering on the edge of my lips, I pivoted to grab paper towels—only to knock over the glass of water I had set on the counter earlier. My crutches ended in the mess of water and egg yolks at my feet, and I clamped the countertop with both hands to prevent my own fall.

Hot tears welled up in my eyes, and I used my shoulder to wipe them off.

My earlier confidence shattered.

Sliding to the ground, I studied the state of the kitchen floor, my shoulders heaving with suppressed sobs.

My tears multiplied, and I choked on them as I hollered Sam's name. A mixture of fury and despair boiled in my veins, and it drained the sound of my voice.

How had I become so dependent on everyone else?

From where I sat, I could hear the steady rhythm of his snoring. I called his name again. Once more, my voice died as it left my mouth when I hiccupped. I had no more fight left in me. I had to go. To leave. To relieve the people I love from the burden I had become.

My heart fractured in my chest.

How would I ever be able to say goodbye?

# Chapter 24
### Sam

I woke up to the sound of pots and pans slamming. It took me a beat to patch together last night's events. Without even trying, my lips drew into a smile I had no intention to conceal.

"Babe, come back to bed," I called out, braced on one elbow, desperate to catch sight of Madison from the comfort of my bed. "We can tackle breakfast later. I wanna cuddle. And do more dirty things to you."

Her figure appeared in the doorway, but instead of a grin shaping her lips, a deep wrinkle marred her forehead.

"Hey, what's wrong?" I asked, taken aback by the fury I could read in her expression. "Come here."

She eyed me, her crutches resting against her ribcage, helping her to keep her balance.

"I'm just done with all this." She pointed around with her hand. "It's not working. I've tried, but it's not."

Her words made no sense. What happened to the comfort and elation we had experienced earlier?

I jumped to my feet, slid into a pair of sweatpants, and neared her. "Hey, hey. Talk to me." I closed both hands on her upper arms, but she yanked free from my touch. I blinked, unsure if I was awake after all. "I don't understand. This morning you were happy. What changed?"

"Sam, I'll never be okay again. Can't you see that? I can't even pour myself a glass of water or cook breakfast without being clumsy and pain paralyzing me. I'm not useful. Now there's an egg and water mess all over the kitchen floor, and I'm one slip away from breaking my other leg. Congrats on getting a crippled girlfriend. By being here, I'll just complicate your life. I won't even be able to watch over the girls on my own. How pathetic have I become? Please don't answer. You should send me back home."

"Home? I thought you said last night your home was wherever I was."

She blinked, and the intensity in her eyes magnified instead of vanishing.

I spoke before she could say something else she didn't mean. "Stop with the bullshit. Sure, we gotta find our footing. You've never lived on a bus before, let alone with crutches. It's not the most practical place to call home in your situation, I agree, but we'll figure it out. Together."

I stepped forward, but Madison blocked me with a crutch. "Don't. Don't come closer. Can't you see it? We shouldn't be together. It doesn't make any sense. I realize it now. Perhaps the accident was life trying to teach me something. To prevent us from getting too deep before it was too late. Whatever the reason, I can't stay here. I'm suffocating. I long for air. And a fucking break."

"Maddie. No. Listen to me." My tone sounded harsh, but I didn't care. She had to hear me out.

She raised one arm and let it fall beside her. "Not now." Her eyes brimmed with tears.

I felt helpless as I watched her. Broken. No matter how wonderful last night—and earlier—had been, reality hit me in the morning light. The situation we were in couldn't be ignored. I could tell the accident had changed her. Some part of me prayed it hadn't changed us too.

Madison pivoted to leave the bedroom when she tripped over her own feet.

I rushed to her and circled her waist with an arm before she could crash face first. I lowered myself to sit on the floor, bringing her with me.

Sitting on my lap, crying as she struggled to escape, her body shook with desperation. I held her tighter, unwilling to let go, even as she fought against me.

"Let me go," she shrieked. "Just let me go." Her punches hit me square in the chest. "Send me back. Send me so I'm not a deadweight in your life."

Her voice cracked.

Sobs rocked her body.

"Maddie. Stop with the nonsense. You belong here. Unless going back to Nashville is really what you desire. Be honest with yourself…and me. If the words you spoke when you arrived last night were true, then you'll stay with us, and we'll find a way to make it work. Together. I'm not giving up on us—on you—and neither should you."

She turned her face away, making sure I wouldn't be able to read the expression spreading across her tear-streaked face.

Her body got rigid against mine. I could feel her drifting away.

I continued, hoping my words would reach her heart

and make her reconsider fleeing. "You said yourself you were miserable on your own. Now that I got you back and we finally have a real chance to be together, when I'm ready to go all in, you wanna ditch me? You wanna ditch *us*? I understand your anger. I do. Remember, I was angry for a long time myself. I kinda get how you feel. One thing I can tell you is that it will all get better. Maybe not today or in a week... Maybe not next month... But one day, you'll wake up, and the pain will have faded. You'll wake up from the nightmare you think defines your life right now and find yourself stronger. You'll see how far you've come—and how much you've overcome—and realize that failure was never an option, and healing was always meant to happen."

She relaxed a bit against me, so I kept going.

"When you're upset or feel like you can't put in the effort anymore because it's just too much, don't keep it all inside. Don't let the hard times overshadow the good ones. Believe me, even the challenges we think we'll lose are worth fighting for in the end. I'm the perfect example... If I had thrown my life away two years ago when I was bathing in permanent darkness, I wouldn't be here today, and I wouldn't have found you. You can be mad as you want, but you gotta open up to me when it gets too tough. It's the only way this is going to work."

She snorted, but there was no conviction behind it.

"If you want to go back to Nashville, I won't stop you. But if there's even the tiniest part of you that believes we're meant to be together, that your place is here, on this tour, with us, then let that part speak up." I paused, letting my words sink in—both into her heart and the analytical part of her mind. "Whatever you decide, talk to me. I'm right here, and I'm not going anywhere. If you choose to leave, I think I deserve an explanation. It can't be just because you dropped a couple of eggs. Don't bullshit me."

Madison ignored me for the longest time, her shoulders heaving, until the fight left her, and she sank into me.

I combed her hair back with my fingers. "Maddie. No one said it would be easy, but it will be all worth it," I repeated. "I swear."

She sniffled, still not looking at me.

"When you came into my life, I was mad most of the time. With your selfless heart and contagious optimism, you pierced through my stony heart. Your kindness seeped through the cracks, and it healed my broken self. You never faltered when I was being a jerk and held your head up and argued when I was being wrong. This time around, you are the one who requires someone in your corner. To help you get back out there. And thrive. And kick asses. Because the Madison Prescott I know wouldn't let some bump in the road set her back. She'd get up and wrestle the shit out of her misfortune."

When she spoke, her voice had lost all conviction—and warmth. "Sam, I'm just tired of the fight. Of the pain. I've been fighting all my life. From the day I was born. I struggled a lot growing up. Nightmares. Making friends. I can't do this anymore. It's asking too much of me."

"Maddie, what happened to you? I'm not a pushy guy, but I gotta know. Please confide in me."

She buried her face in her hands.

I said nothing, wishing she'd let the walls come down around her once and for all.

Swallowing the pebbles growing down my throat and disrupting my normal breathing, I asked, unable to hide the alarm rising in my voice, "Did someone hurt you?"

Her gaze returned to mine, and she shook her head. "No. Not like that. I swear."

Relief washed over me. "Then what?"

Madison inhaled and wiped the traces of her melt-down with the hem of the T-shirt she was wearing. "Remember that time I told you I'd been neglected?"

"Yes. I met your parents when you were in the hospital. We even had lunch together one day. They're nice people, and they love you. That much was evident. I can't imagine them being careless with you as a child."

"Sam… Emily and I were…were adopted. When we were five and three. Our biological parents didn't care for us. I-I spent days in my dirty diaper when I was a baby. I only learned about it because it was written in our file, and our real parents, the ones who raised and loved us, told us much later. The ones who conceived us forgot to feed us or would disappear for a day or two, chasing their next high…or their youth. I don't know. Ems took care of me. She was just a baby herself, but she made sure I had food to eat and rocked me to sleep every night. She protected me. Sacrificed her own needs to fulfill mine."

She fidgeted with her hands, keeping her gaze down.

I remained silent so as not to disturb the story of her childhood.

"One day, I fell and broke my wrist. She…huh…she dressed me up in dirty clothes because that was all we had, and we walked a mile to get to the next house. Our neighbors had never heard of us. We lived in a rural area, and we hadn't ventured outside before that day. Our parents never took us anywhere with them. The neighbor called the cops, and paramedics to care for my arm, then fed us, and cleaned us up. One day, in therapy, they showed us pictures she had taken that day. It was terrible. We were skin and bones, with disheveled hair and ghostly complexion. Not what kids that age should've looked like."

I turned her hand over and threaded our fingers.

"The first family who fostered us—it was a temporary placement—forced me to sleep on the floor after I peed the bed twice. They said they were paid to foster a kid, not a dog. Ems says I was crying all the time, and they wouldn't let her comfort me. After a few weeks, they removed us from that horrible family. But then they failed to find someone who could take us both in, so Emily and I got separated. I don't have very clear memories of that time, but I still can feel the fear twisting my insides when I think about those years. I was all alone and scared. Emily had learned to fend for herself, but I hadn't. I was just a baby... Eventually, I ended up with a nice lady, but no matter how much she tried, I wouldn't let her in. I stopped eating. I wouldn't communicate with her. Emily's and my language skills were so far behind, I had no idea how to express my feelings. I missed my sister, and they wouldn't let me see her."

She closed her eyes, then opened them and continued.

"My adoptive mother…she heard some of the ladies working in the foster care system one day talking about the feral sisters who were raised like animals and had to be separated, and they worried the younger one would never heal from the psychological trauma she'd experienced in her short life. My dad and she had already discussed fostering or adopting children. The idea of siblings enticed them. Ems and I were the perfect match. They found us and brought us home. From the day we met, I've felt a pull toward them. They saved us. They…they saved my life."

I tightened my squeeze on her hand. This was so much worse than any scenario I had pictured in my head. Wrath simmered in me, directed at the people and the system who had failed Emily and Madison at such a young age. But then Madison offered me a small tip of her lips, and my rage evaporated. She was here. With me. None of those people could ever hurt her again.

"My trauma isn't the same as Justine and Mika's, but I can relate to them…even though it sounds crazy."

I resumed my breathing, the knots around my stomach loosening.

"Somehow, I know I haven't landed into your lives by chance. I've cared for a lot of kids in the past, but I never bonded with them as much as I bonded with your daughters. Like we can understand one another. Like we connect on a deeper level. When we were kids, it took years of therapy for Emily and me to come to terms with what we went through. That's why we were so resilient at such a young age—we fought to survive and made a promise to ourselves early on in life that we wouldn't settle for less than we deserved, and we would reach for our goals. Our parents decided to homeschool us because, for a long time, the idea of being sent to a classroom full of students, too many people cramped together, was a trigger for my anxiety. It turned out to be the best decision for us. We healed. We got stronger. I'm not mad at my biological parents. They had us when they were still kids themselves… It didn't excuse their behavior, but I guess they didn't know any better. Thanks to them, we grew up with the parents we were always meant to be with and who couldn't have children of their own. The ones who love us unconditionally."

Madison closed her hand over our joined fingers, and I traced the side of her cheek with my knuckles.

"Maddie, I don't know what to say. It…fuck, it breaks my heart. For the younger version of you. For your sister. I'm so sorry you had to go through this. Wow, I'm speechless right now, and that says a lot… Your story is tragic but beautiful at the same time. How can it be both?"

"I could say the same for you guys. If Lisa hadn't left, we wouldn't be here right now, having this conversation. As I said once before, I believe, you and I, we were meant to meet."

"No," I said. "You and I, we were meant not to only meet, but also to love each other."

"Sam—"

"No, let me finish. I love you. And I know for a fact you love me too. I saw it in your eyes last night. Deny it all you want, but I don't believe the lies you're feeding yourself this morning."

"But—"

I cradled her face and claimed her mouth. Madison stiffened against me, but soon relaxed and kissed me back.

My lips molded to hers in a breathless kiss. She clutched my forearm as our tongues danced together. Shivers traveled through me. She purred against my mouth, deepening our connection, her other arm locking around my neck.

"Do I need more arguments to prove my point?" I asked, pulling back for a split second.

She shook her head.

"Babe, I promise, here and now, you'll never feel like a burden and be alone ever again. You have my word. You've found your place in this world. We'll find all the help you need and get through this. You and me, together."

Her lips returned to mine, cementing the invisible link tying us together.

# Chapter 25
### Madison

Sam's hand wound around my waist as I knocked on Riley and Devon's tour bus door. His lips brushed that spot behind my ear, and I shivered.

"Ready?" he asked. "Let the fun and thousand questions begin." I heard amusement in his voice. We had decided to tell the girls together, hoping it would make answering all their questions a little easier.

After my meltdown earlier, Sam and I had a long and emotional conversation. One where I cried. A lot. Every word he said to comfort me soothed the fears that had tightened my insides. Sam made me believe we could defeat the circumstances that were forcing us to adapt to our new reality. That our love was strong enough to overcome what I had perceived as impossible.

Confiding in him about the doubts weighing on me lifted a burden I hadn't realized was so heavy. I realized that the pressure I'd been putting on myself to rush back to my normal life before my body had time to heal wasn't just unhealthy—it was foolish. I needed time.

I still had a long road to recovery ahead of me, but this time, I had chosen to let him in entirely. My gut told me it was the right choice, and somehow, I felt a quiet ease settle over me once I accepted it.

After I told the man I loved about my childhood, the burden of the secrets I'd been carrying for so long evaporated. It felt right to be completely honest with him, and I realized I should have opened up a long time ago. Even though I'd had my reasons for withholding that piece of information in the past, I knew I had to lay everything out in the open if we were ever going to move forward as a couple.

Mikaella and Justine's screams of joy hit me before the door was fully open. All my cells transformed into particles of glee. Yeah, I was exactly where I was supposed to be. Their contagious enthusiasm, even before they saw me, confirmed every word Sam had spoken to me earlier. For now, I was choosing happiness over despondency. Sam and I had promised each other we'd revisit this discussion later once the emotions of my comeback had settled.

The girls barreled out the door, down the steps, and straight into my arms. Standing with the help of the crutches, I lost my balance, but Sam caught me before I hit the ground. He steadied me, keeping his hand on my waist as I leaned forward to level my face with his daughters'.

"Maddie," Mikaella and Justine both cheered, their arms wrapped so tightly around my neck, I thought I might choke.

From the corner of my eye, I spotted my man beside me, his eyes filled with tears, watching us as if he had just won the lottery.

I wriggled a hand to the side and laced our fingers.

The smile he aimed at me shook me to the core. Drying his eyes, he mouthed, *I love you.*

Justine grabbed my face between her hands and offered me a pointed look. "Why was it so *loooong*, Maddie? I missed *youuuu.*"

Sam helped me to a folding chair, and I sank into the seat, appreciating the rest. The girls eyed my splinted leg and moved closer, careful not to bump into it.

With both arms now free, I fastened my grip around them. "Oh girls, I missed you two so much. I can't wait to hear about all you did while I was away."

Justine placed a wet kiss on my cheek and nestled her head in the crook of my neck.

"Are you in pain?" Mikaella asked.

I grimaced. "Yes. Sometimes. But being with you makes it all better."

"Are you staying with us forever?" she asked.

I nodded, my gaze steady on hers so she could see the honesty in them. "I am. As long as you guys have me, I'm not going anywhere."

Even though I'd tried to convince myself otherwise earlier, and I was sure I would try to leave again from time to time whenever I felt dejected, I knew my place was beside them.

Having them in my arms, I had no more doubts.

"Did Daddy kiss your booboo?" Justine asked.

I heard laughter around me. Adult laughter.

"Yes. He did."

"Did he make it all go away?"

"Not totally, but he's working on it."

"Listen, girls," Sam said, sitting in a chair next to me. "There's something we gotta talk about. The four of us."

That brought their full attention to him.

"Madison and I, we are lovers. It means she is my girlfriend."

We had already decided the terms sounded juvenile, but we hoped it would resonate with them.

A spark of joy ignited in me as he confirmed the status of our relationship in front of everyone.

Mikaella's eyes ping-ponged between us, her features hardening.

"Are you my mama now?" Justine asked, her tone full of expectations before we could clear the air.

Mikaella backed away from me, incomprehension filling her golden eyes. "Daddy, because of you, Maddie will leave. She already left once." Fury distorted her face. "I don't want another mama," she screamed. "And I don't want Maddie gone. You're mean, Daddy. You're not nice. I hate you. I hate all of you."

Before we could react, she went to our bus and sat on the step, ignoring us.

Sam started to stand, cursing under his breath.

"How can she still blame me for her mother leaving? Lisa abandoned them. She quit on them. Without ever reaching out or explaining herself. How can I be the one responsible for her actions? How am I the mean one?"

I reached for his elbow before he could go after his daughter.

"Maddie, I gotta fix this." He dragged a hand over his face.

"Sam, if you're serious about us having a future together, about all you've said earlier, you'll let me talk to her. She's mad at you right now, not that it's justified, but I wanna do this. I'm as deep into this as you are. Trust me."

Before he could argue, I placed Justine in his arms, kissed her cheek, and managing the crutches, joined Mikaella.

Her shoulders heaved with heartbreaking sobs.

"May I hold you?" I asked once I took my place beside her, resting my crutches next to me.

She nodded, and I wrapped one arm around her shoulders to pull her closer, until she sank into my embrace, her small body quivering.

"It's okay to be confused," I said. "It's a lot to take in. Do you wanna talk about it?

"O…kay."

Over the months I'd known her, Mikaella, the angry little girl I had met the first day, had ceded her place to a more trusting and blooming version of herself.

Watching her, I gulped a big dose of air, forcing my racing heart to stay put. "Are you and I okay?"

She nodded, staring at the space in front of her, not sparing me a glance.

"Are you mad at your daddy?"

She nodded again.

My insides clenched as I prayed to find the right words to get through to her.

"You know your daddy loves you, right?"

She shrugged.

"He does. He loves you so much. You and Justine are the most precious people in his life. I swear."

She remained silent.

"Adults like your daddy and I are looking to be loved too. Your daddy knows you and Justine love him very much, but he also needs another adult's love. Someone to be his special friend. Like you and Justine are. You see, like Riley and Devon. They are each other's special friends. And once upon a time, your mama and your daddy were too." I inhaled. "When your mama left, it broke your daddy's heart. Remember when he was grumpy and barely smiled before?"

Another nod—all the encouragement I needed to continue.

"Well, it was your daddy being sad…in his heart. Because he didn't have a grown-up special friend anymore. Someone to reassure him when he was afraid or be by his side when he was having a bad day. Daddies can be scared and have broken hearts too. When I started coming to your house to take care of you and Justine, your daddy was often angry, and it broke my heart. One day, we became friends. Really good friends. We started laughing together, and then, not so long ago, your daddy and I realized we could be each other's special friends, so that when we were together, we didn't feel alone anymore. And we made each other happy."

Mikaella stayed immobile beside me.

"When adults become special friends, they kiss each other. Because we can't go on play dates. Duh, we're too old for the slide or trampoline. Instead, we hold hands. And we have sleepovers. And when we both are so happy that we are always laughing and kissing, we know we have found a very special friend, and we should hold on to them because they make our hearts jump in our chests and send butterflies to our bellies."

Mikaella said nothing, so I kept going.

"Your daddy and I discovered we're very good at being special friends. I'm not your mama, and I will never be unless one day it's you who's asking me to be. Your daddy and I are great together. You wanna know why? He holds my hand when I'm afraid and smiles at me when he's happy. When I'm sad, he pulls me into his arms to comfort me, and when I go to bed, he kisses me goodnight. Remember when I told you that before being your nanny, I traveled the world with other families? Well, I didn't know it back then, but I was searching for my own special friend too." I sighed and dropped my shoulders. "Can I tell you a secret?"

Mikaella nodded.

"I never really felt at home anywhere and didn't have a lot of friends growing up. I thought traveling would help me find where I belong… It turns out that since the day I met you guys, I don't feel lost anymore. I know where my home is. It's with the three of you. It's wherever you guys are. I don't ever wanna go away anymore. Not if you guys aren't around because I'm scared I will get lost again."

"Were you sad when you were hurt and all by yourself?"

"Yes. And I was angry too because I missed you all so much and had no idea when I'd be back."

Mikaella turned her head my way, watching me with interest now. "Daddy and you are special friends? Like Jacob and you were?"

I sighed. "Jacob and I were good friends, but I'll tell you another secret." I lowered my voice to a whisper. "I thought for a moment he could be my special friend, but it turns out your daddy is. A lot, lot, a whole lot more. He is my *true* special friend. And I am his."

"What will happen now? Are you gonna leave us? Because Lisa did." Her eyes, still brimming with unshed tears, studied me closely.

I pulled the little girl to my heart and enveloped her in my arms. "No. It means the four of us will live together and be around one another a lot more. Your daddy and I will also spend more time together. I won't go anywhere. I'll be here with you all the time. And available anytime you need me. Not like a nanny, but more like your *extra* special friend."

Mikaella raised her eyes to mine. "Do extra special friends kiss too?"

I pinched my lips to refrain from laughing. "Nah, extra special friends are best friends forever. They eat tons of pancakes together, sing songs before bedtime, dance in the rain, watch movies with a lot of popcorn on the weekend, and tell each other when they're sad…or afraid…or happy. Do you think you and I can be *extra* special friends?"

She bobbed her head, a hint of a smile grazing her lips. "I'd like that."

"Me too," I said, mirroring the tilt of her lips. "I'd like that very, very much."

I fastened my arms tighter around her, and she hugged me back.

"I love you, Maddie."

"I love you too, Mika. So much, you have no idea."

"Are you going to sleep in daddy's room now?"

I offered her a lopsided smile. "I will. Even daddies are afraid of the dark sometimes."

"It's okay. Daddy is less *grinchy* when you are here anyway. He smiles more. And doesn't burn dinner when you are around. He even sings in the shower or when he's doing the dishes."

"See? All he needed was his own special friend. I guess we've figured out how to keep his grumpy-bear attitude away then."

Her giggles filled my heart with a new sense of purpose, and a lot of calm.

She turned until we faced each other. "Do you *love* love my daddy? For real?"

"I do. Like a lot. So much my heart breaks when he's not around."

"Why did you stay away for so long if you missed us?"

"Because I had to get better so I wouldn't have to leave ever again."

We stayed like that until she broke the silence. "Daddy

was *grinchy* again. When you were gone. He only smiled around Justine and me. The rest of the time, he was unhappy."

"I'm sorry. I'll do my best to keep his *grinchy* side far away."

"Okay. Can I tell you a secret?" She lowered her voice, kneeling to speak into my ear. "Daddy has a hairy chest. And sometimes, he snores and sounds like a bear. Justine and I think it's funny."

I couldn't contain my laughter this time and tilted my head back as my eyes dampened. "I won't tell him you told me. Your secret is safe with me. *Extra* special friend safe." I held out my hand. "Think we should go see him and tell him we're not mad at him? I'm sure right now his heart is sad because he thinks he's lonely again."

Mikaella watched my hand, then her eyes traveled to mine, and after I gave her an encouraging nod, she moved to her feet.

The last bruises of my heart healed.

Her fingers snaked around mine. "Do you think Lisa will come back?"

My heart pinched in my chest. "I don't know. I wish I had an answer for you, but I don't."

She shrugged. "It's okay. Daddy is happier with you anyway. I think he loves you too."

"You think?"

She bobbed her head fast. "Yes. He has shiny eyes when you're here, and he keeps staring at your mouth like he wants to kiss you."

"Oh, I didn't know that," I said, doing my best to look surprised.

"I saw him do it. Many times. Daddy is not good at looking away from you."

I bent to kiss her hair. "I love you, Mika."

"I love you too, Maddie. Can Justine call you Mama? Because if you kiss daddy, she'll believe you're her mama. She already thinks you are. She doesn't understand you're not."

"If she wants to call me Mama and it's okay with all of you, then it's fine with me. Justine is still little and can't understand everything, but I don't want you to be mad at her if she does."

She reflected on what we'd just shared for a minute. "I'll tell her I'm okay with her calling you Mama. I won't tell her she's stupid anymore."

"That's really kind of you. That's your big sister's job. To explain things she doesn't understand to her, like I just did with you, and to reassure her. Emily is my big sister, and she always explains stuff to me too since she's older and knows more."

Glee painted Mikaella's face, and my heart swelled inside my ribcage at the sight, knowing everything would turn out just fine.

Side by side, with my hobbling on crutches and her supporting me, we went back to Sam and Justine. My man moved to his feet, relief loosening his features the moment we neared them.

"Sweet pea," he said, sauntering our way, his eyes asking mine if it was safe to proceed.

I gave him a subtle nod, and he looked at me with so much love and a lot more emotions. Respect, lust, affection, gratitude. The entire cocktail.

Squatting in front of his eldest daughter, he sucked in a jagged breath. "Can we talk?"

Mikaella shook her head, and Sam's face fell. "Sweet pea—"

Her eyes flew to mine, and with a squeeze of her hand and a nod, I assured her everything would be all right.

"Daddy, it's okay if you want to kiss Maddie because you can't stop looking at her mouth, and I think it's because you love her." Her voice dropped to a whisper. "She also said you're less *grinchy* when she's with you. And I agree."

"Did she?" Sam said, waggling his eyebrows when he glanced at me.

Mikaella bobbed her head. "If Justine wants to call her Mama, I won't call her stupid again." She shrugged. "Justine is little. She doesn't understand how mamas and daddies work."

Mikaella said something in her sister's ear, and both girls snickered, watching Sam and me.

"What is it?" he asked after a moment.

They held hands and asked together, "Can you kiss?"

Sam raised an eyebrow. "You sure?"

They bobbed their heads fast.

Before I had time to say anything, Sam cradled my jaw, and his mouth claimed mine, our lips meeting and my heart thundering in my chest.

The girls screamed, bounced on their feet, and clapped their hands, excitement radiating from them. Soon, their arms wound around our legs—careful around my bad one.

Sam's hand splayed across my lower back, steadying me, while he tugged me closer to him. *I love you, Maddie*, he mouthed, kissing me once more.

The girls cheered and hugged us again.

"Can you be my mama now?" Justine asked, and all laughter died down.

"Yes," Mikaella replied before Sam and I could utter a word. "It's okay. Maddie and I discussed it, and we decided it's normal for you to be confused because you are little. She can be your mama if you want her to be."

Justine's eyes brightened, and Mikaella offered me a thumbs-up.

"You're stuck with us now," Sam whispered against my mouth.

"There's nowhere else I'd rather be. Remind me of this moment when my thoughts go dark, please."

"Always."

# Chapter 26

Sam

We were about to cross into Oregon, where I had a series of concerts lined up along the West Coast.

With the woman I loved back by my side, I felt invincible, my level of glee reaching new highs.

Last summer, Riley and Devon had decided to get their own bus and tour the country with us. As my manager, Riley didn't have to be on the road with me, but I was grateful that he had chosen to. The more time we spent together, the more inseparable we all became. I loved having our friends around. For someone who had pushed everyone away for two years, I was now thankful for those who had stuck by my side. Things were running smoothly these days, and it felt like life had finally decided to give us a break.

Right now, my girls were with Devon in her bus, catching up on news about the crew and baking cupcakes, while my friend and I were in my bus, discussing business and going over the itinerary for the next few shows, interviews, and promo requests.

Madison had been back for almost two weeks now, and whenever I had days off, we made sure to spend time with the girls, showing them everything would be all right. That we loved each other, and they had nothing to worry about. Things wouldn't change for them—only get better.

Stud Burgess, Carter and Dahlia's ex-bandmate, had agreed to join me onstage for two songs tonight. He now lived outside of Portland with his wife Belinda and their children. Since he had retired from the music industry a few years ago, he'd been doing woodwork and had started his own business. The guy was one of the most talented musicians I had ever met in my life. He could play any instrument with ease and perfection. Or, I should say, he was talented with anything his fingers touched. Riley, being his ex-manager, persuaded him to make a comeback—for one night only—and he had agreed. We met through video chat earlier, and I had just finished putting together what we had discussed.

At the end of the afternoon, we parked the buses in a rest area, ready to pile ourselves into the SUVs Riley had ordered for tonight when Mikaella and Justine came running in. Dressed in matching silver skirts and white shirts, they halted near Riley, who spun them around and kissed their cheeks.

We were having a pre-show dinner in a fancy restaurant with our friends before Stud and I took the stage together later. Since Doris was still touring with us, she would babysit my girls tonight, so all of us, grown-ups, could enjoy the night together.

"You girls look like royalty," Riley said with a bow.

"*Royalality*? What is it?" Justine asked.

"It means we are princesses," Mikaella added, joy shining in her eyes. My little girl was back. All of her. Gone were the tantrums and bad words. She was glowing and appeared to have forfeited the grudge she had been holding against me for the last two years. Three days ago, we video chatted with her therapist, who had confirmed she was doing a lot better too. I shed tears that day. And kissed Madison senseless that night. Mikaella's victory was all ours. Madison's primarily. It was only thanks to her that my family could get the breath of fresh air it was starving for. The path to move forward, one that would leave the past behind. For good.

"Daddy," my daughters screamed when they saw me, running into my arms when I crouched down before them.

"You girls look stunning. And your hair, wow. It looks fantastic." They both wore some sort of complicated braid on one side of their heads.

"Devon picked our outfits," Mikaella said, twirling on herself.

"And Maddie did our hair," Justine added.

"Girls, I'll go to my bus to get ready. I'll see you later, okay?" Riley said.

"Bye, Uncle Riley," they both hollered.

Frantic energy permeated the air.

Armed with her crutches, the ones she now cursed at only every few days, Madison walked in, sporting the rose-gold sequin strapless dress I'd gotten delivered for her this morning. Tonight was a big night for all of us—our first as a couple and a family. It was also the first concert where Madison would stay from start to finish.

"Wow," I murmured, unable to tear my eyes away from her.

She discarded her crutches and walked toward me. I froze there, speechless. Even though she complained that physical therapy hurt like hell, I couldn't help but be in awe of her dedication and strength. Tonight was the perfect example.

"You look beautiful, Miss Prescott."

"And so do you, Mr. Stevens."

"One day, you'll be a Stevens too."

"Is that a threat?" she asked with one arched eyebrow.

"No, it's a promise."

She swiped her thumb across her phone screen, and music began playing from the portable speaker we kept on the kitchen counter. The girls started dancing around, giggling and singing. For an instant, we watched them.

"Dance with me?" Madison asked when the song switched to a ballad.

"Are you sure it's safe?"

"One song. Hold me tight so I don't put too much weight on my leg." She locked her eyes with mine. "I trust you."

"Then it would be my pleasure," I said, bringing her arms around my neck, my thumb grazing the soft skin of her cheek. "I love you. Thank you for not quitting on me that day at the nanny agency. I don't know what I've done to deserve your love, but you're the best thing that has happened to me in a long time. I can't believe I'm the lucky man who wakes up by your side every morning, and the father to the girls you love as your own. Tonight, I'll show you all over again how gone I am for you."

We kissed some more, and our focus traveled to the girls, carefree and happy.

"Sam, were you serious that night before the accident when you said you'd have more kids one day? With me?"

I drew the length of her spine with a finger, and Madison shivered against me. "Yeah. I want it all with you.

Not now. But in the near future. When we're settled. If that's what you desire too."

Moving to the tiptoes of her right leg, she claimed my mouth. It was slow and tender. A pledge of our love. A promise of our devotion to each other. And the confirmation that our family would be a pillar of our relationship.

---

Thanks to Madison, I gave the performance of my life. Everything shone brighter, smelled better, and tasted fucking amazing when she stood beside me. Her eyes met mine as I sang the last verse, and I swore I could've blown my load right there onstage in front of fifty-thousand people, and no one would have been able to prevent it.

In the rose-gold number that sheathed her curves perfectly, she looked like a vision. My woman illuminated not only my heart, but also the lives of everyone around her. She wet her lips with a swipe of her tongue, and no matter how much I tried to look straight ahead, my eyes always returned to hers. I had never performed a show on this scale in front of her before, and it felt so damn right. I wondered if she had any idea how much better she made me. As a man, and as an artist.

Right now, I was stiff as a pole. Performing for over an hour with a hard-on was possible. I could testify. Uncomfortable, but doable.

Stud joined me for two songs, and together we rocked the stage. Memories of performing at festivals with Carter Hills Band years ago flooded me.

My friend was still the *über*talented musician I remembered him to be.

He clapped my shoulder. "Thank you for this opportunity," he said, before walking offstage. He joined Belinda,

Madison, Riley, and Devon by the side of the stage as I played for another half-hour.

After the last song, I thanked the crowd for sticking with me after my sabbatical, then rushed offstage and pulled Riley into my arms. None of this would have been possible without his stubborn ass and his convincing talent. As it always did, emotions poured out from both of us.

"Thanks, man. You changed the course of my life."

My friend slapped my back, his arms still tight around me, and he repeated the same exact words he always did. "It was all you. Get ready, Stevens, it's just the beginning."

We broke apart, and the need to touch Madison, kiss her senseless, fuck her, and relieve the scorching tension that had been circulating between us all night made me angsty.

The way she watched me robbed me of all common sense.

I found an excuse to bring her to my dressing room, and without a warning, I plunged into her with abandon.

I could write an entire album from just the way she made me feel. How she colored the somber pieces of my life in vibrant shades and hung stars in my darkness.

How every word she spoke added lyrics to the melody of my heart.

"Downtown, our place, or yours?" Stud asked when we met him by the artists' entrance of the venue after I'd changed and we'd made ourselves presentable. "Where's the celebration tonight, Stevens?"

"There's none. I'd rather be home with my girls and be a father in the morning without a hangover than partying all night."

"Yeah, I get it," Stud said. "Where are the buses parked?"

"I've texted you the location," Riley chimed in. "Follow us."

———

Up early, I sipped coffee as I worked on a new song, a pencil lodged between my teeth, ready to note the lyrics that flowed from me as I adjusted the melody. At this rhythm, I'd have enough material to record a new album within a month or two. Creativity had been on my side since Madison came home. Every time we loved each other, a new burst of songs spilled out from me right after.

Tiny feet padded my way, and after kissing my cheeks and hugging me good morning, my daughters hurried to my bedroom where I knew they'd cuddle with Madison for at least another half-hour. Having a woman full-time in our lives hadn't just been beneficial for me, but also for them.

And love from the woman they both considered a mother figure had skyrocketed their confidence too.

My daughters were thriving. Emotionally, physically, and psychologically.

The sound of their chatter warmed my heart. I could hear them laugh as Madison told them something.

They joined me forty minutes later, all dressed and ready to go.

"Are we packed?" Madison asked with a kiss.

"Yes. The rental is parked outside, and our stuff is already in there."

She eyed the pad of paper on the table beside me. "New song?"

"Yep. New material. I'll sing it to you later. Since it's all about you anyway."

She cupped her chest with a hand. "I love the sound of

it. But 'Kissed By An Angel' and 'Maddie' will forever hold the top positions in my heart."

Standing, after I put away my guitar, I faced the girls of my life. "Today's schedule includes a visit to the aquarium. I read somewhere they have a great white shark, and we can pet starfishes, then dinner at that dinosaur restaurant, and desserts under the stars. Who's ready for a day of fun?"

My daughters raised their arms above their heads and screamed, "Me, me, me."

"I made breakfast burritos that we'll eat in the car since it's over an hour's drive. Madison told me you each prepared a presentation. I can't wait to hear all about polar bears and walruses."

They both started talking over each other.

Madison watched me and shrugged.

"Ready?" I asked.

"With you? Always. Show me the way."

With her hand nestled in mine, I led her forward. "The song I wrote this morning, I came up with a dirty version, just for you," I whispered in her ear.

Her face lit up.

"So maybe you'll have another favorite by the end of the day." I winked, and her smile shook me to my core. Like it did every time.

"If it's good enough, I may reward you with a prize. A private show. Since you won't be able to get a music award for it, you better surpass yourself."

"I love you."

"You better because I prepared a presentation too. But it can only be appreciated without clothes on and with a very naughty mind."

I pushed my hardening erection down with a palm. "Now I can't wait for tonight."

"Let's enjoy this day out first. Family day is my favorite day of the week."

This woman, she'd never cease to impress me. Her dedication to us had no boundaries. I dropped a kiss on her shoulder as she buckled Justine in her car seat while I stored her crutches in the trunk.

"Daddy," Mikaella said, tugging at my shirt and putting the brakes on my train of thought. "I'm happy you found Maddie. And I love when you're smiling."

"Me too, Mika. I'm thankful she found us. And I'm happy you're smiling so much all the time too."

I hugged my daughter.

"I love you, Daddy."

"I love you more," I replied, kissing the top of her head and closing the door behind her.

My eyes found Madison's as we both settled in our seats. "Ready?" I asked, leaning forward to tattoo my lips on hers in a bruising kiss that left us both breathless.

"With you? Always. Let's go on our next adventure."

# Chapter 27


At five, I woke up, ready to jumpstart my day. Sam's arms prevented me from moving. He spoke in a hushed tone, his eyelids still sealed from sleep, "Don't go. Stay with me. I need your warmth. Sleeping is pointless without you."

I turned in his arms and kissed him. His hands descended to cup my ass, grinding his morning wood against me.

"If you stay in bed for another hour, I'll make you feel good."

His teeth grazed my neck in a way that had my toes curling.

"Sleep some more. We'll have our fun later. The girls never wake up before nine these days. We'll have enough time. You'll need your strength," I mused.

With one last kiss, I tiptoed my way outside, a yoga mat

tucked under my arm. For the last month, Devon had started practicing yoga with me three mornings per week, stating it helped her to rest her mind. Last night during Sam's concert, we spent the evening together, and she had opened up about her past. The scars that had marked her heart for the longest time. I told her about mine. We hugged and cried together. Cursed and clinked our glasses at how her life had turned out and at the happy ending we both deserved.

The first signs of a new day brightened the sky with pink and orange glaze. We were in Virginia, and even at this time of the year, the crispy morning air wasn't too cool to prevent us from exercising. Still, the coldness stung when it reached my lungs.

Four months after the accident, I had returned to my yoga practice. Even though I still had to be careful and avoid some movements, I felt more like myself as it helped bring balance to both my mind and body—and boost my confidence. I wasn't back to my old self yet, but I was getting there. One day at a time.

My friend joined me, dressed in leggings and a hoodie, her hair messy and eyes still swollen from sleep. "How can you look so awake at this early hour?" she asked, laying her mat next to mine.

"Habit, I guess."

"Riley groaned because I got out of bed and he wanted to snuggle."

"Sam whined too. Said he couldn't sleep if I wasn't around."

"Last night, after he came back, Riley said we should get married," she confessed.

"Ohmygod, did he propose?"

She shook her head, her smile taking over her whole face. "Not yet, but I can feel it coming."

I took her hands in mine. "Do you want him to?"

"Yes. I told him I love the idea. I never thought I'd get married one day. Sure, when I was a little girl, I dreamed of it. Thought some prince would save me and we'd live happily ever after together, but as I grew up, I never believed I was destined for such dreams. That I'd meet someone who would love me unconditionally. So, I kinda forfeited the entire thing. A piece of me has been wishing for it to happen lately. We've decided we'll start trying for a baby next year, but Riley says he's old school and wants to get hitched first."

"You guys have been together for a while, so it's like the next logical step. Baby or marriage. Whatever the order." I pulled her into a hug. "I'm happy for you…if you are."

"I am. Your turn will come next. I've seen how Sam is around you. It's almost animalistic how he watches you all the time. Like he can't wait to have his way with you."

A heartfelt chuckle left my mouth. "Mika once said he can't stop staring at my lips."

"Yes. Imagine, she's six and noticed. He has it bad. I'm telling you."

"He's already hinted about babies and marriage. We'll see how it goes after the tour. I don't have doubts. I know he's the one. I'm not even scared when he talks about the future. It just sounds so…so natural. We're in no rush, though. We must learn to be a family first, the four of us. It's still brand new and already more than what I've ever wished for. I'm ecstatic and perfectly happy with how things are right now."

Bare feet and with our arms stretched over our heads, tickling the clouds, we breathed in the silence and calm of the early hour. I led the session, and Devon followed my movements, her face waking up the more we got our blood flowing. We bent over to touch our toes, letting it all go.

And started over. Until our bodies vibrated with new energy. Sitting, we raised our arms and legs into a boat pose, our toes and fingertips pointing upward. I relished the way my abdominal muscles engaged. Surgery had really thrown off my core stability, but now, I was slowly getting it back.

After a few deep inhales, we switched from one position to another, only to end up in a side plank. This pose hurt my bad leg the most, but I gritted my teeth, breathed deeply, and tried to relax as I counted to thirty.

A shadow hovered over me when I rolled onto my back, and for an instant, I sucked in a rickety breath until I realized who stood there.

"Morning," Sam said, bringing a camping chair next to where we lay, his eyelids hooded. He looked good enough to eat right now. "Mind if I join you?"

"You wanna practice yoga?" I sat with my legs stretched before me, massaging my cramped thigh, curious about his newfound interest.

"Yep. Heard it'd calm my overactive imagination. These days it goes to dirty territories. I share my bed with my favorite person every night, and my body and mind are restless. And you girls look great in spandex."

Seconds later, a barely awake Riley walked out of his bus and took a seat next to Sam. Had they called each other?

"Are you guys ambushing us?" Devon asked, unable to stop grinning at her man.

"Please continue what you're doing," he replied. "Stevens and I have decided we should have our own morning ritual. I'm sure I'm speaking for him too when I say the view is quite enjoyable from where we sit. In fact, it makes waking up at five a little easier. You girls do your thing, and we'll be right here, drinking coffee, in case you need us to intervene or be a partner to help you stretch."

I sighed, but I saw how he watched Devon. If she thought Sam had it bad for me, she was blind to how Riley was head over heels in love with her. "You guys are incorrigible. Next time, I expect you two to join us. It will be good for your stress level. Either that or you can watch from a distance. No more disturbing our moment with your naughty thoughts."

Sam leaned in and kissed my lips. "Oh, I love this business side of you, babe. Careful, Ry will want to snatch you up and bring you on his team."

"I already offered. She's better at working with kids," Riley said with a shake of his head before disappearing inside his bus, only to come back minutes later with two mugs of coffee and offer one to Sam.

Back on our knees, once the tension in my leg had receded a little, Devon and I moved to child's pose, stretching our arms in front of us on the ground and breathing in and out. Beside us, the guys sipped their caffeine, lost in their thoughts and the calmness of the morning.

In silence, later, once we were all done, we watched the night ceding its place to the day, relishing the beauty of nature as it offered a blank page to us—and to our souls

———

The emotions whirling inside me were hard to name. Pride and lust. Or joy and fascination. And love with a capital L. I was madly in love with my country music star boss. The man whose daughters I adored, and the one whose smile grew bigger when I stepped into his vicinity.

Sam strummed the first chord of "You're My Whole World," waiting for the images of the girls and him to start playing on the giant screen behind him. Mikaella and Justine's voices filled the space, and his eyes darted to mine. All night, I'd been sitting on a stool by the side of the stage, my gaze glued to the man performing. He kissed two fingers and sent the gesture my way, though people might interpret it as being meant for his daughters. But I knew better. A mist clouded my eyes, and I pressed my chest with both hands, calming the chaotic throbbing of my own heart.

Kissing my fingers the same way he had, I blew the kiss back at him. My heart went haywire at the sight of the twinkles dancing in Sam's eyes.

In this silent conversation, we exchanged more emotions than any words could.

"He's amazing, isn't he?" Riley asked from my right.

I nodded. "I'll never get used to this. It's breathtaking."

He chuckled. "His *Legend* title fits him more than ever. He was at the top, walked away when he had to, and climbed right back up as if he never left. He's an amazing father, an amazing artist, but more than that, he's an amazing man. I'm glad he finally gave himself the chance to prove it."

Belinda, or Belle as they all called her, joined me. After the success of Stud's surprise appearance back in Portland, her husband had agreed to do a few more shows with Sam.

Our men hugged and performed together.

"They're just phenomenal," she said, watching her husband with so much pride. "I know he misses it. I'm glad he accepted Sam's offer to join him."

I looked at her. "Why did he retire? If it's not too personal."

"Short story. Dahlia quit the band and got married after she learned she was pregnant with Jack. The whole nine yards. It got us thinking. We had talked about having a family of our own and reaching for other dreams we shared. This life isn't always easy. Anyway, the opportunity presented itself sooner than we thought. We bought a piece of property and decided to go for it. During that time, Carter was struggling due to the band breaking up. Timing." She paused. "We never looked back. I'd follow him around the globe if he chose to give it another shot. Music is his passion, but woodwork fulfilled him. He's calmer, more focused, and he gets to be with the kids. I'll always respect his choices, but seeing him rocking a stage fills me with a mixture of nostalgia and elation."

I sighed. "I get what you mean. It's still brand new to me, but I see how Sam thrives. How happy he is when he steps onstage."

Her phone rang. "I'll be right back."

Once she left, I returned my full attention to my own rock star.

The crowd erupted in applause and chanted his name as he walked offstage, after an hour and a half of laying his heart and soul bare in his music.

My body thrummed with its echoes even minutes later.

After accepting a bottle of water and handing the technician his guitar, Sam walked to Riley and hugged him, torrent of emotions bursting out of him. I blinked to keep my own emotions at bay at the sight of this man, strong and hard-working, vulnerable and grateful, facing his friend. None of us would have been here tonight if Riley Burns hadn't made it happen. I was all too aware. Sam knew it too.

Once he collected himself and dried his face with a towel, Sam pivoted until we faced each other. His pupils dilated. Raw arousal radiated from him in waves. Even without touching me, Sam Stevens had total control over my body. It responded to every twitch of his.

With my finger, I pressed the rapid pulse point in my throat, talking myself into calming the fuck down.

I knew that version of Sam Stevens. I'd never be able to resist him when he stared at me as if I was his next meal. This happened every time he exited the stage on the nights I'd come to see him perform.

He neared Stud, and they clapped each other's backs, grinning like fools. Even tonight, I still had a hard time conceiving how I had ended up in the close circle of two of the most talented musicians in the world.

We parted ways, Sam leading me away after telling Stud we'd meet him at his hotel for drinks afterward.

Unable to stay apart, we reached the green room where Sam had gotten ready earlier. His fingers circled my wrist, and he pushed me inside the room, kicking the door shut and pressing my back against it. His lips crashed onto mine. Assertive fingers hoisted my dress up to my hips. Positioning me until my front pressed against the cold surface of the table, he sheathed his erection with a condom, and after ruining my panties with a flick of his wrist, plunged himself deep inside me in one possessive thrust. The earth opened underneath my feet. Every single molecule of air left me. My head whirled. Right and wrong, black and white, up and down, everything got mixed together.

With his hand seizing my ass, Sam pumped inside me, blurring my vision. My hands clutched the edge of the table, and with each piston of his hips, the room spun around, both of us intoxicated with each other.

Adrenaline surged through him, and it left me giddy and ravenous for more.

Our bodies met thrust for thrust. Our breaths mingled. Our hands sought blazing skin.

He turned me around and sat me on the table, positioning himself between my legs. My nails left marks on his shoulders as I gripped him tight, ready for the ride of my life.

This post-concert, aroused version of Sam was my demise. A euphoric demise. Growls—sounding more like guttural barks—blended with the sound of our skins slapping together. Sam rammed into me with purpose, breaking me and gluing me back together all at once. His hands cherished my flesh as he built me to his touch.

"Maddie, you feel so perfect. You are *my* perfect."

He leaned in, and I cocked my head back when his teeth brushed against my right collarbone. The words, *his words*, always brought a fresh batch of dampness to my eyes. Sam pulled me into his arms, spearing into me from beneath, harder, faster, branding me with promises and forevers.

With my arms around his neck, we melt together and reached our climax, our tongues swirling and our mouths starving.

"I love you."

He tugged me closer to his heart. "Maddie, you already are everything I could ever hope for in this life. I waited for you for so long..." His voice trembled. He blew out a hissing breath. "Everything I went through wasn't in vain if it meant I'd find you on the other side. I would do it all over again, just for a chance to be seen by you. To be kissed by you. And to hear those words."

Framing his face between my hands, I kissed the tears building up in his eyes. My beautiful man. Strong and brave. Real and oh so talented.

Sam glided out of me, and the withdrawal sent chills through me.

His lips connected with my bare shoulder. "This was just the appetizer," he said with a wink. "To get the angst out until later when we're all alone."

My pulse turned into an orchestra and fireworks show.

Right now, I had a hard time remembering what my life was like before we became an us, and I wouldn't have it any other way either.

# Chapter 28
### Sam

The girls rushed into bed, wrapping their small arms around Madison's neck and mine, laughing.

"We made breakfast," Justine announced as I ruffled her hair and nuzzled her neck, my eyelids still half-shut from sleep.

My eyes sprang open, and every remaining trace of sleep vanished. "You did?" I asked, exchanging a nervous glance with the woman who shared my bed, now snickering behind her fist.

"Yes. We made *cedredals*."

"Cereals, Justine. Repeat after me. Ce-re-als."

My baby girl's smile widened. "*Cerededrials*."

"We'll practice later," Madison said, nudging my arm.

*I love you*, I mouthed her way.

She flustered. *I love you too*, she repeated.

"Sorry. We never get a chance to cuddle in the morning when they're up early."

She shrugged, then grinned. She looked so beautiful, with wild strands of her hair spread across my pillow. "I'll check on that delicious breakfast of yours, girls," she announced, pulling away from me to get up.

"Can I ask something to Maddie first?" Mikaella's tone had turned serious. Since the day she'd gotten onboard with the idea of Madison and I dating, a permanent smile had taken root on her face. My little girl had never been happier.

The four of us were joined at the hips.

I had everything I wanted in life. For now.

It had been a month since the concert in Virginia, where Stud joined me onstage for a few songs. It was crazy how time flew when you were enjoying yourself, surrounded by the right people—and lots of love.

Mikaella fidgeted with the hem of her blue nightgown. Gone was the black. Now she dressed in colors all the time. I only had Madison to thank for this change. She brought sunshine into our stormy days and planted seeds of love into our hearts.

"What is it?" Madison asked, lifting my daughter onto her lap and wrapping her arms around her. "You can tell me anything. You know that, right?"

Mikaella nodded, her golden irises sparkling. Her eyes drifted to me.

"Whatever it is, sweet pea, you can tell us. We love you both so much. It's okay," I said, trying to encourage her to speak up.

"Huh, can I…can I call you Mama too?"

Madison's eyes rounded, and a pink hue covered her cheeks.

I was pretty sure my heart grew butterfly wings. I tried to talk, but words got stuck in my throat. My vision blurred, and when I cocked my head, Madison had tears shining in her eyes, and she blinked, trying to stop the flow from streaming down her cheeks.

"I already call her Mama," Justine said. "I always call her Mama."

"I know, baby," I said, trying to keep my composure.

Madison fastened her grip around my eldest daughter. "Mika, is this what you want?"

"Yes."

"Mama is fine with me. In my heart, you are my little girl, no matter what. And I love you."

Mikaella rose to her knees and looped her arms around her neck. "I'm sure I love you more."

Right there, time stopped.

How could I ask for anything else in life?

They hugged, and Justine and I joined in, our family bubble filled with so much love and respect for one another. It was rare, unique, and exclusively ours.

"Ready to go back home next week?" I asked once we all stopped crying and took our place around the kitchen table, ready to enjoy our…huh…whatever this was. It looked a bit like cereals after all.

Both girls shook their heads.

Mikaella tugged at my sleeve. "Do we have to go home? Vacations are the best. I love it here."

"I want to stay on the bus. I like the bus," Justine said, pouting.

"I think we should go on a real vacation. All of us."

"Like a princess castle vacation?" my baby girl asked, her eyes big as saucers.

"No, more like a beach vacation. What do you think?"

"I love the beach," Mikaella exclaimed.

"Me too," Justine echoed.

"Me three," Madison added.

I let out a loud chuckle.

"Me four," a voice said from behind us. We all turned to stare at Riley as he took a seat beside us. "So, what are we having here, guys? Cereals? Hmm, that looks…well… yummy." The girls snickered as my friend fixed himself a bowl. "About this vacation, can I come too?"

The girls cheered.

I stared at him with a frown. "And you're crashing our family breakfast because—?"

"Oh, yeah. We gotta meet. And it couldn't wait." His gaze traveled between Madison and me and then the girls. "Justine, Mika, do you want to go to the park with Devon? Hope and she are kinda lonely right now. I think they miss the company."

Justine jumped to her feet. "I'll be *Debon's* friend."

Riley ruffled her hair. "Good, that's the spirit. Let's meet her. She's waiting for you. I gotta talk to your daddy, then I'll come too." Riley lifted Justine in his arms and spun on his feet to face us. "Hey, Mika, you coming?"

Mikaella moved to stand and entwined herself in Madison's arms, who held my daughter in a caring embrace. "I wanna stay with Mama."

Riley's mouth popped open.

His eyebrows bunched together.

He blinked.

"Wow, I never thought I'd see this day coming. Wow, my heart is racing right now. This is huge. Are you guys okay?"

I nodded as Madison dried fresh tears building in the corners of her eyes with her fingertips.

I swallowed my own emotions. "It's new. From this morning. It came from her." My heart bounced in my chest. My daughters never stopped surprising me.

"Can we go now?" Justine asked, cupping Riley's face with both hands. "*Debon* misses me."

"Sure. Mika, come. I'm sure your…Mama will join us later too. We could all go for a picnic or something."

Madison leaned forward and pushed the hair away from Mikaella's forehead. "We'll be real quick, sweetie. I love you. Now go save Devon from her loneliness. I'll be right behind you."

My daughter bobbed her head and circled Madison's neck with her arms. "I love you, Mama."

"Love you too. Now go."

Riley left with both my daughters, and I pulled Madison against me.

My lips found hers, and when she parted them to let my tongue in, I dissolved under the strength of her love. I grabbed a handful of her ass with one hand, winding the other around her neck, keeping her as close to me as possible.

If I could spend my days buried in her warmth, I'd be the happiest man out there.

With her love, Madison not only salvaged my heart, but my soul too."I want you naked. Now."

She raised her glistening eyes to me, overflowing with lust and love. "Can you at least wait until Riley is gone? He'll come back any minute. Ohmygod, I'm so wet I could drench the floor right now."

"Glad I'm having so much effect on you, babe."

I grabbed my phone and texted my friend.

ME

Don't come over just now. Wait.

My palms glided under her shirt, and I lifted it up over her head, exposing her black lace bra. "One day, I want a child who looks just like you, Maddie. Someone with your beauty, your intelligence, your heart," I said, kissing my way down her chest. "You're too good for me. I'll never understand how you can love all of me."

She pulled me up, her lips searching for mine. "Don't ever say that again, Sam. I love everything about you. Your smile, your energy, the way you're a daddy to those girls, even your grumpiness. I want a child who looks like you too. We already have two amazing daughters, but there should be more people like you on Earth. Smart, generous, and strong." Her mouth feasted on mine. "I don't want to wait, though."

I leaned back, just enough to stare into the depths of her eyes. "We have all the time in the world. You're so young."

She shook her head. "Nah. I want our kids to be close in age. I want them to grow up together. To play together. To run around the house together. When you are ready. I know I already am."

"You sure?"

Emotions twinkled in her eyes, making her irises greener. "I've never been so sure."

Riley's words from a conversation we had a long while ago popped into my head. *If I do this, I'll do it right.*

"You know I'll have to ask you to marry me first, right?"

She shook her head.

"You don't want us to get married?" I tucked a strand of her hair behind her ear, wanting to see her whole face.

"Not now. We're good. When the day comes and our family is complete, then our kids—all of them—will celebrate with us. It'll be a family thing. The last piece tying us all together."

I swallowed the lump in my throat. How could she be so selfless? And so amazing? How could she consider my daughters hers so easily? Without questions or demands?

"I just fell in love with you all over again, Madison Prescott. You're one hell of a woman. I'm glad you're mine because I'll never let you go. And I'm gonna get you a ring. To symbolize everything we are. And everything we're about to be."

"Please love me."

And that's what I did. Until we were both panting, our bodies fused together.

"We should call Riley. He must be wondering what's taking so long," she said with a grin.

"Shit, I forgot about him. He must be seated outside, waiting for us to finish." Madison's laughter mixed with mine. "Maybe he'll think twice before playing matchmaker next time." I dropped a kiss on her bare shoulder, and she shivered under me. "Come on. Let's get dressed, or we'll be spending the day in bed."

ME

The coast is clear, man. Come over when you're ready.

Madison carried three cups of coffee and placed them on the table, then sat onto my lap. She could now walk without the crutches, a victory we had celebrated two weeks ago. Spasms still crippled her at night, but they were less frequent and painful. I locked a protective arm around her, keeping her close to my heart. I was nuzzling her neck when Riley peeked inside. "Everyone dressed and decent?" he asked.

"Yep. We're all covered up," I teased.

He stepped closer and studied us, his hands stuffed in his pockets. "Can you guys just break apart for a minute? I can't focus when you have your hands all over each other." He made a gagging sound, and we all burst out laughing.

Madison moved her arms around my neck. "See? My

hands are where you can see them. No funny business, I promise. But I won't move because we're barely ever alone, and we don't get a chance to be all over each other often enough. So don't be the fun police—or rather the love police."

I smiled at my girl's wit.

"Sam, honey, show Riley your hands so he can see where they are."

"My arms are around her waist, don't worry," I said with a wink.

Riley huffed. "Okay, you two, you think you're funny." He sat in a chair across from us. "Here's the deal. We could extend the tour. By three months. Starting in a little over a month. Some pop band broke up, and we could get their dates. We have to move fast, though. The guy called me first because he owes me one, but we need to confirm by the end of the day." I began to say something, but Riley raised a finger. "Think about it. And gimme an answer by two."

My eyes drifted to Madison. She gave me a subtle nod, her eyes shiny.

"We've already decided, Ry. The girls aren't ready to go home just yet. And neither are we. We'll do it. But we'll go on that beach vacation we've talked about between the two legs of the tour."

"One more thing," my friend said. "I talked to Curtis earlier. We were talking about Anderson and his refusal to go on tour. All because of Alexi. Fear of missing out, I guess. Or to succeed at making it work. What if he opens for you? With you guys as an example, maybe he'll realize it's possible for him to combine his personal and professional lives on the road. And with Maddie there, it will help with the transition. I think it'll be the perfect opportunity. What do you think?"

"You talked to your father about your half-brother opening for me?" I bowed my head. "I'd like to have the youngest Burns brother around. See if he's anything like you. I just met the guy once, so it was inconclusive."

Riley sighed, barely hiding his crooked smile. "Stop fucking with me, Stevens. Officially, he's a Ford, and you're well aware. Anyway, Alexi will need some extra help if you don't mind sharing your nanny with him."

Madison's gaze drifted back and forth between us, trying to catch up on the conversation.

"Curtis Burns is Riley's father," I explained.

"*The* Curtis Burns?" she asked with wide eyes.

I nodded. "And Anderson Ford is his half-brother."

"Oh, I see," was all she replied.

My friend dragged a hand over his face. "Our relationship is complicated. Sam will fill you in later. So do we all agree to an additional three months of tour?"

Madison and I said "Yes" at the same time.

"Great. Let me call my guy, and I'll keep you posted. I won't be able to follow you on the road this time, though. Thanks, Maddie, for making this grumpy fellow happy and making my job easier. You should get a raise."

I kicked my friend's shin under the table.

"My heart is full," my woman said, glancing at me. "Money doesn't matter. It's just numbers."

We swam into each other's eyes and failed to notice Riley leaving.

My phone vibrated on the table, breaking the moment.

RILEY

We'll talk later. You two are disgustingly in love, it shouldn't be legal. I'll take care of your kids while you're busy with their mama. (I still can't believe Mika said those words this morning.)

I'm happy for you. You deserve it all.

I put my phone down, unable to tame the grin stretching my face.

"You really want to do this?" I asked.

Madison nodded.

"What about your job? I put you out of work…sorta. You don't need to get a job, but I'm pretty sure you'll want one, and I want you to thrive, not be an accessory to my life. You gotta fulfill your own dreams."

"Well, now that you've brought it up—and it's funny Riley mentioned it—I've been thinking for a while about teaching kids on the road. All these roadies, they miss their families. What if I teach their kids too or find a way to provide them with the curriculum they need when they join their parents for long stretches of time? We could make your tour and others' family-friendly so all those guys wouldn't have to choose between their children and their jobs."

A million thoughts swirled in my head. "Wow, I like that. Also, the girls would have friends. This could actually be great. I already knew you were amazing, but you just proved it to me all over again. You should talk with Ry. I'm sure he would be a great ally in helping you set this up."

"I know nothing about Alexi, but from what I gathered from your conversation, he could be the first one to benefit from this."

"We'll sit down with Riley. I'm sure he'll be ecstatic at the idea. Alexi has special needs. I'm not entirely sure what that involves, but helping him through his struggles could be a new challenge for you to tackle—in a positive and productive way. We'll ask Ry for more details." I kissed her lips, eliciting a moan from her. "Now that we have a few hours to ourselves, what do you have in mind?"

Madison shrugged. "Can we just watch a movie or do something boring together? You know, cuddle under a blanket and nap on the couch. Regular stuff couples do, that we never have a chance to indulge in."

"You want us to be boring, Miss Prescott?"

"My life will always be full of excitement with you guys in it. But yeah, we could be that couple for a few hours to see how it feels. Let's get naked and see how long we can resist each other under that blanket."

"Deal."

We stood up, undressed, and slid under the blanket Madison had brought to the living room section of our bus.

We were just getting comfortable when her body went limp in my arms, her soft breaths acting like a lullaby. My eyes grew heavy.

"Thank you, life, for putting her on my path. I'll forever be grateful," I said. Unable to keep my eyelids open, I capitulated and fell into a deep slumber, the woman I loved nestled against me.

# Epilogue
## Sam

**Three years later**

"Daddy, come see. Come see. Austin is making bubbles with his mouth. It's so funny. He can't stop laughing."

It took me all my will to crack my eyes open. What time was it? I looked to my right. Madison wasn't there. I was supposed to do the morning shift. We'd talked about it last night.

"Where's Mama?" I asked my cheerful daughter.

"With Austin, duh," Mikaella deadpanned, rolling her eyes.

"Come here, you," I said as she neared me and dropped a kiss on my cheek. "I love you, sweet pea."

"I love you too, Daddy."

I felt a rush of warmth in my chest. Seeing the joy pouring out my little girl was priceless.

"Now come and see Austin. You'll miss his show."

"All right. Let me get dressed first."

"Hurry," my daughter said. I was picking up a shirt from my dresser when her soft voice sent a shiver down my spine with her next words. The kind that felt good. "Are you and Mama going to get married one day? All my friends, you know, their parents are married. Why are you not?"

I turned on my heel and sat on the edge of the mattress to level my eyes with hers, weighing my words. "Does it matter to you?"

Mikaella nodded. "I don't want Mama to ever go away. I want her to be in our family forever. I love Austin too, even when he burps all over my shirts or when he stinks."

"Listen, you know the ring on Mama's finger?"

She nodded again.

"It's my promise to her to always love her. But I think you're right. We should ask her to marry us. For real this time. The wedding will have to wait until after the baby is born, though. That's what she wants. All her children here to celebrate with us."

A wide smile brightened my daughter's face. "Can Mama also be our mama forever?"

"She already is, sweet pea."

"But I want to be her real daughter. Like in that movie. Justine wishes it too. We talked about it."

"You did?" I blinked to keep my emotions at bay, not ready to let them out. "You two want Maddie to adopt you?"

Mikaella nodded again, seriousness written all over her face. "Yes, and be a real family. Austin has a real Mama. We don't. Justine and I choose Maddie. Can you choose her too?"

I pulled my now nine, almost ten-year-old, daughter into my arms.

It'd been almost six years since Lisa left, and to this day, she'd never contacted us or tried to make amends with her children. For a short while, I was tempted to hire a **PI** to keep tabs on her, but Madison discouraged the idea. What would it change in the end, except bring more pain to the girls, if she ever came back or approached them? She said she wouldn't want her own biological mother to reach out if she was given the choice. After she shared her point of view, I couldn't agree more with her perspective.

"That's all I've ever wanted, Mika. You sure you're ready, though?"

"Daddy, I've been ready for a long time. I was just waiting for you to make a move. Since you don't move fast enough, I've decided to help you out. We'll bake a cake later and ask Mama, okay? Justine said we should throw a party."

"Oh, I'd like that."

"We'll invite our friends. And Riley, Devon, and little Briana. And your other friends with their kids. All the people we love. We'll call grandma and grandpa and grams and gramps on video."

Madison's family had become ours too. Her parents loved my kids as their own grandchildren.

"Mika, right now, you're making me the happiest daddy on the planet."

"Now hurry. You'll miss Austin laughing."

She tugged at my hand, and I followed her downstairs and into the kitchen.

My pregnant fiancée sat there, looking at our one-year-old son with stars in her eyes. The same stars that appeared every time they landed on the girls or me.

I leaned in to kiss her lips, and like always, my heart

shot fireworks in my chest. Contentment traveled in my bloodstream. These people were my entire universe.

"Oh, you taste good. I could eat you up right now. You know how hungry I am all the time. These damn pregnancy hormones," she said with a wink.

"Let's drop the kids at Riley's later. He still owes us hundreds of hours of babysitting. I might let you sample me afterward. To satisfy your appetite. Because I'm selfless like that. And maybe because I love you a little bit much."

Madison snickered behind her hand. "I love selfless Sam Stevens, always ready to share his essence. He's my favorite."

Austin laughed, bubbles coming out of his mouth. Just as Mikaella had described. He looked adorable in his highchair, clapping his hands before him, enjoying being the center of all our devoted attention.

"I think we've got another performer in the family," Madison said with a dramatic sigh followed by a small grin.

"Babe, you look tired. You should rest. I'll take care of the kids." I dropped my voice to a whisper. "I want you refreshed and relaxed if we wanna play later." I looped one arm around her and helped her up. "I love you."

She buried her head in my chest, the smell of her vanilla shampoo filling my nose.

"If you drive the kids to our friends'; don't go before I get a chance to kiss them goodbye, okay?"

"Never. Now go, take a nap. This baby girl in there is sucking all the energy out of you."

My eyes were trained on her backside as Madison climbed the stairs to our bedroom, my heart pumping heat waves through my veins, every molecule of me at ease—and at peace.

"Okay, girls," I said to our daughters once I heard the bedroom door click behind her. "Time to bake that cake."

———

I brushed my lips over Madison's. Hers still tasted like the blueberries she'd had in the morning. "Hey, babe. Time to wake up."

She stirred in her sleep, grumbled something, and rolled to her side. I grazed the side of her face with my knuckles, relishing the trail of goose bumps they left in their wake.

Her eyelids fluttered open and seconds later, she fastened her arms around my midsection. "I was having the best dream. What time is it?" she asked, her voice groggy from sleep.

"Almost five."

Her eyes sprang open, and she propped herself up on her elbows. "Sam, you didn't wake me up. I asked you—"

My mouth claimed hers, silencing her protests as she melted under my lips. Even after all these years spent together, we were still insatiable for each other. Our honeymoon period had just never ended. Our tongues danced together. I forgot how to breathe or to form words. The entire world started and stopped with us.

She locked her arms around my neck, pulling me closer and deepening the kiss. I was a gone man.

This woman could ask anything of me, and I'd say "Yes" without a second thought. Never in my life had I trusted someone as much as I trusted her.

Madison Prescott owned my heart and every bit of me, my present and my future.

"Are the children still here?" she asked once we broke apart.

"Yes. Downstairs. They wanna see you actually."

"They do? Wait. Aren't they supposed to be at Riley's?"

I shrugged. "No. He had other plans. He promised a raincheck, though." I waggled my eyebrows. "Let's get you out of those pajamas and dress you into something a bit more fashionable. I have great expectations for later."

She frowned. "Why? I love these PJs. They would make a great motherhood fashion statement."

"Suit yourself, babe. I'll never complain, but I thought maybe we could eat out or something." *And because there are people downstairs, and I'm pretty sure you'd kill me if I let you walk down there dressed like this.*

Without asking further questions, she put on the powder-blue cotton maxi dress I brought her. She braided her hair quickly and added a touch of gloss to her lips and a coat of mascara.

"How do I look?"

"Perfect."

Something I made sure to remind her every day. To me, no none had ever looked so beautiful as this woman. Inside and out. The one I still had no idea how she could love an old man like me. Well, not old, but older. Back when we'd started dating, she said age was just a number, and I couldn't agree more. Madison and I, we just fit. From the first time we saw each other, I'd never looked at another woman the way I looked at her. We were two halves of the same heart. If that made sense.

With her hand firmly in mine, we made our way down the stairs. My fiancée stopped on the last step, taking everybody in. Our children. Riley, Devon, and their daughter, Briana. Carter and April, Aisha and Gavin, and all their kids. Emily and Becks, who'd gotten engaged last summer.

And some of Mikaella's and Justine's friends from down the street.

"What did I miss?" Madison asked, strangling my fingers as she squeezed my hand a little tighter. "It's not my birthday." Questions and surprise shone in her eyes. Without a word, I pointed with my chin to the banner the girls had painted earlier, now hanging over the back door.

*Maddie, would you agree to become our mama?*
*For real. And forever.*

The love of my life cupped her mouth as tears cascaded down her face.

"For real?" she asked in a small voice.

Justine and Mikaella, who was holding Austin in her arms, inched closer.

"We do," our eldest daughter said.

"All three of us," Justine added.

"Do you want to be our mama? Like in that movie you like so much? Where the couple adopted those orphan siblings?"

Madison bobbed her head, her emotions preventing her from speaking. She opened her arms and pulled our children to her heart. "Is it for real?" Her eyes met mine.

"Yes. We all agreed it was about time. Also, there's something else we've meant to ask you?"

She arched an eyebrow, drying her tears with her fingers.

"Yes," Justine said, clapping her hands.

I dropped to one knee. "Madison Prescott, I've been loving you since the day we met. I was stubborn and stupid back then and tried to push you away. To keep my feelings tightly chained. Luckily for me, I realized I was being an idiot and came back to my senses just in time. Now that we're about to have four children together, I think we should officialize our love. I know technically we're already engaged, but let's get married—with all our children—so we'll remember this night forever, the one where you agreed to become my wife and the mother of our children in front of all the people we love. Madison, will you marry me?" I took a steadying breath. "Please say yes."

She let out a cry. Then, through sobs, her shoulders heaving, she whispered, "Yes. Oh, Sam. I do. I love you all so much. Official or not, you're all already mine."

"We love you so much," I said as we kissed, her lips trembling under mine. "I love you so freaking much."

Opening an arm to welcome the girls, I lifted Austin from Mikaella's embrace, and we all hugged one another.

"I heard those guys even baked a cake for the occasion. At least that's what they said to convince me to come over," Riley announced with a wink.

"Cake. Cake. Cake. Yes, we baked a cake," Justine singsonged, her happiness still contagious even though she was older. "And we made you gifts."

Their mama squatted and grabbed both our girls' hands in hers. "Justine, Mikaella, I'll always be your mama. Whether or not I adopt you two officially, you'll always be mine in my heart."

"We wished for it. Many times. We asked Daddy, and he agreed we'd wasted too much time already. Do you agree to become our mama, Maddie?"

Another batch of tears filled Madison's eyes. "Yes. There's nothing that would make me prouder and happier. This is the most incredible day of my life. Gosh, I love you two so much."

They all hugged as I stood there, my son in my arms,

wiping my own teary eyes, my heart racing in my chest, blissfully happy.

My fiancée moved to stand up. "Now let's taste that cake. I'm starving."

Carter and April joined us a while later. "Maddie, I got your message. About helping out with our charity. When you're ready to discuss how you see things from your end, just reach out, and we'll set up a meeting," Carter said.

My wife-to-be clasped her hands before her. "I'd like that. My *teaching kids on tour* business is running smoothly. I'm ready to add another challenge to my professional life. Once the baby is old enough for me to resume work full-time, I really wanna help you guys. Be a part of it. Your foundation is doing something meaningful for young artists, and I really appreciate you two including me."

I kissed her temple. "They will be lucky to have you, babe. Please don't spread yourself too thin, though."

"Yes," April agreed. "We'll be happy to have you onboard, Maddie, but don't overdo it. I know how exhausting raising a house full of kids can be. Come on, let me help you out."

They both disappeared toward the kitchen.

"Congrats," Carter said with a smirk. "If only I had predicted it years ago, right?"

I backhanded his chest. "Yeah, yeah, yeah. Throw yourself some flowers, man."

"Are you happy, Stevens? You look happy."

My eyes caught sight of Madison, laughing with the girls about something Justine said. "Like I've never been before. I have everything I've ever wished for in my life."

———

"Did you put the girls up to this?" my soon-to-be wife asked as she exited the shower, enveloped in only a towel.

I neared her, Austin now deep asleep in my arms, sucking on his pacifier, his tiny fist clamped around my finger, and his dark locks brushed gently to the side.

"Nope. It's all their doing. They said it took us too long to make a move, so they've decided to take matters into their own hands. I can't be prouder right now."

Madison rose to her tiptoes. "I never knew how much it meant to me until they asked me. I love our family. It's unique. It's us. We're perfect."

"No, you're perfect."

The towel billowed on the floor at her feet, and she grinned at me. The scar across her hip was still visible. Madison had undergone one round of plastic surgery before deciding she loved her scars because they reminded her of never losing hope and fighting for what you desire the most. The ones along her leg had healed better and faded with time. They were daily reminders that life could be unpredictable and that we should love with all our hearts when given the chance.

"You and I, we haven't celebrated yet. Care to love me, future husband?" she asked, her sultry voice sending electricity up and down my spine and waking up every part of me.

"Oh, you won't need to ask me twice. Let me put this little man in his crib, and I'll be right back." I did a quick tour, making sure all three kids were deep asleep before going back to our bedroom. I almost tripped over my own feet in my hurry to bury myself in my wife-to-be.

I locked the door behind me and prowled in her direction, ditching all my clothes in the process.

"I like it when you're happy to see me," she said as I

moved closer, my throbbing hard-on now pressed between us.

I kissed the woman I loved with everything I had and lay onto my back on the mattress.

God, she was beautiful.

A chime on my phone broke the silence of our rushed breathing. Who would contact me at this late hour? Holding up a finger to indicate one second before kissing her lips, I twisted my body to fetch my device from the nightstand. I blinked. And re-read every line to make sure I got it right the first time.

"Everything okay?" Madison asked, braced on her elbow and spreading kisses in the crook of my neck. "Sam, you have your business face on. Something's wrong. I can tell. Who is it?"

"It's Kiera and Edward."

She frowned. "What happened? Are they safe and sound?"

Eight months ago, we had fostered seven-year-old twins, whose mother had gone to rehab and father was unknown, for five months. A way for us to help children like Madison and Emily who'd suffered from their parents' neglect. Kiera and Edward had fit right in with our children. It was a tough adjustment at first, but we made it work, and it was one thing Madison and I were really proud of. That we brought some light and hope into those children's lives.

"Yes and no. Their mother. She relapsed and…huh… she overdosed. The social worker is searching for a home for them. She asked if we're willing to take them in since they know and trust us. They're affected. They found her unconscious and called 9-1-1 themselves."

"Ohmygod. That's terrible."

"Yep. She said it will be an even bigger challenge this time around."

"Poor babies. Where are they now? I'd never let them go to a stranger's house. They need stability. A loving environment. I want them home, Sam. With us."

"They're at a foster home. For tonight only. All temporary. They could come here tomorrow. Full-time, if we agree to do this."

"Do you?" Madison asked. "We're leaving on a seven-week tour in two months. I want them here, that's not even a question, but we gotta be practical about it."

I rolled to my back, and Madison shifted position until half of her was spread over half of me. "Yeah, I don't want them living with strangers either. I'm sure we can make this work. We'll talk with Shana, the social worker. Last time they traveled with us for a week. I have no idea how we'll do this."

"Raise six kids?"

"That. And making it all work."

Madison's eyes shimmered in the semi-darkness of our room, and her smile split her face in two. "Are we really doing this?"

I mirrored her grin. "I guess we are. They're already family. Imagine how scared they must be right now."

"This breaks my heart. Think we can go get them? Tonight?"

"Let me make a quick phone call and see what I can do."

Madison glowed as she kissed my jaw. Her heart would never cease to amaze me. She watched me with adoration, and I kissed her.

"Sam? I'm happy we're doing this together. It means a lot to me."

"Always. Perhaps we should consider expanding the

house after all like we've discussed. We'll need a few more bedrooms."

"We'll look at the plans the architect drew tomorrow and see our options."

"Gosh, I love you so much."

"I love you more," she said in a breathless voice, the fire re-igniting between us as she coiled strands of my hair around her fingers.

A wave of joy washed over me.

Music had come back into my life, and I'd climbed to the top again. Nothing or no one would ever push me down again. Right now, I had everything a man could wish for and more. My life was about to get even richer in so many different ways and I only had Madison to thank for all of it. Together, we were unstoppable, and I relished every single one of our adventures.

"You're the best man I know. Don't ever stop loving me," she said.

My lips molded to hers in the slowest kiss, injecting her with all the passion weaving through me. "Never. You're my home, Maddie, you're my heart and my soul. And the best part of me. Let's go get those kids."

The End

———

Continue with Anderson Ford's story.
**Read Snowbound**

emmanuellesnow.com/products/snowbound

Thank you for reading
Sam and Madison's epic love story.

———

FREE bonus chapter
Want even more? Your bonus chapter awaits here
emmanuellesnow.com

———

**Want more of Riley and Devon?**
Read Last Hope: Riley and Devon's story
Read Midnight Spark: Aisha Jone's story

**Curious about the rest of their friends?**
Read False Promises: Carter's story
Read Cruel Destiny: Dahlia and Nick's story

# WANT MORE EMOTIONAL
# LOVE STORIES?

## WHICH COUPLE WILL YOU PICK NEXT?

**False Promises**

★★★★★ "The angst, the utter heartbreak, and protectiveness I felt for Carter during this book is unreal!"

★★★★★ "Emmanuelle Snow really knows how to tug at all of your emotions and does such a great job of bringing her characters to life!"

**A gripping story of sizzling passion, lust, and the price of fame.**
**Start Carter Hills's story now**

———

**Sweet Agony**

★★★★★ "If I could give more than 5 stars, I would."

★★★★★ "This is not a romance, it is a story about first love, first heartbreak and growing up."

**A compelling tale of love, friendship, and self-discovery that will tug at your heartstrings.**

**Start Dahlia's story now**

———

**Cruel Destiny**

★★★★★ "Wow. Just wow. If that could be my review, that is all I would write."

★★★★★ "Emmanuelle has done it yet again. She found a way to slip into my mind and heart with her words and the creation of characters you can't help but fall in love with."

★★★★★ "This book broke my heart in the first twenty five percent and sewed it back together."

**A story of healing, second chances, and the risks of opening your heart to someone new. Can they trust each other with their hearts, or will their pasts keep them apart?**

**Read Nick and Dahlia's love story now**

———

**Wild Encounter**

★★★★★ "This is by far one of the most well-written

book I've read this month. It is dynamic, intriguing, interesting, unafraid to go there and most of all touching."

★★★★★ "I personally wouldn't call this book JUST a romance novel because it's so much more. I 100% recommend it no doubt in mind."

**A tale of passion and perseverance that will leave your heart racing and your spirit soaring.**

**Read Tucker and Addison's love story now**

———

**Last Hope**

★★★★★ "This book was not only about the darkness but it was about pure love, hope, spice, family, and friendships on point with just the right amount without overpowering the storyline at all."

★★★★★ "Devon and Riley's story is a beautiful one with a lot of emotions. The subject matter is intense but it is handled very gently."

**A tale of resilience and second chances in a world where love and danger intertwine.**

**Read Riley and Devon's love story now**

———

**Midnight Sparks**

★★★★★ "The characters, the love, the humor, the steaminess, the emotions… it's everything I hoped and more."

★★★★★ "I think that is one Emmanuelle Snow's sexiest novels yet."

**Welcome to the island where Holiday magic meets unexpected romance and a chance at a fresh start.**

**Read Gavin and Aisha's love story now**

———

**Fallen Legend**

★★★★★ ""The love that grows, not only through tough angst but through unconditional moments had my heart. This is a spicy and riveting book"

★★★★★ "Emmanuelle Snow doesn't just tell a story, she creates an entire world."

**A poignant and uplifting journey of hope, love, and the power of second chances.**

**Read Sam and Madison's love story now**

———

**Snowbound**

★★★★★ "5 big stars from me for this amazing story. Absolutely loved it!"

★★★★★ "Emmanuelle Snow's stories are always full of angst, and Snowbound is no exception."

**The intertwined lives of two strangers bound by fate in the midst of a snowstorm.**

**Read Anderson and Abigail's love story now**

———

**All available at emmanuellesnow.com**

# ACKNOWLEDGMENTS

Oh, wow! This book has turned out to be a greater challenge than expected. I have no words to express how happy I am it's now released.

Publishing a book is not a straightforward process, and it's hard to estimate from the first line you write where the characters will take you. And how much they'll complicate your job as an author. I'm a sucker for soulmates, realistic, and emotional love stories, and this book is living proof.

From the first time Riley mentioned Sam Stevens in *the Heart Song duet*, I knew I had to write his story. It was one that stuck with me and wouldn't go away. So, I started writing this book a long time ago. And up until now, it's the one that took me the longest time to complete. Because it had to convey the right emotions and complexities (Mikaella would love the usage of this word here!) to Sam and Madison's story. With Sam being a single father of two, he and Madison couldn't just jump into a relationship without second-guessing themselves in the process since it wasn't just about them. I wanted the story to feel real as much as possible. I wanted the children to play a huge part in their love journey because no matter what we tell ourselves, no parent can disregard the consequences of their choices when little kids are involved.

Sam and Madison's story is filled with uncertainties, challenges, hope, and a lot of love. The simple word, which comes with the greatest powers, can also spin your entire world upside-down when you least expect it.

Children being neglected, no matter the form, is a topic that's often disregarded because it makes people queasy, but it's real. And it's important we address it. Not all stories turn out perfect, but some stories really come with a happy ending. Because there are people who care.

This is not your typical single-dad, age-gap romance, but I hope it'll live in your heart for a long time.

I wanna thank my Snow babies for this one. We've been through hard and amazing times together, and I love you more than words can express. And no matter what, you're stuck with me. Because I'll always have your back. And I'll always cheer for you. To Mr. Snow, I love you. We've proven over the years we make a great team and that no matter what life throws at us, when we're together, I know that in the end, it will all be okay. Because we have each other's backs. You don't write me love songs, but I know that I can always count on you. Even when it gets tough.

Shalini. Where do I even begin? Once again, I'm impressed at the turn-around we succeeded to accomplish for this book. When I set the book up for pre-order a year ago, I had no idea my year would get crazy, and it would mess with my schedule. But you hung in there. With me. And for that, I'm thankful. I can't give you a hug right now, but I'm sending a virtual one. We did it! Hope you are ready for all my new projects lining up and filling your own schedule.

To my friends and family, thank you for encouraging me when I need a little push in the right direction.

To my Snowmate team, you guys are the best. Seriously. You're always so happy when I announce a new release, and you do awesome, sharing your love for my work. Thank you.

To the Bookstagrammers, YouTubers, TikTokers, bloggers, and everyone else who spread the word about my releases and love for my books, I'm thankful. This is the best feeling in the world when I see you posting, sharing, and supporting me. Every time someone tags me in a post for the book they have loved, I do a happy dance. It's worth the world to me.

And finally, to life. When you keep pushing, you should know by now I'll just keep pushing back. That's just how I'm wired. And I'm glad you tested me many times in the past because now I know how strong I can be.

This is a wrap.

To all y'all, cheers!

# ABOUT THE AUTHOR

## Soulfully Beautiful Love Stories

*USA Today* Bestselling Author Emmanuelle Snow is an author of contemporary YA and women's fiction love stories, who gives life to strong characters who'll fight with all they have to reach their life goals and find their own happiness. She loves her characters to be relatable and realistic.

Emmanuelle is in love with love. Especially complicated, deep, and passionate feelings that make a relationship extraordinary and complex all at the same time.

In her spare time, when she's not writing or reading, she likes to go on road trips—with her four kids and her own soulmate—watch movies, paint, or do some DIY, always with a cup of green tea in her hand and listening to country music.

She splits her time between beautiful Canada and the small US towns she adores.

### Find all of Emmanuelle's books here:

emmanuellesnow.com

———

**Want to connect with Emmanuelle online?**
YOU CAN FIND HER HERE:

**Website**
**Author's bookstore and merch store**

**Snow's VIP newsletter**
emmanuellesnow.com

**Readers' VIP group Snow's Soulmates**
facebook.com/groups/snowvip

amazon.com/author/emmanuellesnow

goodreads.com/emmanuellesnow

bookbub.com/authors/emmanuelle-snow

facebook.com/esnowauthor

instagram.com/snowemmanuelle

x.com/snowemmanuelle

pinterest.com/snowemmanuelle

tiktok.com/@snowemmanuelle

# ALSO BY THE AUTHOR

## CARTER HILLS BAND UNIVERSE

(suggested reading order)

### Carter Hills Band series

False Promises

Heart Song Duet

Blindsided

Forevermore

### Whiskey Melody series

Sweet Agony

Second Tear Duet

Cruel Destiny

Beautiful Salvation

Breathless Duet

Wild Encounter

Brittle Scars

### Upon A Star Series

Last Hope

Midnight Sparks

### Love Song For Two Series

<u>LONESOME HEART DUET</u>

Fallen Legend

Rising Star

<u>TWO OF US DUET</u>

Snowbound

Wicked Love

**MEDORA BEACH UNIVERSE**

**Wrecked series**

Cast Away

Ride for a Fall

**Touchdown series**

Kickoff

**Read them all**

emmanuellesnow.com

**All available on author's bookshop**

# EMMANUELLE SNOW

USA TODAY BESTSELLING AUTHOR

# SNOW BOUND

*a love story*

Love Song for Two series - book three

# PROLOGUE
## ABIGAIL

My eyes hurt from the lack of sleep. I'd been up all night, searching the internet to find the one person on this Earth I didn't know the name of. I rubbed my heavy eyelids with the sleeve of my hoodie, hoping to clear my now cloudy vision. I swore my brain had decided to see everything in dual frames. A thick fog enveloped my mind, making it hard to think straight.

Every social media platform I could think of, I'd checked numerous times.

How many Andrews about my age lived in this country? Way too many. It was a lost cause. A conclusion I'd come to minutes ago. He could be anywhere around the world right now.

I sighed.

Soon, I would have to resign myself to my fate and go through this alone. *On. My. Own.* I scanned the space around me and took in the pile of boxes my best friend Ellie and I had emptied last week, and my eyes brimmed with hot tears. A wave of sadness washed through me. Exhaustion settled in.

I had promised myself I would find him. And I had failed.

Rivulets of my sadness cascaded down my cheeks, and I let them flow freely, too tired to even patch the broken pieces of my heart and the dam that had ruptured.

How had I become such a failure at nineteen? I wasn't even out of my teen years, yet my life seemed all set to derail—in more ways than I could count—and I was all alone for the ride.

Ellie had left before dinner. She had taken a flight back to campus.

She didn't have to come all the way to Tennessee for me after I'd broken the news to my parents that I'd withdrawn from college. For now.

She didn't have to help me set my new life on track either. Or even fly here once more to unpack my things after I'd moved.

Three months ago, my parents gave me an ultimatum and threw me out without a second glance. For eleven weeks afterward, I'd been living someplace I never thought I'd consider home in this lifetime. But what other options did I have? Zero to none.

Deciding not to let life have the last word in my future, I worked double-time—even when exhaustion got the best of me—and so far, it had paid off, because now I had a place to call mine. A home. Or more like the only non-dump I could afford.

Ellie didn't have to fill the refrigerator of my new apartment with healthy options. And she didn't have to stop by the store to pick up colorful decor items to give this place a little character and make it lovelier than it was. I had told her I'd pay her back. Eventually. One day. She'd brushed the idea away with a flick of her wrist. "My treat," she had said. Something that she often repeated these days whenever it concerned me. Or my screwups.

No, Ellie didn't have to do any of those things. But she did them anyway, out of the selflessness of her heart. And I would forever be grateful that she'd stuck by my side, because no one else did.

To add misery to my already complicated existence, I was now failing at the promise I'd made to myself: to get hold of the one person I needed to talk to, to confide in about everything. Be honest. And tell the truth. And yet, he was the one who didn't seem to exist. As if my brain had created him one night. And he'd evaporated in the morning light.

Fresh tears blurred my vision.

Pulling the fluffy purple blanket Ellie had gotten me to cover the not-so-pretty brown couch that came with the apartment around my heaving shoulders, I curled up on the worn wooden floor that must have looked fancy in its earlier years. Now it just looked old. And sad. Like me.

Even though I tried, I had no more fight left in me.

These days, every effort felt harder than it really was. I was constantly exhausted, but I always tried to push a little more because I only had myself to rely on. And being tired wasn't an option.

My body let go first. But even in my dreams, my mind was restless.

Images of our time together waltzed behind my closed eyelids.

"I'm sorry," I murmured through the raw lining of my throat. "For everything."

That was when my brain lost the fight too.

I would be all right. I had to be. What else could I do?

His name fell from my lips as his handsome face, brightened with joy, formed in my mind, the sparks in his eyes aimed at me. He smiled and whispered, "I'll never forget you, Abby." The last words he had spoken to me.

How I wished it were true. The image dissolved, and there was nothing left of the man I'd been thinking about for months now.

I begged my mind to bring him back. Not a flicker. Nothing. Even the dream version of him had abandoned me.

For the first time, fear made me a prisoner, its steel claws digging into my heart.

I wouldn't let it win. I had to fight back. To make it work. Somehow.

Oblivion filled my head, my heart heavy with tears.

# CHAPTER 1

## ABIGAIL

**Present**

All my life, I'd been wanting to work in the music industry and after everything that happened, I never thought I'd see this day coming. Or that my dream could become tangible one day. For more than three years, I'd worked my ass off as a virtual assistant while juggling home, college, and all the other responsibilities a twenty-three-year-old woman shouldn't have had to deal with all by herself. But hey, I was now ready to prove to Mr. Burns I could be the assistant he was looking to hire.

Three months ago, I had finally graduated with a dual degree in business administration and music management. One I'd worked my ass off for. Days and nights. Literally. I was overqualified for this position, but I didn't care. I would be an assistant any day if it meant I could prove my value. Climb up that career ladder until I reach my ultimate goal. Yeah, anything to bring me closer to my dream job.

In the full-length mirror in the entryway, I glanced at

my power outfit one last time—white blouse and red pencil skirt—my first impulsive buy and the most expensive one to date. Along with matching heels. Money had been scarce in the past few years. But I had always made it work somehow. I smoothed the fabric over my thighs with trembling fingers, doing my best to calm the jitters invading me.

Tears pooled in my eyes, and I felt a little pinch in my heart.

"I can do this. I will do this. I deserve this." I repeated my mantra over and over. Nothing like a little pep talk to put me in the right mindset.

I blinked hard to chase the moisture away. Now wasn't the time to think about every bump in the road, all the things that needed to be done to reach where I was today. Instead, I focused on Aisha Jones's country song "In Your Dreams" playing in the background. A reminder that the Holidays were seven weeks away. And a nod to the best night of my life.

Two weeks ago, I had celebrated my birthday with Mixchos—reinvented nachos—and the biggest mug of hot chocolate I could find. Ellie, my best friend, had sent me the new pair of heels I was wearing today as a present and told me they would bring me luck. I hoped she was right.

From my spot near the front door, I surveyed my small apartment, the single main room, two closet-sized bedrooms off to the side, and an open kitchen. My eyes caressed all the furniture and the mess around it lovingly. It had been hard, but totally worth it.

A hint of a smile peeked on my lips. If I'd come all this way, the interview would be easy-peasy. I crossed my fingers, hoping it wasn't wishful thinking on my part. I'd been learning all about CB Music for the last month, from the awards Mr. Burns had won over the years to each page of their corporate website. A girl couldn't be prepared enough. The guy was a household name on the international music scene. I wouldn't let his credentials and achievements intimidate me. I would be the professional he expected me to be. Even though, deep down, I was kind of amazed by his career and success.

Every day, I listened to each of his songs, just in case they quizzed me on them.

Back when I was nineteen, I used to be a music encyclopedia. I knew every artist, even the emerging ones, and could recite by heart every award they'd won in their careers and all their biggest hits. I could tell which songs would be chart-toppers and which ones would be misses. Over the last few years, I'd lost my magic touch, too busy with the numerous curveballs life had thrown at me. Now I was ready to take my power back—to get to the top of my game and dig up the version of me I had somehow lost along the way.

Looking in the mirror, I wiped the tears from my eyes with my fingers and swiped a hand through my hair. I was ready. I would get this job. I could feel it. Today was the day my life would change for the better. It was about time. I huffed. Yes, the stars would finally align themselves. It was my time to shine.

At the front door, with a hand around the doorknob, I closed my eyes. This job, this opportunity, would mean the world to me if I got it. I believed in the magical power of the holidays. A girl could always hope for the best. Growing up, my grandma had told me multiple times that all the best things happened around this time of year. I could tell she spoke the truth, because I had already experienced a Christmas miracle four years ago. Now I craved a second one. If it wasn't too much to ask.

Locking the door behind me, I exited the building with a pep in my step. All week, I'd been walking around my apartment in heels to get used to their feel and look confident wearing them.

On the sidewalk, I let a full breath out as I glanced at the sky. An immaculate blue canvas and glittering sunshine. Yes, today would be a good day. A great day. One to remember.

A prayer to the Gods above and I climbed into the backseat of the idling cab that would drive me to Nashville's tallest building where I would meet some of the most important music executives in the country.

*Wish me luck.* No, not luck. I knew I'd be the best at that job.

*Go, get them, tiger.* Yeah, much better.

I exhaled. This position was mine. I was ready to hustle for it. Whatever it took, I'd be the newest CB Music employee by the end of the day. I, Abigail Peña, would be a rising star on the Nashville music scene. One day, I would sign the biggest artists under my management and would become a household name in this industry.

———

One breath in. I passed though security, filled the logbook, hung the visitor pass around my neck, and made it to the twenty-sixth floor. Yes, I belonged here. I could feel it deep in my bones. Goose bumps spread on my arms, and excited flutters danced around in my stomach. This was my chance. And I wouldn't miss it.

I checked my outfit and makeup one last time and smoothed a hand over my hair in the mirrored wall of the elevator. Satisfied, I rubbed my clammy hands on my skirt discretely and steeled my shoulders.

A woman in her fifties with a businesslike demeanor

gave me a not-so-subtle once-over when I exited the elevator.

I cleared my throat softly before approaching her, hoping my voice wouldn't squeak.

"Welcome to CB Music. May I help you?" she asked, lifting a dark eyebrow.

I breathed out. "Yes, I'm here for the interview. For the assistant's position. I'm meeting with Mr. Burns and Mr. Jacobson at ten."

The woman tapped something on her computer before bringing her attention back to me. "Ms. Peña. You're early. That's good. Just take a seat. I'll call out your name when they are ready for you."

I nodded and sat on a white leather chair in the small waiting room, crossing my feet at the ankles.

To avoid freaking out, I grabbed a magazine and pretended to glance through it.

I had an interview with Curtis Burns, one of Nashville's most famous country music stars turned record label owner slash manager.

If he were as good a manager as his son Riley, this was promising. Riley Burns had signed many upcoming country rock stars over the years. He was as famous as his dad, even though they chose different career paths. One day, I'd play in the big leagues. Just like him.

The receptionist called out my name, and I jumped to my feet, adjusting my top before following her to the conference room. My breath hitched when I took in the view. The room had a floor-to-ceiling glass wall, offering the best view of the Cumberland River and the football stadium on the opposite shore.

Curtis Burns and Gregory Jacobson rose to their feet to shake my hand as I entered, and I took the seat they pointed me to, a genuine smile plastered on my lips. I finally had my chance to shine.

Deep down, I urged my throbbing heart to take a rest.

Confidence spread through me. It spurred me to talk slowly and show them I was the real deal. That I was the perfect—no, the only—valuable choice for this position.

The interview passed in a blur.

If someone had requested me to write down the questions they'd asked, I couldn't have done it. The words had flown out of me with ease before I could think them through. Every time the men exchanged nods and took notes, I high-fived myself in my head. I could do this. Excel and take the first step toward making my dreams a reality.

"Before you go, Ms. Peña, I want you to meet the first artist we've signed under our label," Mr. Jacobson said. "Being Mr. Burns's assistant means you'll work closely with our artists." He pressed a button on the speaker set in the middle of the table. "Laura, please send Mr. Ford in. We're ready for him."

Laura said a few words and hung up as we waited.

Moments later, a discrete knock resonated through the room, and the door opened to let the man in. I moved to my feet, ready to greet him and introduce myself. Longish brown hair, dark enigmatic eyes, nonchalant gait.

Our eyes met, and air froze in my lungs.

"Ms. Peña, this is Anderson Ford," said someone in the background.

I tried to speak, but words refused to make their way up, my feet glued to the floor and my arms hanging at my sides.

Then a rush of air along with a single word. "You?"

———

Read Anderson and Abigail's story,
**_Snowbound, now_**

emmanuellesnow.com/products/snowbound

Author's bookstore at emmanuellesnow.com

"I'll tell you this; if you're looking for a book that will make you ugly cry but leave you with your heart full – look no more; <u>*Emmanuelle Snow*</u> is the right author for you." (OMGreads)

*"Be ready with a box of tissues because this is gonna tug at your heartstrings from every possible direction. I was ugly crying so much the whole day and even now." (OhMyWordMelly)*

**_Snowbound_** is book one in the **_Two of Us_** duet.
Read the first part now

Dad
#1
Dad
SAM STEVENS
ECHOES WORLD TOUR
FEBRUARY 16, 20
SAM STEVENS
SAM STEVENS